Finding My Way Home

Finding My Way Home

Magic in Realism
The Intrinsic Nature of True Love
and a Remarkable Journey Home

V. A. COLUCCI

Rock's Mills Press
Rock's Mills, Ontario • Oakville, Ontario
2024

Published by
Rock's Mills Press
www.rocksmillspress.com

Cover design: V. A. Colucci
Cover image: Natasha Pelley-Smith

This is a work of fiction. Any resemblance to actual events or persons, living or dead, is entirely coincidental.

I am you

You are me

We are the universe

And the window opens …

Love, because of its purity of being and clarity of mission, is the oldest and most resilient of human emotions.

Some believe in a broad interpretation of love, a regatta of sorts, others prefer the notion of fewer ships, and still others cherish the idea of a very exclusive journey in a vessel for two. Although all ships will ultimately be lifted by the same tide, only true love in a vessel for two can safeguard the journey.

As to when hearts actually unite—that is contingent on how long each takes to emerge from the surrounding tempestuous waters. Once arisen, the heart glows more vividly, uniting itself with its companion heart and together cross-stitch a clear passage for two on a fresh, new sail and set course towards a more permanent sunset.

"How did Mo and VC know their hearts would be each other's sanctuary?"

"The jewel that is love is hidden in all of us and shines most radiantly in our hearts when companion hearts decisively touch. Theirs touched and converged early in their journey."

"Is the heart indestructible?"

"Yes."

"Does love ever die?"

"Once lit, the light that is genuine love never dies."

"Is the search for one's true life-companion long?"

"Depends."

"On what?"

"On when that special voice in another's heart speaks to yours."

"Can there be many that speak to one's heart?"

"Many talk, but only one will speak truthfully of love to your

heart, and if you pay close attention, amidst the perplexity of it all, you will hear the soft calling of your name."

"I have."

"Then you know. The heart is a formidable vessel with love as its most precious voyager. Love's only mission is to merge with that of its true companion. Love is not bound by seasons, time, speed, gender, colour or shape. Love can experience joy, tears and joy again in a single moment. Committed love can create dreams with a warm touch, a loving whisper, a soft kiss, a simple smile. Love is resilient and at its pinnacle is the rhythm of life, and although the time signature is different for everyone, once that love rhythm is synchronized in the heart and soul the music chart is complete.

"Is it true, once hearts genuinely merge, eternity for the new entity as one begins?"

"Yes, that is the time when unfading love for one another is born. It can take place on Earth or in the Constellations, and only true love for one another can evolve into pure love. Only pure love can take you to become an attribute of One."

"Is the journey to One long?"

"Once transitioned from the physical, you depart the Great Earth and journey towards a purer state of being, absolutely essential in the reunification.

"The Great Hall is a galaxy of globular Chambers and it is your first non-planetary stay. It consists of the Chamber of Planet Earth where the chronicled events of one's life on Earth are examined and evaluated by the Tribunal.

"The next step is directly to the Chamber of Enhanced Understanding and Wisdom unless obligatory time is first required in the Chamber of Amendments.

"All Chambers lead to the Constellations, and in doing so the human form becomes less prominent as it is increasingly shrouded by a veil of subdued light. This is where all lights begin to animate more vividly, as their journeys continue.

"The Constellations is a supreme assemblage of entities."

"*Can you explain?*"

"*Certainly.*

"*The Constellations are comprised of Restored Radiance, Healing Lights, the Emerging Glow and the Festival of Lights. The Festival of Lights is a vibrant reassembly of colours. It's the only location other than Earth where those who initially travelled as one on Earth and now seek to travel with a loving companion may do so and continue their journey as two; those who travelled as two and had the misfortune of losing their true companion on Earth may wait here, reunite and continue as two; and those who arrive as two continue as two.*

"*This all-embracing glow then continues its journey to the Constellation of Restored Souls, then to the Constellation of Healing Souls.*"

"*And from there?*"

"*From there, this reunited entity of Light and Soul journeys to the Great Constellation of Souls Pristine, then to the All-Encompassing Festival of Souls. From there, this glowing integrated entity of Light and Soul, this now Supreme Glow, resumes its journey as a singular, complete and absolute entity, ultimately ascending to the place from where it once emerged.*

"*This ultimate setting at the centre of all universes is where all attributes of eternity merge and re-enter, One Love, One Light, One Soul, hence One, much like the dispersion and reassembly of light in a spectrum.*

"*There is no darkness in The Constellations because the lights intensify, as their Epic Journeys continue towards becoming One.*"

"*Do we remain as One Light?*"

"*We do, but there is talk of emitting prominent rays from the One, providing humans with a more effective glow while on Earth.*"

"*There is so much darkness.*"

"*Doesn't need to be.*"

"*I know, I have also been blinded by it for so long.*"

"*I know. After the tragedies the deep sorrow ... the loneliness, the light of hope within your heart ebbed and you permitted darkness to reign. The moonless skies overshadowed your only guiding star and you lost sight of home."*

"I so wish to feel the touch of home again … gently kiss her tender lips, softly caress her face, look into her eyes and say 'I love you.' Can you help me?"

She takes his hand and slowly walks him into her glow. She places her fingers on his long-abandoned lips and whispers, "I will, for I am the glow from which the light in your heart first ignited, and you mine. I am the one I have always been, my love, I am me; I am you; I am us."

CHAPTER ONE

In the year nineteen sixty-six of the Common Era … *the global land-scape* … Camelot and all that might have been soon to be forgotten … equilateral triangles of the republic give way to acute isosceles as political and corporate power remains in the hands of the elite. Wall Street rolls unapologetically down Main Street all the while leisurely sipping Dom Perignon. The poor become increasingly invisible and children go to bed hungry … the marginalized build more cardboard shelters under bridges … the ostracized overdose in rodent-infested alleyways … America learns little from the Watts Rebellion … and the Wolf Clan struggles to protect its own. Orange is the new colour in Vietnam, Charlie Company takes heavy losses and humankind eats its young.

The Industrial Average walks into Bear territory and front-page news increasingly reads like the obituary… But eh, Hollywood is experiencing a renaissance, Ford beat Ferrari at Le Mans and the Rat Pack is doing just fine at the Sands.

The movie *A Man for All Seasons* took the Oscars in the land of la-la and Edyie Gormé stole the spotlight with her rendition of "If He Walked into My Life Today."

Out of the ashes, oaks of virtues rise. Nineteen sixty-six was also the year when Mo's and VC's passionate hearts spoke to each other. They intuitively harmonized their particular rhythms of love and life and the eternal part of their journey rose from their subconscious ashes and consciously began voyaging as one.

"Do you remember our first dance?"

"I do."

Mo's and VC's hearts effortlessly guided their love for each other towards the long-awaited path to a life resonant with their convictions. They lived and loved life fully and were happy. Life became increasingly esteemed, particularly with the birth of Aila.

Then tragedy befell this young and vibrant family. Holding desperately onto each other, Mo and VC were able to briefly calm the winds of mourning for their precious little one. Then tragedy struck again, hurling their restored vessel viciously against the rocks. Water savagely rushed in and when it receded it took Mo with it.

The once cherished first dance had lost its most precious partner and their once harmonious musical score for two, then three, had now become an irrevocable collection of nonsensical notes for one. VC's once healthy arteries of life quickly hardened, home as he knew it was now inaccessible. Darkness prevailed, and he lost his way.

METAMORPHOSIS: PART ONE

VC was a precision young fighter, *"Climbing too fast,"* some would say. He was creative with his combinations, highly successful, and surely headed for the championship, but after a few years in the ring he could no longer ignore the internal bleeding. It was a slow bleed, the type that left unattended would ultimately hemorrhage.

He knew his longing heart was becoming a distraction. He also knew, as everyone in his corner knew, that sooner or later unresolved emotions in the ring will make you choke on your own blood on your way to the canvas.

He had hit the canvas before but was never down for the count. He had bled before, but never from the heart.

The only letters he chose to have sewn on the back of his boxing robe were VC. He could have consented to "The Kid" for his youthful looks but that's not who he was or wanted to be. Or "Kid Lightning" for his quick hands and rapid combinations, but he declined. He just wanted to be known for who he was, VC. His uncle Lou, however, endearingly referred to him as "The Kid," and it remained.

The Kid liked colours. He selected red letters on a blue robe. Red, fire and determination, intensity, passion and true love, the last of which still absent in his life. Blue, tranquillity and calmness often pursued but seldom achieved; a colour embodying truth, trust and loyalty, which he possessed in abundance; a colour that spoke of the unending sky and his desire to know and see beyond what the eye could see and the heart could feel. Often thinking of his past and present led him to develop a series of "files" under the heading "Life Files," an appraisal of sorts for the purpose of reviewing personal life's events.

Lying on his bed, frequently looking through the large skylight into the night splendor, he was increasingly becoming a dreamer of the heart and for that he created a separate file aptly named "The Love File," a file void of notations, until he met Mo.

"Can dreams come true?"

The night he believed his dream of love could come true, entries in the Love File promptly began, quickly surpassing those in the Boxing File, but they were only dreams, yet sufficiently distracting that the promising career of this skilled young boxer inched closer to the ropes.

THE BOXER

THE MATCH ... THE INJURY ... THE HOSPITAL

"The Kid will take it in six, eight max, maybe KO."

"The money is on the Kid."

"Nah, the Kid is not on his best game, hasn't been for a while, rigor mortis will set in by the eighth, and the brawler will take it on points ... possible KO, it won't go the full."

"He can do it, I know he can," said his corner man, who was also his uncle Lou. Alone with the Kid in the dressing room, Lou places his hand on his nephew's shoulder and says, "Relax Kid, you're too tense, loosen those arms up, let the juice flow. You haven't been yourself lately, is everything okay?"

"Yes, Uncle Lou, all fine," the Kid answers, trying to convince himself and his uncle that he was ready for the match.

"I know you can take him, but you have to focus on the match; the only distraction I can think of is a girl. You didn't get a girl in trouble, did you?"

"From a distance? Right, Uncle Lou. I hardly go out, boxing is all I do."

"Maybe in a way that's the problem. You need someone else in your corner besides us old guys, you need someone special to cheer you on. Life is not just about boxing and fixing Mustangs."

"Do you think I'm losing my nerve, Uncle Lou?"

"You'll never lose your nerve, Kid, you're a natural, but it seems to me that lately the stars in this profession are not lining up for you, and to be at the top of this game you have to be at the top of yours. If not, you're leaving yourself wide open, and then anything can happen. I don't want to see you hurt or worse. If this is no longer working for you, as your uncle, I say, time to hang up your gloves, Kid."

"I don't want to let anybody down, Uncle Lou."

"I love you, Kid, but it's your life we're talking about here, not mine or anyone else's. You know you can never disappoint your uncle, and as far as your parents go, they never liked you taking up boxing in the first place. You broke your mother's heart when you dropped out of school. If boxing has run its course, know that you cut an honest path through any jungle out there and that says a lot. You're a class act, Kid, and you can go out on a high note."

The Kid closes his eyes and takes deep breaths.

"That's it, breathe and think of how you're going to take out the brawler tonight. Now go in the other room and do three in front of the mirror. Start the juice pumping and flowing in the right direction, come back, I'll wrap your hands."

The Kid comes off the table, walks to the other room, faces the mirror and begins to shadow box slowly, picks it up, up, up, and by the time the bell rings in his head he's totally ready. The rush, the speed, the drive to win, it was all coming together. He walks back, sits down at the table and puts his hands out for his uncle to wrap. His uncle dries the Kid's forehead and begins wrapping his hands.

After a brief silence, the Kid says, "I'm ready."

His uncle smiles and says, "I know, I can feel it."

The Kid had never been knocked out, lost a few on points but always walked unaided back to his corner.

"Your father will be here tonight, rare, so no showboating, okay, just get the job done, and your mother—my wonderful sister—you know she will never attend, but she cheers for you."

"And prays."

"And prays not for a win, but for you not to get hurt," replies Lou.

The Kid nods.

"Ready?"

"Yes, I am."

The sixth round came and went, as did the eighth without a knockout. The brawler is ahead on points, drops the Kid on the ninth but he gets up just under the count and stays up. The bell of the tenth and final round was about to ring and only a knockout would assure a win for the Kid.

"The most important three minutes of your career are coming up, Kid," says Lou. Towelled down, jelly reapplied to his face, mouth guard secured, the Kid stands, hits his gloves energetically while staring down his opponent, and nods.

"He's going to come out with all he's got, but you've got the reach, the speed, don't let him get close, double up on your jabs, follow up and stay away from the ropes, take the fight to the centre of the ring, own it, make it yours and take the bastard down."

The two boxers come out, face each other and tap gloves. The bell rings, the referee steps out of the way, and the last round begins. Immediately the brawler comes at the Kid and unleashes. The crowd cheers. The Kid is on the ropes, protecting himself, and as soon as the frequency and strength of the opposing punches lessen, the Kid launches a relentless offensive and his opponent backs off. The crowd cheers louder.

A determined Kid mercilessly forces his opponent further into the centre of the ring with his quick jabs, setting him up for power punches and unrelenting combinations. The Kid delivers. The brawler staggers, looks for the safety of the ropes, but the Kid quickly blocks his path and continues with combinations. His opponent takes and gives, it could have easily turned into a brawl, but the Kid remains in control. The brawler hits the blood and sweat-soaked canvas hard and the crowd cheers loudly.

The referee immediately begins the dreaded count. The almost lifeless fighter lifts his head and eventually stands at the eighth. The referee briefly speaks to him, nods, the Kid leaves the neutral corner, arms up and both boxers resume. The brawler's attempt at forcing the Kid to the ropes fails and the Kid drops him in the middle of the ring. He tries to stand but falls back down. The referee counts him out, waves both arms and the fight is over. He raises the Kid's arm in victory, everyone invades the ring, the microphones come out and the first question is "What's next, Kid, the championship?" to which there is no reply. Lou removes the Kid's gloves, drapes the robe over his shoulders, and leads the way to the dressing room, avoiding the lights, cameras and reporters.

Victory in the ring is normally followed by fiery celebrations. For some warriors, cold packs on swollen eyes, temporarily crudely-stitched flesh, battered and bruised body in a stench-fraught dressing room make for a long night of agony. For others, pain-concealing ecstasy. For the bookies, grins and sneers, and for the Kid, often a shower, clean clothes and a ride home. Tonight, the hard-fought win brought him a step closer to the championship bout, if he so wished, but that discussion never took place because he never made it back safely to the dressing room.

A man associated with the betting world who lost a considerable amount suddenly came at the Kid as they walked to the dressing room and viciously hit him over the head with a steel chair. The full impact was lessened by Lou's defending arm, but the Kid tumbled down the cement stairs rendering him unconscious. The shock discharged a frenzied retaliation and by the time the ambulance arrived, there were two bodies lying on the cold cement floor. The Kid, in his father's arms with Lou desperately trying to stop the bleeding from the head wound, and that of the barely recognizable attacker.

THE HOSPITAL

Several weeks later, sitting on either side of their son's hospital bed holding his hands, Augie and Sarah look at each other and Sarah with tears in her eyes asks if their son will ever regain consciousness.

"I wish I knew. What I do know is that I should have put a stop to this long ago," he replies.

"And how would we have done that, Augie? How?"

After a brief silence, Augie looks up at his wife, sees tears covering her face, gently wipes them and says, "Our son will wake up, Sarah, we know he will, just needs time."

Mike, VC's cousin, enters the room filled with flowers, get-well cards and balloons, embraces his uncle and aunt, and Augie says, "Good to see you, Mike."

"Good to see you too, Uncle Augie, Aunt Sarah. How's VC doing today?" To which Sarah answers, "A little better, I think." She looks at her husband and he nods.

"Been here all day?" Mike asks, and both his uncle and aunt nod.

"Why don't you two get something to eat, I'll stay with him for a while."

"Thanks, Mike," says Augie, "You and your parents have been such great supports, you're here as often as we are, thanks Mike, thanks."

He then walks to the other side of the bed, places his arm on his wife's shoulder, she reluctantly stands and both leave the room. Mike moves one of the chairs closer, kisses his cousin, his best friend, on the cheek and sits. He holds VC's hand and says, "Is this your good hand? It is, okay, then I won't squeeze it too hard."

After a brief silence, Mike says, "I know what you're thinking VC, I do, and no, pugilists aka boxers cannot beat martial artists in a contest, they can't, well maybe you can, but I can kick your ass any day, you know that don't you? Of course, you do, and the last time at the dojo, well, truth be known, I let you win, but I am ready for a rematch. So as soon as you get out of this bed, we'll have the re-match… I can see the headlines now," Mike says looking upward and motioning with his hand as if he was pointing at a billboard, *The Kid "The Fast Hands" versus Mike (Bruce Lee) "The Feet"*… the Hands and Feet bout of the century. No contest, I mean how can you guard against my double spin and hook kick … you can, you say? Maybe you can because you know a little karate, all right, black belt, but unlike me, you still have a ways to go before you reach the upper echelons of karate as moi. That's French for *me*. What's that you say? Your spin kick? Are you kidding me? I can count your toes by the time you land your kick."

Mike squeezes VC's hand, and says, "Squeeze my hand, VC, squeeze it hard … toes, wiggle your toes." He looks closely, hoping, but neither sees nor feels movement. Continues holding his cousin's hand and says, "You know, in the grand scheme of things, this is just a brief stop over, much like switching tires on the track, but don't let this life-choking demon interfere with your tomorrows. Once the door is open, you know more will come in, and it's not easy to get them out."

Following a brief silence he adds, "VC, you have to come back to us, you have to fight this demon, and hard. Fight, VC, fight!"

He looks at his motionless cousin, hoping for some kind of move-ment, and no matter how intently he looks, there was none to be had, not today. Soon after Augie and Sarah return, Mike stays a while, then stands and says, "I'll be back tomorrow."

He kisses his cousin on the cheek, squeezes his hand, hugs his uncle and aunt and leaves the hospital room.

Into the third week of the coma and VC failed to respond to all known medical treatment, therapies or prayers. Hoping for a full recovery was gradually becoming hoping for any recovery. No one spoke of the long-term consequence but it was increasingly on ev-eryone's mind.

Day eighteen, Mike walks into the room with a bouquet of freesi-as in a glass vase and holds the flowers under VC's nose.

"VC," he says, "These are freesias, they are as you have said to me, from your reading of course, the flowers of courtship. So, inhale deeply and think of summer, think of the beautiful woman, the one you've been dreaming about these past few weeks, the one you will be taking to dances, extravagant dinners, on long Sunday afternoon drives in the country on main roads, no side roads, no detour to green fields, the one with whom to walk hand in hand to your favourite café… Think about all those possibilities … to be continued."

Day nineteen. Mike returns, takes in the aroma permeating the room and says, "The scent of a flower enriches the soul, don't you agree, VC?"

He sits next to him, and while holding his hand says, "So tell me, VC, what is she like? Smart, beautiful, classy, but with a great sense of humour … what did she think of the freesias? Always a big hit. So, I know, I know, you snuck out last night with her next to you in the Mustang, moonlit country road, howling at the moon, right?"

After a brief silence, Mike squeezes his cousin's hand and says, "All armours have a chink, VC, find the fucking chink in this one and break out, I know you can."

Day twenty-two. Mike enters, immediately embraces his cousin and sits next to him. "Good morning, Cousin Extraordinaire," he says, looks at the freesias and adds, "Look at those flowers, still bold and beautiful. Tell me, VC, did anyone visit you in the midnight hour? Nothing you can talk about? Okay. I have been thinking, when this is over and done, you may wish to consider law school and come back with me. You're an old guy, I know, but I'll put in a good word for you … and consider this, when you graduate, we can start our own law firm … of course me being handsomer and smarter, my name would be first on the plaque, something like Mike and the Other Guy, Attorneys at Law, what do you think? Okay, how about Mike and VC? No? Okay, okay, VC and Mike, like that? I know you do because I think I saw a little smile, yes, I did, done, Mike and VC, all right, all right, VC and Mike. And you know when business is slow, I figure we can do some work for "Uncle Guido," our go-to

"*Uncle*," but he's so cheap and never pays on time and when he does, he always wants the brown envelope back, I don't know if it's for re-use or recycle, I think the former, can't mistake Uncle Guido for an environmentalist, can you? Didn't think so."

Suddenly Mike stands, stares at VC's face and says, "Holy shit, VC! I think I saw that fat lower lip of yours move ever so slightly." Leans forward, looks more closely and says, "I did, VC, I did."

Mike pulls the chair closer, sits, grabs his hand and says, "I know what I saw, VC, and I'm going to sit here until I see it again."

After a while, he felt VC's fingers twitch. He gently squeezes and feels a slight response from VC's hand. He squeezes again and again but VC's response was inconsistent and barely noticeable … but in his heart, he knew it was there. He stands, looks directly at his cousin's eyes for another indication of recovery just as Augie and Sarah walk in.

Mike turns and says, "Uncle Augie, Aunt Sarah, just in time."

"Oh?' replies Augie.

"I'm going to get some coffee, need to celebrate," Mike replies, walking towards the door.

"What's there to celebrate, Mike?" asks Augie.

"Life," answers Sarah, "We should celebrate life every day, Augie. We are blessed that VC is here with us, and that's all that matters."

While Sarah and Augie move their chairs closer to the bed, Mike notices VC's hand twitch again and as he's leaving the room says, "Stay close to VC, I'll be right back."

"I have a good feeling today, Augie," Sarah says, but he doesn't reply.

Mike leaves the room and waits in the hall just outside the doorway. He could have easily shouted the great news as they walked in, or acknowledged Aunt Sarah's feeling that today was indeed a new day, but chose not to. In his heart, he felt it would be more profound, more miraculous for his uncle and aunt, particularly his aunt, to be the first to experience the rebirth of their son.

Several minutes later he hears his aunt loudly say, "Augie, Augie! His eyes moved, VC's eyes moved, they moved!"

Augie moves very close to VC, looks at him, looks at his wife and says, "I think they did, Sarah, I think they did." He then takes his hand and says, "VC, it's us, can you open your eyes? Can you squeeze my hand? Try, son, try." After repeating it several times, he looks at his wife and says, "I felt something Sarah, I did!"

Mike follows the nurses in, they take VC's vitals and one says, "Quick, call the doctor."

METAMORPHOSIS: PART TWO

To no one's surprise, the once judiciously nurtured goal of the championship ended on the blood-stained stairs the night the noble art of pugilism displayed its dark side, forever sealing shut the door to VC's return to the ring. A decision considered weakness by some, strength of character by others, to VC a mixed bag of emotions he had to work through, to his parents a blessing in disguise.

"I told Helen, Lou can watch the fight at his own house," says Sarah while preparing dinner.

"Sarah, he's your brother, stop blaming him, it wasn't his fault," replies Augie while setting the table.

"Brother or not, he needs to clearly understand that VC is done with boxing."

"He does, Sarah, he does, and he was devastated by the incident as we all were. This family has suffered long enough, I think you have been unreasonable and should reach out to him."

"My mind is made up, Augie. No more boxing!" she shouts. "We went to hell and back with VC in a coma and thank God, he made it through. I will not, will not have him or us go through that again, ever!"

"Sarah, please lower your voice," says Augie.

"He's downstairs…"

Suddenly VC appears in the doorway and says, "I'm here, Mom, and I heard much of the discussion."

Sarah and Augie look at each other, she looks at her son and says, "That's how I feel, VC, boxing came close to being the end of you, of us, and I won't have it."

"You're right, Mom, but it seems that's all I have been thinking about these past few months. All the roads lead me back to Rome, to the Coliseum, the gladiatorial contests, I seem to be drawn to battle."

"Drawn to battle? In a past life maybe, but not for you today. Leave those battles to the movies, you, my son, have different fish to fry. I could not live with myself if I consented to you boxing again, I couldn't," she angrily replies.

"Mom, sit down, please."

"Pour me a wine, Augie, please, and fill the glass," she says as she sits. VC sits next to her, places his hand on her shoulder and says, "I feel that reaching this decision seemed so natural, as if it was made for me."

"But why, VC, why? Didn't you learn anything in these past months? You could have died, or still be in a coma, so why do you want to put yourself in the same situation again? Augie, talk some sense into your son, will you, please."

"Wait, wait, Mom, I think you misunderstood me."

"What's to misunderstand, you just said you wish to continue these gladiatorial contests, to me that means returning to boxing. What does it mean to you, Augie?"

Augie remains silent and VC continues, "Mom, I have a question, have you ever had a situation where making a decision came so naturally you felt that somehow someone helped you?"

"Yes, occasionally, why?"

"And what do you attribute it to?"

"Guardian angels, and sometimes to your father, why?

"Well, that happened to me in deciding whether to return to boxing or not."

"And?"

"And, as you say mom, when one door closes, another is bound to open," VC replies.

"And?" she repeats.

"And, I am ready to take that wobbly walk down that uncertain hallway towards that, hopefully, bright new door."

"Don't play word games with me, VC. Are you saying you are definitely done with boxing or not?"

"No more boxing, Mom."

Sarah looks at Augie, back at VC, smiles and tears. She embraces her son, Augie joins them and she says, "Thank you, VC, we know it wasn't an easy decision to make, but we are so happy for you. Our prayers have been answered, thank you, God."

"You should feel very proud, son," adds Augie.

"I am, Dad. Mom, there is another matter that I need to discuss with you, and this is the perfect time to do so."

"Sure, anything, what is it?" she replies.

"I need you to know that what happened is not your fault, nor is it dad's, nor Uncle Lou's, nor mine, nor anyone else from our family. So, Mom, I hate to think that you would hold a grudge against Uncle Lou, your only brother who means so much to you, for something he didn't do."

Sarah remains silent, and VC continues.

"Mom?"

"Yes, VC?"

"Would it be too hard for you to invite Uncle Lou, Aunt Helen and Mike over for the match?"

Sarah shakes her head several times.

"Mom," says VC, "I think this is the right thing to do for everyone's sake. You have hardly spoken to Uncle Lou since the incident, our families don't get together anymore, we can't go on like this, Mom. We all need to reconnect, forgive each other, and give each other the permission to move on. We all need to heal and it needs to be done, Mom. You want to have a fresh beginning? Well, this is where it starts."

Sarah looks at Augie, but he remains silent. She looks at VC and quietly says, "You're right, VC, give your uncle a call."

"I prefer you call Uncle Lou, Mom," he replies.

"I will, and you're right, time to move on. Augie, while I'm on the phone, please set the table for six."

"Six?"

"Yes, Augie, three for us and three for them, oy."

Shortly after, Sarah returns and says, "Spoke with Helen, and they're not coming."

"Not surprised," says Augie.

"Lou doesn't want to come and Helen and Mike won't without him."

The three look at each other and VC asks, "What now?"

"I'll tell you what now," Sarah says, while walking decidedly towards the door, "Augie, watch the roast, I'm going to pick that stubborn man up myself."

"Stubborn? A family trait no doubt," he says. She looks, smiles, puts on her coat, picks up the car keys and says, "I'll be back soon."

Since they lived minutes away, it didn't take Sarah long to return. She opens the door, enters and closes it behind her.

"Are they coming in their own car?" asks Augie.

"Not coming. Lou answered the door, we talked briefly and I said I forgive him, he said he appreciated what I had to say, then said another time and closed the door."

"Not unexpected, Sarah," says Augie.

"Why would you say that?"

"Really, Sarah? After all these months of blaming, ignoring and hardly speaking to your only brother, after all that outrage, you go over, ask him over to dinner as if nothing happened and he should reply, sure Sarah, be right over."

"I said I forgive him."

"Forgiveness has a time and place and can be the pathway to emotional freedom but is time sensitive and sadly, often missed by many of us. And since we're on the topic, he doesn't need your forgiveness, Sarah, he is struggling with forgiving himself, as we are. He knows it wasn't his fault, yet feels the same pain we feel, and you have never acknowledged his pain, or the hell that he, Helen and Mike underwent throughout this entire ordeal. He was the first to say no to VC when he wanted to join his boxing club, so give him some credit, and give him a break for everyone's sake, Sarah."

"You're angry," she says.

"Of course, I'm angry, enough is enough. We have been so self-absorbed with our own pain and never noticed anyone else's. It's time to look beyond ourselves, we all need to stop focusing solely on pain and look to healing and help others do the same. The healing circle is missing comforting hearts, Sarah, and they all must be brought back into it."

"Dad is right, Mom; everyone's healing hands must be on each other's cuts for the larger wound to seal properly."

After a brief silence, Sarah stands and says, "I'll be right back."

"Where are you going?" Augie asks but Sarah was already out of the door.

She rings the bell and Lou answers. She steps inside, opens her arms and embraces him. They remain embraced for a long time, neither spoke amidst the tears, but it was clear, their new road to healing had been set alight.

"Coats on everyone," says Helen and on their way out the door, Lou asks his adoring sister, "What's for dinner?"

"Your favourite," she replies while getting into their separate cars.

"This I got to see."

The night of the greatly anticipated fight between Muhammad Ali and George Chuvalo on this blistering 29th day of March in the year 1966 had arrived and by the time the night was over, the outcome would forever be branded in history. Although this epic collision of two stories, of two lives, this clash of two titans would, at a different time, have been the centrepiece at the dinner table, not tonight, not at this table of reconciliation and reunification.

The television was on, but it was downstairs in the family room. The dinner took place in the dining room upstairs. The loud cheers from the television, barely audible upstairs, distracted at times but no one left the table.

The breaking of the bread at the restorative table slowly brought back the joy of life these families once knew and frequently shared.

When strangers are in a strange land, family ties are the ones that bind best and most securely. They are the ones that are strong enough to weather the storms of heart-wrenching yearnings for their native home.

They ate traditional soul-soothing food, drank Uncle Lou's homemade wine, recounted stories short and tall and tears were shed, but laughter and good will won the evening. This family re-union, long overdue, revitalized the unyielding love for each other as they walked hand in hand through the oftentimes perilous jungle of forgiveness into a clearing of a richer life that only healing can bestow.

It wasn't until later that night, when everyone had left, that VC and his father caught the late news.

After a truly epic, full fifteen-round battle, Ali was given the win on points—a questionable decision to some—and retained his title. Chuvalo never stepped back, and in the end walked freely and tall back to his corner. When it was all said and done, Ali spent the night at the hospital and Chuvalo went dancing with his wife.

Augie and VC return upstairs, Augie looks lovingly at his wife sitting on the sofa in the living room with a glass of wine listening to Antonio Vivaldi's *The Four Seasons*.

"Spring?" he asks.

"Spring eternal," she replies, motioning him to sit next to her. He looks at the gently falling snow through their bay window, walks to the kitchen and returns with a glass of wine of his own. He sits next to her and says, "To Spring."

"To Spring," she replies.

"VC, come sit with us for a while," says Augie. VC, standing in front of them, says, "Thank you both, particularly you, Mom, I know it hasn't been easy on anyone," and sits on the recliner across from them.

"Never again," says Sarah.

"What do you mean, never again?" asks Augie.

"Never again will we allow tragedy come between members of

our families. Love and caring for one another should define who we are, not pain and blame."

"Literature is you, Mom, always has been, so why don't you teach at the university?"

"Another life, perhaps, now I'm happy with what I do. So, VC, after the winter thaw, what's your next season to explore?"

"Fall."

"Fall?" replies Augie.

"Fall as in…?" says Sarah.

"Yes, Mom, as in school."

"Does this mean…?" asks Sarah beaming.

"Yes, it means I am going back to school…"

Sarah jumps up, spills her wine, says "Allegria," then hugs her son and says, "We are so, so proud of you, VC, so very proud."

"Wait, wait, Mom, there is more."

"There is? Oh, I know, you will graduate, go to university, law school, and become a famous litigator, correct?"

"Well, not quite."

"Heart surgeon, yes?"

"Well…"

"A doctor of philosophy, of letters, that would suit that keen mind of yours," says Augie.

"Well, Mom, Dad, you may not like what I'm about to say, but after I get my diploma, I'm going back to boxing," says VC while winking at his father.

"Pardon? What did you just say?" asks a shocked Sarah. She looks at Augie, and as he begins smiling says, "You two, I should have known … just kidding, right?"

"Yes, Mom, just kidding. School in September it is."

The three embrace and VC says, "Thank you both for always being there for me."

"And we thank you son, for being the stand-up and courageous young man you are. You will make someone very happy someday," says Sarah.

VC smiles, walks towards the upstairs staircase and bids them a good night. Augie refills Sarah's glass, they raise their glasses and Augie says, "To life."

Old dreams rest, new ones emerge.

The Kid from the West End Boxing Club suspends his heavy bag in the corner of the basement, and his prized red 18-ounce gloves on the back of his bedroom door. Sitting at his desk, he turns his chair, looks at the posters around the room, reflects on his boxing career and thinks of what it was, and for the first time, doesn't ask himself what it might have been.

THE WEEKEND BEFORE SCHOOL RE-ENTRY

Spring and summer came and went at a neck-breaking speed. Mike got his feet wet at a law firm downtown. VC worked long hours at the lumberyard unloading boxcars and on weekends gave free lessons on self-defence at the community center. Most Sunday afternoons were basketball days. He, Mike and friends never missed a good, hard-fought, friendly and sweaty game with the emphasis always on friendly.

Sunny, warm, Monday afternoon of the Labour Day weekend, the last such amnesty before Thanksgiving. Vagabond leaves in their pre-golden hues ride the early winds of change, late dandelions re-bloom revivifying green lawns one last time, and black-capped chickadees acrobatically flip through small branches for that elusive afternoon treat.

Basketball under his arm, VC walks alongside his most trusted and only cousin Mike to the nearby court. Cut from the same cloth of honesty, integrity and good will, neither ever strayed from their roots of justice and the courage to uphold it.

"Mike," says VC, "I must apologize."

"For what, brother?"

"The focus of these past few months has been on me, and I have neglected to ask about you. How is law? Will you be the consigliere for Uncle Guido?" and both laugh.

"Graduated top of the class, VC."

"That's terrific Mike, expect nothing less. And how is Maryanne?"

"Well, VC, may as well tell you. It's a story of B and D."

"B and D?" asks VC.

"Life as I see it is about Being and Doing. You, for instance, looked at life primarily within the construct of Doing, of achieving set goals, and that's perfectly fine. I also looked at life as Doing, as achieving goals as we all should, with the proviso we give as much attention, if not more so, to Being."

"Meaning?"

"Maryanne is not ready for Being, as in love, took the path of Doing, relocated to the west coast to study and our Being died of slow abandonment. I can do Being and Doing as long as the balance is in favour of Being. Good person, Maryanne, and I miss her. Regrettably we allowed the forces of Doing to reign over the splendor of Being, and we will never know."

"I am sorry to hear that, Mike, I know how much you two meant to each other."

"Thanks, VC, the stars didn't quite line up for either of us this time, but you, my dear cousin, are now at a point of Being, as in a relationship, as in love."

"I'm not sure love is going to simply fall on my head, Mike."

"It's not your head that needs a hit, VC, it's your heart."

They reach the court, and instead of playing, both sit inside the basketball court against the wire fence and continue talking.

"Big day tomorrow," says Mike.

"Indeed."

"Butterflies?"

"A few."

"Normal."

After a brief silence, Mike asks, "What was it like being in a coma? Do you remember anything?"

"Some, but not sure what was real and what wasn't."

"As in…"

"As in me opening my eyes and seeing Mom and Dad sitting next to me. It felt like a rebirth, and somewhere in the transition I heard your voice, were you there too?"

"I had just entered the room."

"Fascinating, I feel you were there all along."

"What else do you recall?"

"I recall a group of people standing next to my bed and referring to me as Mr. C. Who is Mr. C.?"

"Did you know any of them?"

"That's the thing, Mike, I felt I did, but I'm not quite sure."

"Any romantic adventures while you were out there?"

"I don't believe so, but there was this peculiar pull towards school and it felt good," replies VC while slowly standing up looking at the approaching group. "Who are these guys?" he says.

Mike sees the group of high-school age young men coming towards them, immediately stands and says, "Don't know, maybe they're looking to play."

"Somehow I don't get that feeling."

"Whatever it is VC, we, especially you, can't get into it."

The group stops, the bully moves closer, chest puffed up and says, "Are yous wops or heebs?"

VC and Mike look at each other and VC says, "What's it to you?"

Mike immediately steps between them and says, "How about a game, fellas. Five of you, two of us, we'll start three on three and one can sub, what do you think?"

"Fuck you," replies the bully.

"Not quite the answer I was expecting," replies Mike.

"Fuck you, asshole," the bully says.

"Look, fellas, we don't want any trouble, we just want to play some ball and you're welcome to join us. Should you choose not to, that's fine, just walk away, but if your intention is to make things worse, I must disclose, we are proficient in boxing and martial arts, so do yourselves and us a big favor and let us be, okay?" says Mike.

The bully kicks the basketball into the field and says, "Let's see what you got, kung fu man," and throws a punch that fails to connect. Mike backs up and says, "Whoa fella, didn't you hear what I said? We don't want any trouble."

The bully comes at him again and Mike's powerful kick to the head connects causing the bully to stagger backwards, then he says, "Fellas, let's call it a day, okay? C'mon, VC, let's get out of here."

"This is not right, Mike."

"I know it's not right, but you're still getting over your injury, so let's just go."

The bully bleeding from his nose heard and says, "What do we have here, a lame duck pussy and some kind of kung fu asshole."

VC stopped, but Mike kept pushing him towards the exit. Then they heard, "Thought so, you fucking wops, tell your sister I said hello," followed by laughter from the group.

VC turns, pulls away from Mike, walks up to the bully and says, "Apologize or I'll shatter your jaw."

"Hit a nerve, did I," replies the bully, grinning, and takes a swing, but a fast, powerful strike from VC, as warned, broke his jaw and the brawl began.

Mike and VC tried ending it several times by backing away, but they kept coming. In the end, Mike and VC were the only two standing.

Mike looks at VC and asks, "You, okay?"

"I'm fine, you?"

Mike nods, picks up the basketball, and again asks if he was okay. "I'm fine, Mike, let's go before the cops show up."

They look back and on the ground in some considerable pain were the five boys who, with a more welcoming attitude, could have enjoyed a friendly game of basketball on a pleasant sunny afternoon.

"I shouldn't have let you get involved, VC."

"We tried, Mike, but there is painful history I can't shake sometime."

"Referring to your first day of school in Canada?"

"And subsequent days. Three weeks after we landed, my first day of school in this strange and often inhospitable land ... eleven years old, you lived uptown, no friends, there I was alone in the schoolyard leaning against the wall waiting for the bell when some thought I was standing on their little patch of dirt, so this punk ass kid and his two cronies came up and started hassling me, nobody did anything, so I did, got a fat lip and a few bruises but I decked all three, was taken to the principal's office, given the strap on both hands and sent home. I did have a choice, then I asked myself, what if I let them continue intimidating me? What would after school look like for me? or tomorrow? or the next day? So, I did what I had to do, Mike. High school? Well, not much changed there, it got to the point that if I didn't leave, I was going to get myself into big trouble, and you were a great help steering me towards taking my anger out in the ring as you did with karate."

"And look at how that turned out," replies Mike.

"Mike, what happened to me is no one's fault. This incident today no longer angers me as much as it saddens me as I continue asking myself, when will *all* good fists rise against injustice? Then and only then can we bury hate instead of each other."

"Evil triumphs..." Mike says to which VC adds, "'*When good men and women do nothing*.' We were raised to never look the other way Mike, that's who we are."

"I was born and raised here, VC, and get the same treatment."

"Not surprised, Mike. Imagine what people of different cultures, races, particularly the visible minorities must go through every day. Fucked up world, Mike."

"That's why I went into law, VC, big downtown firm during the day, and community outreach on weekends."

"I'm going to work for Uncle Guido," says VC.

"Too late," replies Mike, "He already hired."

"Who?"

"Me," replies Mike.

They reach Mike's driveway, and he asks VC to show him the cut.

"What cut?"

"The cut you're hiding with your hand, the one that's bleeding through your t-shirt."

Mike looks at it and says, "Jesus, VC, we got to get you to the hospital."

"It's okay, Mike, I'll take care of it when I get home."

"No, VC, I'm taking you to the hospital. You cannot, I repeat, cannot do this anymore, it's too risky. Fuck those assholes, we should have walked away, we should have."

"I was protecting my head, Mike, didn't see the blade coming."

Mike presses his head against VC's and while both hide their tears says, "No more, VC, hear me, no more, I don't want to lose you. Okay? Okay?" VC nods and Mike says, "Wait here." Runs into the house, quickly returns, gets into his car and backs up. VC gets in, they drive off.

"Here," said Mike, "A towel and one on my best t-shirts. How are you feeling? any dizziness? Feel nauseous?"

"Feel okay, Mike."

Leaving the hospital, driving home, Mike says, "Surface cut, VC, but still, fifteen stitches. Little sore, but you should be able to go to school tomorrow, what do you think?"

"Wouldn't miss it, Mike."

Mike drops VC off at his house and says, "Call me when you can, and keep the t-shirt, looks good on you."

VC looks at the writing again. Peace. Love. Karate. Smiles and says, "Good stuff, Mike."

"I knew you'd like it, so, thinking of becoming a lawyer?"

VC places his hand on his wound and says, "I can't laugh, Mike."

"You know they're going to hit the roof."

"I know."

Mike drops him off at the end of his driveway, and before driving off, says, "No more, VC, no more, promise?"

VC nods and Mike adds, "Seriously, VC, if you can't do it for yourself or for me, do it for her."

"Pardon?"

"Wait until you meet her, she will change your life," replies Mike.

"Who?"

"You'll know."

VC smiles, waves and walks with some discomfort to the back of the house. There, to his surprise finds his parents sitting at the picnic table enjoying a coffee al fresco. He joins them and after a long, emotionally charged, upsetting exchange, VC leaves his speechless parents sitting on the bench, enters the house and walks directly to his bedroom. He slowly lies down on his bed trying to suppress the inevitable but can't. Tears eventually pause and he falls asleep, only to be wakened by his father standing in the doorway asking him if he could join them for dinner.

Dinner was less of a rehash of the incident and more focused on the day to come. After dinner, while Sarah is changing the bandages, Augie looks at the wound and says, "Nasty cut, it'll heal quickly. Take my car tomorrow, I'll go in with Mom."

"Thanks, Dad, I think I will."

"Lie still, VC, Augie, the ticker bandage please."

When done, Sarah says, "Walk slowly tomorrow, should be fine, could have been worse, VC, a lot worse."

MO AND VC

The fall of nineteen sixty-six was the year when their singular-purpose hearts led them to each other. They both grabbed the same stalwart life branch over the raging waters of stop-start relationships and pulled each other safely to shore.

Once on solid ground, with ancestral resolve from the mighty Romans and that of formidable Gaels warriors firmly imbedded in their genetic make-up, embracing a true lifelong commitment to each other was effortless and immediate.

INSTITUTE OF YORK

The week before school began VC met with both Mr. B., the principal, and Ms. E., the career counsellor, and felt genuinely welcomed.

Ms. E. looks at VC, they shake hands and she welcomes him to the school and to the new community.

"Read your file, from the big city, I see."

"Yes, ma'am."

"Like it here?"

"So far."

"Judging from your previous marks, albeit from a few years ago, impressive, you should have no difficulty doing the prep work for university. You mentioned you wished to focus on lit courses, correct?"

"Yes, I do, ma'am," he replies.

"Ms. E. will do."

VC nods and Ms. E. continues, "You're very strong in math and sciences, you sure you don't want to continue with those courses?"

"Although I enjoyed those courses, I do feel my interests have changed, Ms. E."

"Very well then, you'll find all you need in this package, courses, programs, schedules. Any questions, do not hesitate. Mr. B. is expecting you in the main office."

She stands, shakes VC's hand and says, "Again, welcome to our York Institute, Mr. C., and we wish you a very successful year."

"Thank you, Ms. E., Please, VC is fine."

"Very well, do you speak Italian, VC?"

"Yes, I do."

"In bocca al lupo," she says smiling.

"Thank you for the good wishes, Ms. E.," he replies. "Your Italian is remarkable."

"As they say, lingua Toscana in bocca Romana," she says with a smile.

"So true, the ever-romantic Italian language on the lips of a Roman."

"Is your family originally from Rome?" she asks.

"Yes, and yours?"

"Born and raised in Canada."

"Where did you study Italian?"

"I did my Masters at the University of Siena, International Studies, a stone's throw from Montepulciano, whose beauty is a feast for the senses. Beautiful, beautiful country, miss it. Someday."

"You will, Ms. E.," he says while opening the door.

"Thank you, VC."

In Mr. B.'s office, sitting up straight, perspiration in check and heart rate soon to be … he hoped. "It has been a while," he thought, "Deep breaths, VC, deep breaths."

"Welcome to our school, VC, and congratulations, we don't have many that return, certainly not after a highly successful career, albeit too short, as yours. Some feel you could have been a real contender, as the saying goes."

"Thank you, sir, life does have a way of bending straight lines."

"And if I may, straightening bent ones," replies Mr. B.

"Indeed."

"As you know, our Institute is a university preparatory school, high academic standards, well balanced with arts and athletics, and zero tolerance for unruly behaviour. I appreciate the fact that returning may not be easy, but I am confident you'll address any obstacles in a sensible manner, yes?"

"Yes sir. I want to be here and graduate from here, and thank you for giving me the opportunity."

"You're very welcome. Before you go, are you planning on keeping your hair long?"

THE FIRST DAY AT YORK

On the first day of school, he could have driven his one and only gift to himself for the years spent in the ring, but he didn't. He wanted to fly under the radar and in view of his recent injury chose to take his dad's car, leaving his brand-new, dark metallic green 1966 Mustang Shelby GT-350 Fastback under a soft cover in the garage. A much beloved car that Shelby, it was his car, and although not as quick as the GT 500 KR or the Cobras, it was, as he, unassuming but with one hell of a powerful iron heart under the hood.

"Nothing compares with the intoxicating sonorous, throaty burble of a V8 Mustang. Detroit iron, American muscle at its best," VC frequently thought during his persistently solo drives on open country roads. That treasured small block Shelby and four on the floor, when on rare occasion pushed, could hit sixty in mid-fives, and a quarter-mile in high thirteens. Not bad, not bad at all. There was only one addition that would make any of his drives perfect. No, no mods to an already great machine, but someone special sitting in it next to him.

Walking up the steps of the forty-year-old heritage building as just another student, his mind, as with his first fight, although eager and ready to go, still had to remind his legs that he couldn't face his opponent from the safety of his corner. Ready or not, he had to walk to the middle of the ring. Ready or not, he had to re-enter school, and ready or not, he had to relearn that particular walk up the steps, down a corridor and into a classroom, this time one filled with younger students.

He bravely enters the school building and stops in the middle of the foyer. It felt like the middle of a boxing ring, no one was throwing actual punches but he couldn't avoid feeling the imaginary combinations from passersby.

He walks towards the wall, stands and looks at his timetable … 9 a.m., English, room 211. Suddenly he feels a tap on his shoulder and immediately turns.

"Excuse me, are you lost?" she asks.

"Good morning," replies VC.

"Good morning. May I be of some help?" she asks, but all he could do is stare at her.

"Do I know you?" he asks.

"I don't know, do you?"

"I think so, maybe, don't know."

"You must be the new teacher."

"Teacher, no, no, I'm the new student."

"Really?"

"Yes."

"Well, new student, welcome."

"Thank you."

"New to the area?"

"Yes, we live on Peacham Crescent."

"Upscale, are you a snob?"

"No, no, of course not. Came from downtown, my Uncle Lou is now a realtor and found us the house."

"Like the area so far?"

"So far."

The warning bell rings and she says, "We best get to class, what room?"

"Where is Room 211?"

"Normally on the second floor," she replies, smiling. "Take the stairs at the end of the hall, up a level, midway down the corridor and you have arrived, are you ready?"

"I think so."

"Then good luck," she says and begins walking away.

VC follows and says, "Wait, wait, my name is VC and you are?

"VC, does that stand for say, Velocity Cruising? Or Victoria Cross?"

VC smiles and says, "Whatever you want it to mean."

"And it's only your first day, my. I'm Mo and what took you so long?"

"Pleased to meet you, Mo, what took me so long?"

"Well, in case you haven't noticed, you do look just a tad out of place."

"What gave it away?"

"Your formal outfit and your short, short hair. An ultimatum from Mr. B. no less, but you didn't have to buzz it. You could have told him you played in a rock, no, an R & B band, or blues, you have more a blues, jazz persona, drummer quite likely, and your hair needed to be long."

"Really? Would that have worked?"

"No."

They both smile and he asks, "Tell me, Mo is an abbreviation for…"

"Moreen."

"Pleasure to meet you, Moreen…"

"You can call me Mo."

"Very well, where are you off to?"

"Class, silly."

"Yes, I know, but what room?"

"Room 210, class 13A1, and you, my lost friend, if you're in 211, you must be in the other, albeit less, 13A2."

"Yes, right next to each other, may I walk with you?"

Mo looks at VC, and after a brief silence says, "If you wish, are you able to walk up the stairs?"

"Of course, what makes you ask?"

"In case you haven't noticed, you're walking rather awkwardly."

"A little, it's an old sports injury, acts up once in a while," he replies.

"Are you an athlete?"

"Of sorts. You?"

"Love the piano, but swim competitively."

"Piano is good, I like piano too, piano, bass and drums, ideal trio, but you're a competitive swimmer, quite an accomplishment."

"Takes a lot of training," she says, waiting for him to catch up, and when he does, she asks, "The scars around your eyes, been in a few fights? Box? Martial arts?"

"You are so astute."

"I am. Well, here we are," she says approaching her room. She stops, looks back at him and says, "Thanks for walking with me, VC."

"My pleasure, and thank you."

Standing at the entrance to her room, looking profoundly at each other, he reaches for her hand. They touch, hold, and he immediately feels a most unusual sensation, a subtle life energy force, a warmth, never felt before. She leads his mesmerized stare from her eyes to their hands, he apologizes profusely while slowly releasing his grip. She smiles and says, "One small suggestion."

"Yes, please."

"Lose the tie."

"Thank you," he replies and while quickly removing his tie, says, "By the way…" but before he could ask her if he could see her later, she had entered her room, closing the door behind her.

He walks into his class just as his teacher was about to close the door. The teacher looks at him and says, "You're late," but VC walks past her without saying a word, not out of disrespect, but because he was totally preoccupied thinking of Mo. While trying to sit down comfortably, he realizes what the teacher had said, stands and says, "Sorry, ma'am," a comment that prompted laughter by some jocks, peculiar looks by some girls, and indifference by the rest.

Lunch came, and after he looked and couldn't find Mo anywhere, he walks out to the football field and sits alone on the bleachers until the next bell.

At the end of the day, he waits outside room 210 for Mo, but she never appears. He looks inside the room and sees a student writing on the board.

He enters and says, "Excuse me, has Mo left?"

The girl turns and asks, "Are you VC?"

Surprised that someone other than Mo actually knew his name, replies, "Yes, I am, and you are?"

"I'm Martha, Moreen's friend. She told me the new student with a buzz cut may be dropping by," she replies while walking towards him.

"Has she left?"

"Her father picked her up just before lunch, they have an appointment with her specialist."

"Is she all right?"

"I'll let her answer that question."

"Will she be back tomorrow?"

"Possibly, but I'll tell her you were asking."

"May I call her?"

"I'll let her know you were asking of her, now if you'll excuse me, I must finish putting tomorrow's quiz on the board."

"Of course, I'm sorry, thank you."

"Welcome to our school, I'm sure you'll like it here. Careful going down the stairs," she says and returns to the board.

"Thank you, nice meeting you too," he replies and leaves.

"Mo seems so nice," he thought, walking through the student parking lot at the back of the school towards his father's car, looks back at the school and thinks, "I like her, like her a lot."

VC's first day back at school was nothing he ever imagined. Teachers are teachers, students are students, but Mo, he did not expect to meet someone as captivating as Mo, someone with whom he could so naturally engage, easily relate and fall in love.

That night at the dinner table, Sarah asks VC about his first day at school.

"Yes, son, how was your first day back?" adds Augie.

"Interesting, uplifting, I want to go in early tomorrow," he replies.

"Our son, the comedian," says Augie.

"So, who is she?" asks Sarah.

"Mom, how did you know?"

"Ask your father how I know."

"Dad, how does mom know?"

"Don't ask, she just knows."

"So?" says Sarah.

"Well, I met a wonderful, witty, and bright girl on my way to class."

"And?" asks Sarah.

"There I was, standing in the middle of the hallway looking perplexed when she came up to me and asked if I was lost, to which I answered yes, and she showed me the way to my first class that happened to be next door to hers."

"If I may, what was so peculiar about the encounter?" asks Augie.

"Strangely, I felt I knew her, maybe in a dream or something, but there was a calmness about her, an aura of kindness, of good will. Anyway, I felt truly wakened to the possibility of a whole new world for me this year."

"We hope so, son," he replies.

"Then I looked for her at recess and was told by her friend Martha that Mo, her name is Mo, stands for Moreen, had left for a medical appointment."

"Hopefully nothing serious," says Sarah.

"I hope not, I like her. You know, I feel as if I've always known her, yet I just met her, today, at school of all places."

Sarah places her hand on her son's and says, "A great first day, VC."

Augie stands, takes a glass from the hutch, places it in front of VC and pours their favourite full-bodied red from the Tuscany region. They stand, raise their glass and Augie says, "I know you only sip on special occasions, son, and this, as we all agree, is such an occasion."

September came and went. VC immersed himself totally in his courses, and the few verbal skirmishes with some of the boys were frequently diffused with VC respectfully walking away. The word that he had been a professional boxer kept most wannabes on the sidelines, but there was always that overly cocky gunslinger aka the school bully with exaggerated fighting skills trying to prove that his dick is bigger than his fist, the type who, VC knew, sooner or later would have to have a face-to-face at the O.K. corral. And, like that legendary shootout in Tombstone, Arizona, on October 26, 1881, if engaged in, it would also be over in thirty seconds, but for now he had to walk away. VC's efforts were now essentially on his studies and his sole preoccupation was with Mo and her state of health.

Being unable to speak with or see her only heightened his longing for her. He often communicated with Martha and she kept both updated on each other's status, but that was not enough.

"Still not a good time to see or speak with her?" he asks Martha on an early fall Friday afternoon while walking out of the school.

"Not just yet, VC, but she said to tell you, it will be soon."

"Can you please tell her I miss her, give her this get-well card?"

"I will, VC. Review your notes, standardized tests on Monday, but I'm sure you'll ace them."

"Thanks, Martha, you too."

The only time VC joyfully hit the canvas was when he first saw Mo. His heart pounded, legs trembled, and vision blurred, but he felt alive. He couldn't identify the type of punches being delivered, but courageously continued walking to the centre of the ring. Once there, she looked deeply into his eyes and his arms dropped. His heart now exposed and defenceless, she smiled and delivered the haymaker. He went down for the count, closed his eyes, smiled, happily stayed down and said to himself, "This is where I want to be."

Then he asked, "What exactly happened? Have I died, gone to heaven, met Mo, lost her and now I find myself back in hell?" *Throw cold water on your face, VC. You may be new at this, but she's not gone and you're not dead, so get back in the ring. How? You'll figure it out.*

It was mid-October, on a Friday afternoon, the senior team was playing basketball against the teachers, a friendly fund-raising match, and VC, now in top physical condition and coming just under the age limit, was granted permission to play.

Going into the third quarter, teachers leading by six ... by eight. VC quickly takes the ball up into the teachers' territory, sets up the play, passes, and as he positioned himself for a possible shot, he looks up at the balcony, sees Mo, and his heart immediately hits the red line. His legs lock and he stands still.

Is it her? Is it really her? Is she really here watching the game? I must be imagining it? No, I'm not; it is her, it's Mo!

He looks closely and next to Martha stands a tall young woman with deep blue eyes and short blonde hair smiling and discreetly waving at him.

He regains some composure but too late to catch the hard pass. The ball hits him squarely in the face. Immediately, his eyes water, feels blood coming down and instantly pinches his nose, walks to the bench and sits down. He takes a towel, wipes blood and sweat from his face, looks up at Mo and both smile.

The ice pack placed on the back of his neck helped, and he was soon ready to go back in the game. His coach nods, VC places the blood-stained towel under the bench, stands, looks up and sees Mo smiling. He walks up to the time keeper and is subbed in.

After the game, Mo waits down the hall from the change room as he so desperately wished she would. Several players come out, acknowledge her and walk on. Then Damien and two of his friends come into the school from the side entrance and stop in front of her.

"Can't say I missed you," says Damien while grinning.

"The feeling is mutual, airhead," she replies.

"So, who are you waiting for?"

"None of your business."

"Probably waiting for that new guy, what's his name?" said Tommy, one of Damien's friends.

"Are you going to the fall dance?" Damien asks.

"Drop dead," she quickly answers.

"Want to be my date?" he asks, turning and smiling at his friends.

"You must be delusional if you think I would ever go anywhere with you, delusional, want me to explain what it means?" she replies.

Damien grabs her arm, causing her books to fall to the floor. "I know what it means, and you're a little too smart for your own good," he states, clenching his teeth.

"How were the three of you ever permitted to attend this school? Pre–Mr. B., no doubt. Now, let go of my arm if you know what's good for you."

"Or what, you're going to hit me?" he laughs. "Or are you going to get your father after me?" all laugh.

"I don't have to!" she replies and attempts to kick him in the groin, but Damien steps back and she misses. He lifts his arm to strike her, when suddenly he hears VC yell from down the hall to let her go.

Damien stops, looks, and sees VC and Mike walking towards them. VC stops next to Mo and asks her if she was all right.

"I'm fine, thanks, VC," she replies.

"Get lost, this is none of your business," Damien says to VC.

"But it is my business."

"And how do you figure that, are you her boyfriend?" asks Damien and VC replies, to everyone's surprise, perhaps not to everyone, "As a matter of fact, I am."

"Well, I don't like you," Damien says.

"I can say the feeling is mutual," replies VC.

Damien looks at his friends and says "Big shot, this new guy, eh fellows."

VC remains silent. Mike gently nudges Mo out of the way and flanks VC.

"Who the hell are you?" asks Damien.

Mike looks directly at Damien and says, "I don't know what your problem is, and frankly I don't care. So, leave us alone, let's call it a day and go our separate ways."

VC looks at Mo, she nods, he relaxes his stance, loosens his fists, and says, "Okay."

"Figures," says Damien.

VC steps closer to Damien, Mike pulls him back and Mo says, "C'mon, VC, let's go home."

"Do you know who Benjamin Disraeli is?" asks VC.

"What is this, a history class? Who is he, some famous Jew or something? Is he coming to this fight too?" replies Damien.

"Well," Mike continues, "He's not coming to this fight, he's got more important things to do, besides there isn't going to be a fight, right, VC?"

"You think you're funny, don't you?"

"Look," says Mike, "Just trying to diffuse a tense situation that could turn pretty ugly fast."

"If I may, Disraeli once said, 'Courage is fire, and bullying is just smoke,'" says VC while picking up Mo's books and his gym bag.

"This is not over," says Damien.

"As far as I'm concerned, it is and should be. We can still walk away and should while we can. We are never going to be friends, but no need to be enemies. We can coexist, let's just stay clear of each other," replies VC, and as the three walk away, midway down the hall towards the exit, they hear Damien say, "You're all washed up, pretty boy."

They continue ignoring Damien's incendiary remarks while walking away, and VC says, "I'm so happy to see you Mo, you have no idea. Are you all right?"

"Much better thanks, and it's so nice to see you too."

"This is my cousin Mike, Mike this is Mo," says VC.

"Pleased to meet you, Mo," says Mike and while shaking her hand adds, "He's told me so much about you."

"Really?" replies Mo.

"Yes, all good, Mo, actually exceptionally so."

"And how would you know, VC?" she asks and he smiles.

"I asked him the same question, and his reply was simply, I just know," says Mike.

"You just know?" she asks VC.

"Something to that effect," he replies.

"Strangely, I seem to feel the same way," she says.

"Okay then, is this my cue to, you know, leave?" asks Mike.

"Don't be silly, Mike," she says.

Mo intuitively places her arm under VC's and all three continue walking, ignoring the unending verbiage from the other end of the hall.

"I'm sorry you had to witness all that nonsense, Mo, really am," says VC.

"I understand, VC and you two handled it very well. Consider other students that are not able to defend themselves like you two, or too afraid to tell their parents or their teachers, think of what kind of days they have. Kick Damien and his likeminded friends out, I say."

"Believe me, Mo, Mike and I are with you."

"For sure, VC, and Mo, you're right, just think of how many students have been victimized by the likes of Damien and his friends."

"And now, Mo, how have you been?" asks a most exuberant VC.

"I'm fine, VC, really, you?"

"Good, good."

"So, Mike, career in law I hear," she says.

"Yes, enjoying it very much."

"Great lawyer in the making, no doubt."

"Thank you, Mo."

"Enjoyed the game?"

"I did, and good game, VC, too bad about the nose, you would likely feel no pain had your team not lost … and by one point!"

"Them's the breaks, Mike."

"Maybe, but that last foul sealed your team's fate."

"Next time, VC," says Mo.

Mike stops, looks at VC's nose and says, "Here let me take a look at your nose, VC." He grabs VC's nose tightly, and with a quick twist, sets it back in place.

"Shit … Mike," says VC. "Sorry, Mo."

Mo looks at the two of them and says, "Well done, Mike, you okay, VC?"

"I think so, thanks a lot, Mike," says VC while wiping fresh blood trickling from his nose.

Mike looks and says, "You'll be fine."

VC pockets his handkerchief, and the three resume walking.

"Mike is one of the judges at the black belt tournament on Sunday, Shodan, first dan. Mo is a champion swimmer, not sure about any self-defence stuff," says VC.

"Not to worry, Mo, VC can help, besides from what I saw, you already know where to aim. If I may, it doesn't have to be hard, just swift."

"Thanks, Mike, will keep that in mind, besides, my dad taught me a few things."

"Proud dad no doubt, keeping his precious daughter safe," says VC.

"I think so."

The three exit the front door and are immediately drawn to the flashing lights across the street where they see Damien and his two friends getting into the back seat of a police cruiser.

"I'm sure it's not for skipping church," Mo says and the three laugh.

"Cool fall evening, you two want a ride?" asks Mike.

VC looks at Mo and she says, "Thanks for the offer, Mike, we'll be fine."

"Thanks, Mike, we're good," replies VC.

"Again, pleasure meeting you, Mo," says Mike, and walks towards his car.

"Pleasure meeting you as well, Mike, goodnight."

THE WALK HOME

Mo places her arm under VC's and both begin walking away from the school and in the direction of her house.

"I cannot tell you enough how happy I am to see you," he says.

"I am so happy to see you too, VC, missed me?"

"I did, and the thought of never seeing you again, it was just … just…"

"Unbearable?" she adds.

"Yes, unbearable," he replies holding her tighter, adding, "So what have you been doing these past few months?"

"Speaking with Martha about you every day and keeping up with my assignments. You?"

"I always look forward to speaking with Martha, about you of course, but she is so clever, gives me just enough information so not to break confidentiality, as long as I know you're okay, that's all that matters."

"You really care about me."

"I do, Mo, and this is no flash in the pan, I really care about you."

"I feel the same way about you, VC."

"So, keeping up with your assignments?"

"Actually, I find myself way ahead in all subjects."

"You're beautiful, Mo."

"Thank you, VC, so are you."

"I don't mean just in looks," he says.

"I know what you mean. Your routine?"

"Yes, so, after school, practice, then straight home, hit the books, work out, still do some road work, good for the heart you know."

"I do. Many things are good for the heart. Love is exceptionally good for the heart."

"In your opinion, is the heart the ultimate destination?"

"No, love is. Once in love, true love, your star among stars will shine forever."

"But it has to be true love."

"Of course. Ever look up at the night sky and notice some stars are brighter than others?"

"I have been looking at the night sky lately, and yes, I have noticed that some appear brighter than others. Is that because they are closer to earth? Or more powerful than the others?"

"Both. They are closer to earth because they have found their true love, hence together more powerful, hence brighter as they journey together to the heavens."

"I like that explanation, Mo, I do. It certainly makes much more sense than the scientific one."

"What does science know about matters of the heart, other than it pumps blood," she replies.

"What else, in your opinion, does the heart do?"

She stops, pulls him closer and looks directly into his eyes. After a brief silence he asks if this is all a dream. "It is not," she replies, and both resume walking.

"How is your health?" he asks.

"I had several lumps removed, more treatment this fall and so far, so good."

"Sorry to hear that, Mo, but you're a warrior and can wrestle any demon to the ground that comes your way. And if you need help, I'm here for you, I mean it."

"I know, and I thank you, but the unpredictability of this disease frightens me."

"It would frighten anyone, but here is what I see…"

"And what do you see," she asks, pulling him closer and looking affectionately into his eyes. He looks at her, leans and kisses her gently on her lips. They resume walking and she says, "What do you see?"

"I see a beautiful person who doesn't get defined by anything or anyone, I see a warrior, a slayer of demons, who carves her own path through the complexities of life; I see an oracle, a mentor in all that is life and love; I see a woman I hardly know, yet I do know; and I see a companion without whom I would surely lose my way, and I feel so blessed to have her in my life."

He stops walking, looks at her and is about to speak, she embraces him and says, "Don't talk, just hold me tightly."

They embrace tightly for a while, then resume walking hand in hand and he says, "How do you explain this development in our relationship, so profound and so immediate?"

"Unexplainable, as yet anyway," she replies.

"So, we are not fictional characters in some romance novel? Aliens?"

"Just two people in love, VC, two people that have been blessed with the gift of the same compass, and for the very first time, I can genuinely feel I'm in love with another true heart."

"I too, and I am in awe, Mo, I am, and feel honoured, feel so special in a profound way, and in some mystifying way, I feel a sense of peace never felt before, and I know, it has everything to do with you, Mo."

"Thanks for the compliment, VC, but I'm sure what we're both feeling may be more complicated then either one of us can explain."

"Could be. Tell me more about you, your family."

"Very well. I am my father's daughter, named after my mother Moreen, it means 'great' in Gaelic and my grandmother's granddaughter, and we all miss Mom, sadly, she was killed in a motor vehicle accident, near the Castle in Edinburgh."

"I am so sorry, Mo, a tremendous loss no doubt. How did it happen?"

"Thank you, VC. It was a beautiful August morning, and Mom and I … walking hand in hand to the school supplies store. I was so excited about starting school, as we crossed the road a car … going too fast … Mom managed to push me back onto the sidewalk but she was hit and succumbed to her injuries."

"How sad, I am sorry, Mo," says VC, drying her tears with his hand.

"Thank you, VC."

"Gran, Mom's mom, and I were speaking of her just last Sunday, her birthday. Dad still has moments of darkness about it, and when he does, Gran in her wisdom reminds him that he won't be able to join Mom with all this darkness besieging him. He needs to walk the path of forgiveness, to which he replies, he has no intention of forgiving anyone for putting a hole in his chest."

"The road to forgiveness can be long and treacherous when the heart is under siege."

"Can also be the road to healing."

"True."

"Do you believe in God, VC?"

"I learn from all the virtuous teachings of those on whose shoulders we stand."

"And who may they be?"

"Our loved ones who have gone before us. I call upon them to light my path. Are they Gods? Do they collectively form the entity we believe to be God? I look at you and I feel so blessed. You can easily be a God, are you God?"

Mo smiles, kisses him on the cheek and says, "Tell me about your studies."

"Enjoying the courses. We're covering the works of Beckett, Ionesco, Pinter and many others, but I keep coming back to the works of Luigi Pirandello. In my view, he was the precursor of the Theatre of the Absurd, truly a creative artist, a genuine visionary with an uncanny aptitude for bridging what is, what is not, what it can be, what it should be, why it is and why it isn't. He *is* the Theatre, and most definitely my preferred author."

"Yes, I'm beginning to see why he would be."

"How so?"

"Well, you seem to be not too dissimilar from those aforementioned authors, mainly how you perceive characters on a page to be … so, so real, definitely out there, VC," she replies.

"You're very kind in saying that Mo … but wait, is that a compliment?"

"It is indeed a compliment."

"Thank you, Mo. You know, I must humbly disclose I have recently begun writing a tale on that plane of being, with characters having a strong voice regarding their path to realization."

"May I ask the title, do you have one?"

"I do, well, in a way."

"Tell me, oh bashful one, spell it out."

"'A-R-E Y-O-U M-E?'" he replies, smiling.

"Cute, VC. 'ARE YOU ME?' Is that the title?"

He nods and asks if she likes it. She nods but looks rather perturbed, to which he asks if she didn't approve.

"No, no, VC, I very much like the title, so personal, so, so straight to the heart, no, I'm trying to figure out how a prospective customer would go about buying a copy. I would imagine, said customer would perhaps shyly, ask the salesclerk in a manner much like someone purchasing personal items at a drugstore … said customer waits until all the other customers have left, tip-toes up to the clerk and says, in a deep voice of course, says, excuse me ma'am or sir, 'ARE YOU ME?' Where is the paddy wagon when you need it, right?"

VC looks at Mo in amazement, and asks, "Do you play poker?"

"Never touch the stuff. So, VC, are you considering writing full time?"

"Who are you?" he asks.

"No, no, love, it's Are You Me?"

"How's this, I LOVE YOU!"

"I can live with that, sure."

"By the way, aren't you cold?"

"Thanks, VC, I'm fine. You?"

"How can I possibly be cold standing next to you."

"Correct answer. I want to ask you, I know you and some like-minded others meet twice a week with Miss Flynn on the stage to discuss the Theatre of the Absurd and speaking of such, is that the focus of your little group or is it Miss Flynn?"

"As you know, Miss Flynn is an authority on the concept."

"Oh, I'm sure she's an authority on many a concept."

She then turns, faces him and says, "VC, place your lips gently on mine and kiss me."

"Right now? In front of your house?"

"No, next week, on the moon. Here and now, my darling," she replies, pulling him closer, and after a long, soft kiss Mo asks, "How did we get here?"

"We walked."

"Brilliant, VC," she replies and both burst into laughter, bringing tears to their eyes.

They resume walking in silence for a while then she says, "You and Mike are a breath of fresh air, VC."

"You mean, being of Italian descent, we exude that much sought-after Continental flare easily recognizable, but not necessarily embraced in a stuffy Victorian neighbourhood?"

"Imagine what an exceptional member of a supreme Scottish clan, more precisely the Walker clan, could add to that Continental flare," she replies.

"That combination could easily take us to the moon," he replies.

"And beyond," she adds.

"I so feel I have always known you, Mo, and I like feeling that way."

"I have never been as happy as I am now, VC."

Approaching her house he asks, "Do you want to go in or shall we walk speedily by your house, again." She pinches his arm, smiles and they continue walking.

"I meant to ask you, how is it that we don't have any classes together?" he asks.

"Simple, you're somewhat of a renaissance man, immersed in art and literature, you know, the bird courses, and I'm in math and science, you know, the brainy courses."

"That makes sense. What led you to science?"

"Gravitational pull," she answers.

"Gravitational pull, does it also apply to love?" he asks.

"Well, in my view, Newton's law doesn't go far enough, it does not include the heart, and it should."

"I agree."

"I mean, does the heart care whether the ball you threw up in the air comes back down or not? Really?"

"Unless, of course, it's a balloon with congratulatory phrases on it, like Happy Birthday. By the way, when is your birthday?"

"Nice try on the birthday question, but my lips are sealed."

"And very nice lips at that, particularly that deliciously corpulent, sumptuous and courageous lower lip," he says, and quickly kisses her.

"I have a question," she says.

"Shoot."

"Clearly, you're a couple of years older, what happened?"

"I was born earlier than you."

"Brilliant, VC, so what happened?"

"I left school to pursue a boxing career, got injured, went into a coma, saw the light, came out of the coma, and here I am."

Mo stops, looks at him and with angst in her voice says "Pardon? Coma? How dreadful, how did it happen? How long were you in a coma?"

"A super-sized thesaurus with riveted metal corners fell on my head," he answers, smiling.

"Stop it, seriously, VC, what happened?"

"All right, there once was a young man in a coma," he says, smiling. Mo smacks him on his arm, he smiles and says, "All right, true story, there was once a famous boxer and his lady, you know, one of those rags to riches tales."

"Aren't they all? Untiring plot, and who knows, there may be a movie from them scribbles, maybe two, or three or … certainly eight at the very least. Anyway, you have a five-minute interlude to tell me of your rags to riches, then must return to telling me about the coma, agreed?"

"Yes."

"All right then, knock yourself out, oops, sorry, poor choice of words, go Kid," replies Mo, smiling.

"How did you know I was known as the Kid?"

"Gravitational, knowledge just comes to me," she replies smiling.

 "I bet, anyway, I'm this great boxer see, aka the Gladiator…"

"Should I refer to you as Mr. Gladiator?"

"You may. So, the Gladiator…"

"By the way, Mr. Gladiator, it's been done," Mo adds quickly, "The lions won, and about time, too."

"All right, next, so, I'm this great boxer aka the Roman Warrior, has it been done?" he asks.

"Don't think so, but I'm sure it's in the works somewhere with umpteen sequels, no doubt."

"I'm in this championship match, and you would be my dame cheering me on ringside."

"Are we in Casablanca?" she asks.

"No, in downtown Las Vegas," he replies.

"Casablanca or no fantasy," she says.

"All right, Casablanca it is. So, we turned Rick's bar into a boxing ring…"

"Pretty small place for a boxing ring, don't you think?" she says.

"Yes, but I can work the tight corners," he replies.

"I'm sure you can. Tell me, how's your Shelby?"

"How did you know I own a Shelby?"

"Gravitational."

"This gravitational all-knowing thing you possess, although terrifying, is growing on me."

"I bet," she says smiling, "Stay with the story."

"I'll try, but this gravitational pull is just, just too strong … how's this, *Here's looking at you, Kid.*"

"Just stay with the story, Mr. Kid," she replies.

"All right, so, back in the groove," he says.

"Yes, so tell me, in this, shall we say, shady setting, are there any you know, dames, with googly eyes, bright ruby red lips all puckered up, winking and blinking their false lashes seductively at their man, you being THE man of course, the great pugilist, right? Am I getting it right?"

"Yes and no. Yes to googly eyes, and no to dames winking at me," he replies.

"All right then, do you miss all the celebratory shenanigans that normally follow a win?"

"Never participated."

"Right. On to floozies. Let me understand floozies, I imagine you came across a few of those in your day as a young, virile and handsome combatant."

"I'm sure floozies are nice people, just not for me, and they always accompanied Suits smoking big cigars, never liked Suits or big cigars."

"Really?"

VC nods, "Yes, really. I got in the ring, boxed and after listening to my Uncle Lou for an hour following the fight, showered, got dressed and went home."

"A typical day at the office type of scenario?" she asks. "Tell me, how old were you when you first started boxing?"

"Not long after we arrived to Canada. Immigrants are always easy targets, new kid, gave a few, took a few, lots of anger to work out and the street was not the place, so I started working out at my uncle's gym."

"Do you still carry a lot of that anger?"

"At first, but learned that if you don't control anger, it controls you. Relentless anger doesn't motivate, it skews perception and behaviour follows accordingly. If you need anger as a motivator, you're relying on the wrong emotion. Boxing and karate taught me how to be methodical, disciplined, and how to park the anger … and how to walk away with dignity."

"Did your parents speak English when you came here?"

"Yes, fluently."

"Tell me more about your family."

"My father worked in Foreign Affairs with the Italian government. Incidentally, that's where he met my mother, and both speak multiple languages, including German. My father began learning it when he was a prisoner of war in Germany."

"Really?"

"Yes, my father, a captain in communications stationed in Trieste along with his younger brother, a lieutenant whom I'm named after, both at the same headquarters, but they did not fare very well."

"Why not?"

"Because like many others, they were men of conscience, and when they discovered classified information indicating their allies had committed atrocious acts, some were quickly silenced, others taken to prison camps."

"How in the world did they survive?"

"Some did, many didn't. In December 1944, a group of prisoners that included his brother was sent to the Russian front never to be seen again, and two weeks later, on a cold, blustery, snowy January night in 1945, my father, along with a small group of prisoners also destined for the Russian front, escaped, some were hunted down, some were killed, but some others, including my father and Mike's dad, Uncle Lou, got away, and here I am."

"Is humanity ever going to know peace?"

"Good question, Mo."

After several minutes walking in silence, firmly arm in arm, she says, "You should know that I, at our dinner table, following that fateful day in September, spoke about you."

"And what did you share?"

"I spoke of this charming new boy at school, that's you, my grandmother smiled and my father asked questions. The first of which was, how could I know you were thoughtful and considerate if we had just met? To which I replied, I just know. Now Gran seemed to understand, but Dad, well, he said he reserved judgement. Then surprisingly, at last Sunday's dinner an epiphany, he asked me if you and I had spoken, and of course I said not since the first day, to which he asked why you hadn't called, and I replied I did not want you to call me in my time of illness."

"What did he say to that?"

"He said I was deciding for you, and not to be so protective. Then he said that if I felt strongly about you, and you seemed kind and caring and were not a jock, musician, pothead or someone not anchored in reality, little did we know of you then, of course, I should take the lead and call you, and I would have, had I not returned Monday. I was shocked to hear my father speak that way, I think it was because he saw how I came alive when I spoke of you."

"You have a wonderful and caring family, Mo."

"I like to think so, VC, as you and yours, I'm sure"

They stop, face each other, she places her arms on his shoulders and asks, "Have you ever been in love before, VC?"

"No, never," he replies.

"Last year at this time, thinking of graduating, of university, of where my knight in shining armour was, and a year later here I am and here you are."

"Not sure of a knight in shiny armour, but I truly care about you, Mo, from first sight."

After walking in silence for a while, she says, "Tell me, VC, this remarkable force of unknown yet familiar quantity, this firestorm of true love … this unique path to our hearts that has lit up our lives with such adoring fury, what does it all mean?"

He stops, gently pushes back her hood, looks directly into her eyes and says, "In my humble opinion, it means we can now begin leading with one heart and speak with one voice."

They resume walking, she holds on tighter and says, "This has certainly been a night to remember, VC."

"No doubt about it, Mo."

"Do you dance?" she asks.

"I do."

"Are we going to the school dance?"

"Of course we are," he replies, "Casual?"

"Casual yes, but certainly more than jeans, white t-shirt and jacket."

"Well, I'll have you know that I own a dark pin-striped suit, actually it's my Sunday suit."

"Sunday suit, tailor-made no less."

"Tailor-made. Dark, thin-striped, single-breasted, wool blend, always vested, solid blue shirt, contrasting tie, belt, socks and shoes to match. Would that be too formal?"

"A smidgen too formal, yes."

"So, how about you?" he asks.

"I make my own clothes, I'll have you know."

"No kidding!"

"No kidding!"

"Who taught you?"

"After my mother's tragic passing, my grandmother taught me all things woman. She and my mother had sewn a beautiful little dress for my first day of school, but I never got to wear it. I did not go to school that entire year, and by the following September, the dress was too small. Gran offered to enlarge it, but I didn't want her to, it would not have been the same."

"I am sorry, Mo."

"Thank you, VC."

"What happened to the dress?"

"Gran kept it for me in case I get married someday and have a girl, then she can wear it on her first day of school."

"That is so moving, I'm sure that little girl would be so thrilled."

"Do you like children, VC?"

"Very much, why?"

"Just asking."

"So, you live with your father and grandmother?"

"Yes, with my father, Ferguson Walker, and my maternal grand-mother, Claire. My father is a good man, with a bit of an edge, but fair. He'll like you a lot, he likes people 'of substance' as he puts it. He's stationed at the West Precinct and will be receiving his ten-year pin this year, we're very proud of him."

"Also proud of you, I'm sure."

"He is."

They stop, face each other and their lips touch again ever so gently. They resume walking and stop in front of her house.

"How is it that someone as beautiful as you, clever, funny, and great to be with, is not being chased by every senior student in the school?" he asks.

"I kept it to a minimum, how about you?"

"Same."

"Why do you think that up to now we kept our social life consciously or subconsciously to a minimum?"

"Maybe someday we'll be able to answer that question," he replies.

"I must confess, I am seeing someone special," she says.

He stops, looks at her with apprehension and says, "Wait, pardon, are you?"

"Yes, you," she replies caressing his face.

"Thank you," he replies, takes her hand, kisses it, adding, "Is this the *beginning of a beautiful relationship*?"

Suddenly she pinches his cheeks with both hands, he smiles and says, "Yes, Mo, I am as real as you."

He then caresses her face and says, "It's getting colder, maybe you should go in or at least let them know you're here."

"I mentioned to Gran I may be late, besides they know exactly where we are."

"They do?"

"Yes, my father has parted the curtains in the basement window several times and Gran is watching from upstairs."

"See you tomorrow, then?" asks VC.

"No, no, let's go and sit in the enclosed porch, it's heated, it'll be fine, c'mon."

"You sure?"

"Of course I'm sure, c'mon."

Both walk in, Mo opens the door to the house, places her books on the floor, and loudly says, "Be in soon."

They sit close to each other on the settee, Mo leans over, kisses him and says, "We're fine, VC, sit back, relax, warm up."

They sit back, Mo rests her head on his shoulder and closes her eyes. Not long after, Gran is at the door with a tray of two cups of cocoa and homemade cookies. VC quickly stands, holds the door open and says, "Good evening, Gran."

Gran smiles, hands him the tray and says, "Good evening, young man, I'm Moreen's grandmother."

"Pleased to meet you, Moreen told me a great deal about you."

"Has she now."

"You're her heroine," he replies.

"I'm flattered, and she's ours. Not many of those left these days."

"That's for sure, I'm VC by the way."

They shake hands and Gran says, "Pleased to meet you, VC."

She looks at Moreen and as she opens the door to re-enter the house, Mr. Walker comes out, greets them, walks up to VC and says, "I'm Mr. Walker, VC."

"Pleased to meet you, sir," he replies, extending his hand.

They shake hands and Mr. Walker says, "Firm handshake, I like that."

"Thank you, sir."

He looks at Gran and says, "C'mon, Mom, let's go back inside and finish the game. Don't stay out too long."

"I won't, Dad."

"We won't," replies an anxious VC. "Thank you again for the cocoa and cookies."

"You're welcome," replies Gran. Mr. Walker follows her inside and closes the door behind him.

Mo looks at him, smiles and says, "They're wonderful."

"Yes they are, Mo, good, good people. I'm happy I met them."

Mo stares at him and, after a brief silence, asks, "Who exactly are you?"

"I ask the same of you, yet we seem to know who we are."

"And who are we?"

"We are two hearts speaking as one."

They hold hands tighter. She leans her head on his shoulder, both close their eyes and fall asleep. A brief time later, VC suddenly wakes and says, "Mo, we fell asleep, what time is it?"

"Eleven twenty-two," she replies.

"Eleven twenty-two? How do you know that?"

"There," she says, pointing to the clock on the wall.

He smiles. "And I should go, my lovely."

They stand, kiss softly and Mo asks, "How many times did we kiss tonight?"

"Not enough times," he answers.

"I must ask, I know, again, the way we feel, so quickly, so deeply, so genuine in such a short time, is this normal?"

"Normal for us, Mo."

"I am simply amazed."

"And I am simply speechless," he adds.

"Call me later?"

"Yes, but it might be too late to call, in case everyone is asleep."

"Not very likely, but thoughtful of you, first thing tomorrow?"

"First thing tomorrow."

Mo opens the door to the house, looks back at him and steps inside. VC picks up his gym bag and leaves. He reaches the sidewalk, looks back and sees Mo waving at him from the living room window, just as she had from the gym balcony hours before. He waves back, and as he approaches the bus stop in front of the school, he hears a car screeching to a halt behind him, turns and sees Mike.

"Eh, VC, frozen yet?"

"What are you doing here, Mike?"

"Came looking for you, get in."

VC gets in the car, thanks him and they drive away.

"I called close to eleven and Uncle Augie said you weren't home yet, so I got a little worried and came looking for you."

"Thanks, Mike, sorry I inconvenienced you."

"Don't give it a second thought, I often drive around late at night, cold, snowy, slippery roads, great fun." They look at each other and laugh.

"So how was your evening?"

"Unbelievable, Mike, really. Walked her home, met her family, gave her the engagement ring, sat around the kitchen table and planned the wedding."

"Not surprised," replies Mike.

"Really?"

"Look, VC, there are cosmos and then there are cosmos—this cosmos pertains only to you and Moreen."

"What are you saying?"

"Moreen radiates wisdom, intelligence, confidence, great sense of humour, boundless personality, is beautiful, and I'm sure very well liked at school, should be fending them off, but not seeing anyone, clearly, she's been waiting for that special one and that special one is you, my fine cousin. You. The same can be said about you, a Renaissance man of sorts, smart, not bad looking, unattached, and now that you two have found each other, you should marry and live happily ever after."

"I'm in love, Mike."

"I am very happy for you, cous, extremely happy, she seems to be such a unique woman, and if I may add, she never took her eyes off you."

"How did I get so lucky?"

"Not sure luck has anything to do with your encounter, and you know, you never took your eyes off her either. Meant to be, VC, meant to be."

Meanwhile, Mo walks into the kitchen where both Gran and her father are sitting having tea, and Gran asks if she wishes her dinner heated.

"Thanks Gran, not very hungry," she replies.

"Have some tea with us, soothes … everything," Gran says, smiling discreetly.

Mo joins them at the table, sits, hands around her warm cup, looks at her father and couldn't quite determine if it was a smile emerging from his rugged and weathered face or the suppressed apprehension that every parent must feel when their young begin spreading their wings, soon to soar.

"What do you think, Dad?"

"And you two just met, as in since this September? And have seldom seen or spoken to each other until now?" he asks.

"I know, Dad, we can't explain it either, all we know is how we feel towards each other. We shared so much about ourselves, our goals, our families, it all came so naturally."

"And you know all this by walking and talking tonight? Mind, you did walk for hours."

"Yes."

"Always trusted your judgement, Moreen, and if you believe, truly believe he's the one, you have my blessings," he says.

"He seems to be a fine young man," adds Gran.

"Respectful, caring, and his affection for you seems genuine, and that's what your mother, Gran and I wish for you, to be happy."

Mo turns to Gran and asks for her thoughts. "What is important is how you two feel about each other, and it's very clear to us, Moreen, that with all you're going through, you are so happy, it makes us so happy to see you embrace life the way you should, and what I find remarkable is that he, knowing all that, told you he loves you and will call you tomorrow."

"Thank you, Gran."

Then with tears in his eyes Ferguson adds, "There is a glow about you we have never seen before."

She stands, walks over and embraces him, then does the same with Gran. He stands and says, "You are an exceptional person, Moreen Walker, I don't know how it all came to be, and it really doesn't matter. Mom is smiling, Moreen."

"He asked me for coffee tomorrow night, but I said it would have to be next Saturday because you're doing a double shift this weekend and I should be here with Gran."

"You needn't do that, dear," replies Gran, "I'll be fine."

"I know, but I want to, Gran, so we settled on next Saturday, and I did say that I would have to be home by ten, that's when you leave for work next weekend and you don't like me to be out when you're not home, right?"

"Yes. I'm off the next two weekends after that, you may wish to consider inviting him over for dinner."

"Thanks, Dad, I will ask him. I know you two will get along greatly."

"I'm sure we will. Interesting ideas discussed out there."

"Mr. Walker! Have you been privy to the whole conversation?" asks Mo.

He raises his eyebrows and says, "Just enough to form an opinion."

Gran smiles and begins tidying up, to which he says while helping, "Might as well, Gran, I doubt anyone will be able to sleep tonight."

"I can help," says Mo.

"We won't be long, dear," says Gran, "Pleasant dreams."

"Thanks, Gran," and while walking out of the kitchen she turns and says, "By the way, Dad, are you going to look him up when you get to the station?"

"Don't have to," he replies.

It was the last week of October and the second full week Mo and VC had spent together at school. They met at different times of the day when schedules permitted and, of course, after school when he walked her home. Being physically together wasn't what gave the magnitude of the relationship away, it was the aura, and the notion that they both walked the corridors without touching the floor.

Friday of that week, VC had a doctor's appointment and his teachers knew he would be absent in the afternoon. He, unbeknownst to Mo, picked her up in his Mustang. Walking out of the front doors as she always did, she immediately sees VC, white t-shirt, jeans and sunglasses leaning against his ivy green 1966 Shelby GT 350. She stopped on the top step, looked at him and smiled. This was the first time he had taken the car to school, and there was no shortage of observers, particularly gearheads, enthusiasts and all-around car guys, who stopped, looked under the hood, walked around the car, and talked shop. Mo, observing VC proudly speaking of his prized possession, took her time.

Nearing the group, she smiles at VC, acknowledges those she knew, he opens the door for her, she settles in and he closes the door. He walks to the driver's side, waves at his car buddies, enters, fires up the Mustang and pulls away slowly … second a little faster, between third and fourth, midrange, she's a climber, but can't hit her true stride on city streets. Looks in the rear-view mirror, sees the car guys standing and waiting, floors it, the torque kicks in, tires spin creating just enough smoke for a loud cheer, then eases off and settles, "Burn and coast as they say," says Mo smiling.

"You are remarkable," he says.

"I am," she replies. Looks around the inside of the car and says, "I like this car, VC, I do." Looks at him, smiles and says, "You know, rolled-up sleeves with a bulging pack of smoke and trilby hat would have heightened the suspense." It was that remark that kept them laughing until he stopped in front of her house.

They got out of the car, and Mo walked around it several times, sat in the driver's seat and VC says, "Want to take it for a spin?"

"You're such a gem for picking me up in the Mustang, VC. I love this car, the colour, the burble, great choice."

"Can you drive a standard?"

"Of course I can, my dad taught me."

"All right then, take it for a spin."

"Oh, I don't know, VC."

"Of course, you do, c'mon, Mo."

"All right, just a short drive."

He hands her the keys and says, "So you know, you are the only other person to ever sit in this car, let alone drive it."

"Thank you, VC."

They get in the car, Mo adjusts the seat, mirrors, and her sunglasses, fires it up, revs it, and before moving says, "You know, VC, I could say hang on lover boy, rev it higher, skip first gear and slip it directly into second … tires squeal and smoke … grip and this beautiful machine would take us to curve at the end of the street in seconds … stomp on the brakes, Mustang drifts, I straighten her out, floor it coming out of the curve and we fly … but I won't."

"No doubt in my mind you could do just that, but then your father would have to bail us out … but what the heck, right?"

She smiles and says, "Hang on, lover boy."

Slowly turning onto the main road, gears in waiting, car set to sprint, VC says, "Are you going to take her out of first?"

"I thought you'd never ask," she replies. She floors it, tires grip, the car bolts like a thoroughbred, jumps second and shifts directly into third, whips her around the corner, brakes, drifts, and cruises. She taps the dashboard and says, "There, there, Shelby, settle, settle," looks at VC and smiles.

"She sure can fly in midrange."

"Yes, she can, maybe on the track someday," he replies.

Half an hour later and no speeding ticket she came to a screeching halt in front of her house.

She lets the engine idle for a few minutes, rpms settle, then turns it off. She removes her sunglasses, looks feverishly at VC and says, "Some machine baby, lots of torque, I feel so, so energized. Dad is at work and Gran volunteers at the hospital and won't be home for a while … want to come in?

They rush through the front doors, and to their surprise, Gran was heard greeting them from the living room.

"Gran, you're home," says a surprised Mo, to which she replies, "Yes, lots of volunteers today, finished early."

"Hi Gran, how are you?" says VC.

"I'm well, VC, you?"

"Well thanks, I am happy you're here because now I can show you my car," he replies.

Gran steps out onto the veranda, looks at the car and says, "Oh my, is that your car?"

"Yes, it is, like it?"

"I do, very much, Mustang Shelby GT 350, ivy green, Le Mans stripes … cool … let's see, 289 hi-po iron block, overhead, single Holley four barrel, four on the floor, dual exhaust, top speed 117 at 700 rpm, yeah, I can dig it."

Mo and VC slowly turn and look at each other in amazement. VC takes out the keys, and says "Would you like to take it for a spin, Gran?"

"I would, but you can't really take it to the limit around here, fine machine, six to sixty?" replies Gran.

"About that Gran, 15 quarter mile," he replies. "You know a lot about cars."

"Some, enjoy, but always drive safely."

"Thank you, always do," he replies.

"Don't forget dinner."

"Looking forward to it Gran, have a good evening."

"You too."

Mo walks VC to the car, and neither could stop smiling.

"She's incredible," says VC.

"Yes, she is, and she can drive a standard and fast, but hasn't driven since Mom passed," she says and he nods.

"Before you go, tell me about the appointment."

"All good, Mo, X-rays, MRI clear, blood tests normal, and heart pumping overtime, so, you know, I'm ready…"

"Great news VC, and ... take a cold shower."

"Love you."

"Love you, too. Drive carefully."

She walks into the house, hugs Gran, tells her how truly wonderful she is, and asks how she knew all about the Mustang, to which Gran answers, "Read it in the car magazines you left on the living room table."

COFFEE

Mo and VC walk hand in hand into Locale Dei Celebrati. All the tables are taken except the one at the very back he had reserved. They are warmly greeted by his good friend and son of the owner, Steven, and on the way to their table they walk past a wall of pictures of celebrities who had dined at the Locale. Mo sees a picture of VC and Steven, stops, looks at VC, he smiles and gently pulls her along. Steven shows them to their table, looks at Mo and says, "Moreen, is it?"

"Yes," she replies.

"Welcome," says Steven.

"Thank you, good to be here."

Once they're sitting, Steven takes a chair from the back and straddles it facing them.

"Good to see you, man. Feeling okay? School? All good?"

VC nods and replies, "Better than expected, much, much better."

"Happy for you, man, really great to see you, VC."

"Likewise, Steven, always good to see you."

"Moreen..." says Steven.

"Please call me Mo," she says.

"Thank you, I will. I know you're here only for dessert tonight, so you may wish to try our made-on-the-premises chocolate and vanilla ice cream with ingredients imported directly from Italy. We also have such eccentricities as torrone, pistachio, lemon and the like, but those are more appropriate when strolling on a hot summer evening in Frascati. I'll do the choccolate-vanilla creation for you here, and

VC will do a Negroni, which is gin, Campari and red vermouth, in Rome. Deal?"

"Deal," she replies, and all three smile.

"You should know, in order to maintain the utmost purity of taste, we serve our ice cream primarily in a decorative Venetian glass bowl, unless, of course, atonement of sins is of concern, in which case we have wafer cones for such occasions, and if the concern is of, say, a more serious nature, only vanilla can accompany the unembellished cone."

"Fascinating tradition," says Mo.

"Allow me to explain. When no atonement is required, definitely use the bowl. When sins are involved and one is too embarrassed to show up at church and confess their wrongdoings, as if they ever tell the truth—it seems to me there is no shortage of people trying to enter paradise through the back door—they come here and order vanilla ice cream on wafer cones, and occasionally, they order just the wafer cone without the ice cream. That usually indicates they're carrying big, big no-no's."

"Interesting, and what is the correlation between sins and wafer cones?" asks Mo.

"Italians prefer wafer cones because it reminds them of the Holy Communion wafer, do you know what that is?"

"I do," replies Mo.

VC shakes his head and smiles, and Steven continues, "You see, Catholics of Italian origin attend church twice a year, Christmas and Easter, often standing room only and normally before the big meal because after those meals topped with several slices of our specialty cakes, they nap until it's time to eat again. The rest of the year, they come here, order a triple scoop, all vanilla, with the occasional small chocolate scoop, you know just for the hell of it, on wafer cones of course, and smile while eating because they feel just as absolved of their sins as if they had confessed to the priest in the confessional. No one likes the confessionals, they're like penalty boxes, the only difference being, athletes are happy to leave the box, have you ever seen anyone holding their heads up high and smiling when they exit the confessionals?" says Steven.

"Really?" says Mo.

"Yes, and I must add, there are those who come in and buy a box or two of cones for use at the office, in their cars, wherever, for immediate consumption after sinful behaviour. VC, what's the name of your uncle?"

"Uncle Lou."

"No, the *other* uncle."

"You mean Uncle Guido?"

"Yes, him, anyway, his driver comes in weekly and buys two boxes, one for him and one for Uncle Guido. And that's all she wrote, all good, Moreen, all good."

VC looks at Steven and breaks into silent hysterics, followed by Mo and Steven.

"Haven't changed at all, Steven," says VC, still trying to contain his laughter.

"So glad to see you recovered well, VC."

"Thank you, Steven, I see you're on the mend too," says VC, prompting another bout of laughter.

After they settle, Steven turns to Mo and says, "Did you know that I brought him boxes of pastries when he was in the hospital?"

"Yes, he did mention you brought him a few boxes of wafer cones," says Mo, trying to contain her laughter.

"You are indeed a quick study," says Steven.

"While we're confessing, just how much vanilla on wafer cones have you consumed this week, Steven?" she asks, prompting the three to laugh loudly.

"I can see why this guy is head over heels with you, Mo, truly."

"Thank you, Steven," she replies.

"VC tells me you're studying hard sciences, so, free ice cream for every distinguished Italian scientist, astronomer and other such notables you can name."

"Free dinner for me and VC?"

"Very well, but a small dinner."

"Shall we begin with the usual suspects, say da Vinci, Marconi, Galileo, Avogadro, Antonelli…" says Mo.

"The last one you mentioned, wasn't Antonelli a priest prior to creating the periodic table?"

"Nice try, Steven, Antonelli did come from the Church, but it was Dmitri Ivanovich Mendeleev who created the periodic table, and I don't think he liked ice cream, vodka maybe," she replies.

Steven nods, smiles and says, "All right then, for a free dessert…"

"Also for two," quickly interjects Mo.

"All right, also for two, the world's first female chemist was … Marie Currie … or Tapputi-Belatekallim?"

"Marie Curie was the first woman to win a Nobel Prize, twice and in two different sciences, but it was Tapputi who was deemed to be the first female chemist. Who, by the way, was Babylonian, but for the sake of this discussion, we'll make her an honorary Italian."

Steven shakes his head and says, "I think I best stop here before I lose my restaurant." He then turns to VC and says, "You're in good hands, my friend, and don't let the Theatre of the Absurd get in the way," then turns to Mo and says, "Mo, it is a pleasure to meet you, and thank you."

"Thank you for what, Steven?"

"For saving my friend from himself."

VC stands and the men give each other a hug. "So good to see you, Steven," says VC.

"And you, my friend."

Mo also stands and Steven kisses her on both cheeks, "Good to meet you, Mo, never seen him this happy."

"Thank you, Steven, pleasure meeting you."

"So treasured friends, what will it be? On me of course."

"You don't have to, Steven," says Mo.

"But I do."

"All right then I'll try the chocolate and vanilla in a Venetian glass bowl."

"Perfect choice with a tall cappuccino, and for you, Mr. C.? Same, with a double espresso? Yes? And two cannoli di sfoglia, it's a wafer shell filled with freshly made secret recipe, light cream, big, big seller Sunday mornings, not before or after church, but instead of church."

"Wafer shell?" asks Mo.

"Yes, but for you two, it's more like a get-out-of-jail-free card, you know, in case you need it," replies Steven while leaving.

Mo looks directly at VC and squeezes his hand. After a brief silence, she looks around and says, "You're right, VC, this is a very nice place, and Steven is a blast."

"Has a business degree, worked downtown, after his father had a stroke took over here, hard work and long hours but loves it. Do what you love, right?" says VC.

"And what do you love, VC?"

"It's not what, it's who, and I love you, Mo."

"And I you, VC."

They continue holding hands across the table until Steven returns. He places the ice cream, coffee and cannoli in front of Mo and says, "Enjoy."

"Thank you, Steven," she replies.

He does the same with VC's order, he thanks him and Steven says, "Enjoy my friend. I'll try joining you two a little later," and leaves.

Mo tastes her ice cream and VC asks, "How is it?"

"Heavenly," she replies and both smile, then she says, "The picture of you and Steven, never seen you in your pugilistic form, I like it."

"Another life."

Nine-fifteen came too quickly, he looks at her and says, "Unfortunately, it's time to leave, Bella."

"Beautiful, thank you, VC. It seems we just got here, and it'll only take us fifteen, twenty minutes, no rush, Bello."

"I promised your father you would be back home safely before he left for work. A word is a word, Bella."

"You certainly are a gentleman, VC."

Steven walks up while they're putting on their coats to leave and says, "Sorry I couldn't get back to you two, Mo, it is truly a pleasure meeting you."

"Steven, my pleasure as well, thank you for everything."

"By the way, have you sat in his Shelby?"

"Yes, I have," replies Mo.

"And driven it?"

"And driven it."

"Well, you are right up there with the Gods because no other mortal has been allowed to even sit in it for more than a couple of seconds, and when allowed, he holds the keys.

"Please take this home, Mo," adds Steven, handing her a box of pastries.

"Thank you, Steven, VC is correct, you do have the best pastries in the world in this jewel of a café."

"Thank you, Mo, all family recipes from the country of love, food and vintages, in that order. No doubt VC will take you there someday."

"At the top of our list, Steven."

"So is Scotland," adds VC, looking at Mo.

He reaches into his pocket to pay and Steven says, "Eh, eh," and shakes his head.

"Take the lady safely home, Vinny."

Walking towards the car, Mo says, "Vinny?"

He smiles, opens the car door for her, settles in, and while they're driving home in his father's hardtop Impala Super Sport sedan, Mo slides over the bench seat and rests her head on his shoulder.

"Is this why you didn't take your Mustang?" she asks.

He kisses her on her forehead, and continues driving. Soon they reach the house and he escorts her to the door. She opens the door, and just inside is Mr. Walker, readying himself for work.

"You're home early," he says.

"Good evening, Mr. Walker," says VC. "Call you later, Mo?"

"Yes, of course," she replies.

"Good night, Mo, Mr. Walker, have a safe weekend at work," says VC and leaves.

"Hope you two had a good time," he says while closing the door, "By the way, where is that Mustang of his? Not too grippy in the cold and wet, I'd imagine."

"That's what he said. This is for you and Gran, Dad."

"Thank you, what's in it?" he asks.

"Pastries from Locale Dei Celebrati, VC's friend Steven gave them to us to take home."

Mo opens the box in the kitchen, he looks at the pastries and says, "They look so mouth-watering, which one should I take?"

"This one, it's called cannoli di sfoglia, cream-filled wafer pastry, specifically designed to cure what ails you."

"Really? I'm sure there is a story that accompanies such a brave little pastry," he replies, bites into one and says, "It's delicious."

"Here, take one to go, you never know when you may need it," she says while containing her smile.

"No cannoli for Gran?" he asks.

"No, she doesn't need them, the tiramisu is for her."

"See you tomorrow."

"See you tomorrow Dad, and…"

"I know, be careful," he says as he leaves.

Mo sets the pastries on a plate, makes Gran tea and calls her to the kitchen. She comes from the living room, where she had been nursing her migraine, and sits at the table.

"How's the headache, Gran?"

"Nothing that a shot of that single malt wouldn't cure. Your grandfather started me on it when he worked at the distillery, and he was right, nothing else will do."

"You miss home, don't you Gran?"

"The bricks and mortar, streets of cobblestone, ancient buildings with tales to tell, yes I do, but home is you and your father and those in our hearts, that's home."

Mo places the tea pot and cups on the table, and gives her a long embrace. She then sits across from her and passes the pastries neatly placed on a platter.

"Such nice pastries."

Mo tells her Steven's take on the pastries and Gran smiles and asks, "Did your father have one?"

"He had two of the cannoli."

"Had a few sins to sack, did he?" replies Gran, and while both laugh Mo says, "Gran, you're incredible."

"That's what your mother used to say about you, bless her soul."

"I miss her, Gran," says Mo, as her eyes fill with tears. "I wish she was here."

"She is Moreen, and she's so proud of you."

The telephone rings, and Gran says, "I'm sure you two have a lot to talk about, I'll take my tea upstairs."

"No, Gran, I know you like your tea in the living room, I'll take the call upstairs."

THE DINNER

Saturday night, precisely at seven o'clock, VC knocks at Mo's door with a red rose for her, freesias for Gran and a bottle of single malt for Mr. Walker.

Mo eagerly answers the door, smiles and says, "Thank you, and please come in," followed by a quick kiss.

"You look beautiful, Mo," says VC, and follows her into the living room where Mr. Walker and Gran are sitting. They stand, VC shakes hands with Mr. Walker and kisses Gran on both cheeks. He then gives her the flowers and Mr. Walker the scotch.

"Thank you, VC, lovely freesias, such fragrance," says Gran, and she and Mo proceed to the kitchen to place the flowers in vases.

Mr. Walker looks keenly at the bottle and says, "Thank you, VC, from the same distillery that employed my father-in-law back home. I like it slightly chilled as in a wine cellar, and in a shot glass. I know, sacrilegious, but that's how I prefer to drink it. You?"

"The odd celebratory drink, or the occasional glass of wine with meals, other than that, never really took to drinking or to smoking."

"I can appreciate those restraints, especially as an athlete."

VC nods and says, "I try. Mo tells me you have a wonderful flower garden in the back."

"Thank you, I started planting flowers after my wife Moreen was killed in a car accident … in her memory, and continued the practice when we came here. I plant a new kind every year, we have a small backyard and I think it's getting overrun, but we like it."

"Mo spoke of the accident, enormous loss I'm sure, my condolences."

Mr. Walker nods and says, "Thank you, VC," and following a brief silence asks, "How is your re-entry into the world of academia?"

"A little bumpy at first, but going very well, thanks to Mo."

"She's special, like her mother."

"Very special," says VC, and after a brief silence says, "You're a police officer."

"I am, have been all my life, but I don't normally bring work home, too disruptive to one's psyche and to the family's well-being."

"I can appreciate that, but hard to do I'm sure, so what do you do to unwind?"

"Gardening of course, rain or shine, read when I can, work out when I can, but I also meditate," he replies. "You know, I thought police work and meditating could never be on the same page, but they can be, a mutually beneficial co-existence, a Ying and Yang in a way."

"The focus, the silence, serenity, I can see the benefits," says VC.

"I thought I could never meditate, but my wife, bless her, showed me the way. I still feel she meditates with me, she brings me clarity of mind and of heart, emotional calmness and, best of all, spiritual composure, it keeps me close to her. It helps me get me through the rough days. What do you do?"

VC's answer would have been "I work out, write, but mostly think of Mo," but they were called into the dining room.

"On our way," replies Mr. Walker, and as they both proceed to the dining room, he says to VC, "To be continued."

"Looking forward to it, maybe on one of your days off, on a dry day, you can try out the Mustang."

"That would be magnificent, VC, I would like that very much. Sunny and dry tomorrow according to the weather report," he replies, placing a hand on VC's shoulder.

"Afternoon?"

"Around two?"

"Will pick you up at two."

They walk into the dining room, VC looks at the beautifully set table and says, "This looks wonderful, Gran."

"Thank you, please sit down, Ferguson," says Gran. All sit, Ferguson carries out the blessings, then turns to VC and says, "This is our national dish as it were, haggis is a meat pudding, very nice, accompanied by mashed potatoes and neeps, also known as turnips, in a whiskey sauce, and at Mo's insistence, a side order of fettuccine alfredo."

"Thank you, you didn't have to go to all this trouble," replies VC.

"Well…" says Ferguson looking at his daughter and smiles.

"And for dessert, an old family rendition of the traditional Scottish cranachan."

"Looking forward to it," says VC.

"How's the haggis, VC?" asks Ferguson.

"Fine, sir, unusual but very interesting taste," he says, looking at Mo holding back a smile.

"An acquired taste, VC," says Gran.

"Yes, very good though," he says, then Ferguson adds, "Now VC, for the next part of the test, please describe in detail, your true palate reaction to such a delectable dish."

After the laughter subsides, conversations touched on a variety of topics in keeping with the evening's good will.

Somehow, this small group, who until three months ago, had never physically met, has so naturally come together to break bread with such familiarity and ease.

"I will have you know," says Ferguson, "VC has invited me to take a drive in his Mustang tomorrow afternoon."

A pleasantly surprised Mo looks at VC and smiles, Gran looks at Ferguson and smiles.

"Moreen," he says, "Is there anything I should know about how VC would like me to drive his car?"

"Feed it power gingerly, Dad, don't nail it."

After dinner, Gran and Mr. Walker moved to the living room and Mo and VC insisted on tidying up.

While sipping at his scotch and Gran at hers, he asks, "What do you think, Gran?"

She lifts her glass, he his, and she replies, "Their hearts sing, Ferguson."

"As do ours, as do ours."

While clearing the table and doing the dishes, all they could do was smile at each other. Once done, VC thanks Gran and Mr. Walker for the dinner and lovely evening, reminds Mr. Walker of the drive and Mo walks him to the door. They kiss, and she says, "Safe home, love you."

"Love you too, Mo. Call you later?"

"Yes."

On the drive home in his father's car, his unbroken smile never left his clean, twice-shaven face. Normally no aftershave, for the occasion a little, very little, Old Spice.

He was exceptionally pleased with how the evening evolved and couldn't wait to tell Mo. In some respects, he was surprised that he was not more thoroughly "interrogated." Mr. Walker and Gran, he felt, must have the same confidence and trust in Mo as his parents have in him.

Turning into his driveway, VC drives the car into the garage, closes the door and hurries in, eager to call Mo.

Meanwhile, in the Walker household, Mo joins her father and grandmother in the living room and thanks them for the wonderful dinner and their kind hospitality.

"You are very welcome, dear," says Gran, "It's our pleasure, he's so thoughtful and appreciative, and certainly madly in love with you, Moreen."

"Looking forward to the drive tomorrow," adds Ferguson. He

then he stands and asks, "Anyone for another slice of that wonderful dessert VC brought from his favourite bakery that according to him, and I agree, makes the best Italian pasties in the world?"

"No cranachan?" asks Gran.

"That's the nightcap, Gran, nothing like the taste of home to soothe the soul," he replies.

Later that night, during their telephone conversation, the evening was discussed in minute detail, leading VC to ask the crucial question, "So, did I pass the litmus test?"

"You did very well, VC, but—" she replies.

"There is a but? What's the but?" he asks with some anxiety in his voice, but she remains silent.

"All right, on a scale of one to ten, with ten being exceptional, where would you place your father's and Gran's impression of me at dinner?"

"Truthfully VC, your rating was…"

"Yes?"

"Off the charts!" she exclaims.

"Really?"

"Yes, you are so well liked here, my man."

"That's a huge relief, thank you, Mo, and I so like them, really do."

"So did you enjoy that little bit of passion in my drama?"

"Speaking of passion…"

"Good night, VC."

"Good night, Mo."

"VC, VC, don't hang up."

"Change of heart … about the passion I mean?"

"The passion is unmistakeable VC, I do have a question, are we behaving in, for the lack of a better phrase, a silly, early adolescent manner? I mean, do others in love of similar age behave the same way?"

"I don't really know how two people deeply in love behave or are supposed to behave, Mo, what I know is that my heart sings constantly, and I will always tell you how much I love and care for you anytime, anywhere."

"I feel the same way, VC."

"Life has its challenges and I suspect the journey of love has its own set of hurdles, but I do know there is nothing you and I together can't overcome."

"Thank you, VC, goodnight."

"Goodnight, Mo."

THE DRIVE

VC arrives promptly at two. Mo answers the door, Gran is in the living room, and Ferguson is putting on his jacket. After the greetings, they leave and walk towards the car. Normally under cover by this time of the year, but this occasion couldn't wait until spring.

Once both are in the car, Mr. Walker adjusts his seat, mirrors, turns the ignition, the irregular firing sequence of the GT gives it its distinctive guttural sound, and both smile. He revs it slightly and the hot pipes clear the exhaust, shifts it into first, and the car slowly moves away from the house with Mo and Gran watching.

"May I take it on the highway?" asks Mr. Walker.

"Of course, please, not a cruiser but it will keep the adrenaline circulating."

Once on the highway, Mr. Walker keeps it within the speed limits and on the outside lane.

"Great machine VC, you'll enjoy it for many years to come."

"I'm sure we will. What did you drive back home?"

"Well, liked but couldn't afford a Rover, even though they look like a Saint Bernard on wheels, so we drove a Ford-made Anglia, and heaters were optional. Good car but far from being an enthusiast's car like this one."

"It did the job, right?"

"That it did. So, what do you see as your next car, besides Mustangs?"

"Mo loves this car, and if the opportunity comes up, I will get her a Mustang of her own, put some work into it, but will have to install a speed limiter in it," replies VC, and both laugh. "Other future cars could include a station wagon," says VC, again prompting laughter.

Following a brief silence VC says, "Great evening last night, Mr. Walker."

"Great. That's how I described you to my daughter."

"Thank you."

"Paraphrasing Gran's opinion, and one I share, '*He seems like such a fine young man, respectful and appreciative, and certainly madly in love with you, Moreen,*' to which I would add, for your sake and hers, and I say this caringly, if you have no intentions of going the distance with Moreen, back out now."

"I appreciate your sentiments, Mr. Walker, and as a father I would feel the same, but please know, I am so fortunate to have Moreen in my life, so much so that words cannot describe how her smile makes my heart sing, and I know I do the same for her. We were meant for each other. How do I know? I just know. How did it happen? And how did it happen so quickly? I don't know, I do know that I would be lost without her in my life."

Mr. Walker takes the next turn off the highway and soon after they arrive back at the house. They exit the car, he returns the keys to VC and both shake hands.

"Thank you, Mr. Walker."

"Thank you, VC."

Mr. Walker proceeds towards the house, and just as VC is about to get into the car, Mo appears, waves at VC and stops on the top step of the veranda. Mr. Walker joins her, and both wave as VC slowly drives away. Mo looks at her father and asks, "Well?"

He embraces her and says, "He loves you very much, Moreen, I know he'll do right by you, and that's all a parent needs to know."

VC's parents extended an invitation to Mo and her family to come together and break bread closer to Christmas.

CHAPTER TWO

Friday afternoon, school's out, no basketball practice. Mo was participating in a swim meet at the nearby municipal pool and VC was getting ready to leave. He had offered to pick her up, but arrangements had already been made for her and Martha, who was also at the trials, to be taken home by Martha's mother, one of the meet organizers.

The halls were almost empty and while at his locker, VC caught a glimpse of Damien and his friends, who had been recently expelled and prohibited from being on the school grounds, waiting behind the double exit doors at the back.

He considered his options and none was good. If he avoided them and exited through the front doors, he would be considered less than brave by some, and smart by others. If he exited through the back doors, he would be considered an instigator looking for trouble with the possibility of being expelled.

He closes his locker door, locks it, picks up his gym bag and begins walking towards the front door. Suddenly he hears chicken sounds, first from Damien followed by Derek and Tommy. He stops, the cluck and cackle stop. He resumes walking, so does the cackling.

The hall quickly became spine-chillingly silent as the eyes of the few students still at their lockers followed VC. He continued walking and as the cackling got louder, he stopped, took a deep breath, turned, and proceeded walking towards Damien and his cowardly cronies, hoping that a face-to-face talk would be sufficient to end it. As is often the case with bullies, talking doesn't go very far.

As expected, Damien, Tommy and Derek defiantly block his way.

VC stops, looks at the three of them and after a brief silence says, "Fellows, why don't we just all go home," and as he tries walking between them, Damien immediately steps in front of him and, with a smirk on his face, says, "Not this time, pretty boy."

VC looks at them, and says, "I want you three to understand something, there are fights of necessity and then there are fights of choice, you three are making this a fight of choice. I don't want to fight, but if you leave me with no other choice, I will, and this time you're going to needlessly get hurt, some badly."

"You think you're so tough," says Derek.

VC offers no reply, instead begins walking away. Damien immediately lunges and punches him in the back of the head. VC missteps but remains upright. He slowly turns, drops his gym bag and says, "I really wish you hadn't done that."

"We're going to teach you a lesson, wop," replies Damien.

Wearing brass knuckles, Damian is the first to take a swing and misses. *Keep your distance Kid, he's a dirty fighter, don't exchange punch for punch ... pull back, let him come to you ... stay loose ... use your long reach ... load up and deliver your famous left hook ... he lunges when he throws his cross and gets off balance, he's exposed ... combination ... but don't underestimate him ... keep your feet planted on the ground, no spinning hook kicks, he'll rush you and take you to the ground, box him hard ... and remember, eyes in the back of your head for the other two, they're just wannabees but still dangerous.*

Damien pushes Tommy at VC, a lightning right, left, upper cut, Tommy goes down but quickly stands back up and rushes him. VC delivers a throat strike, side kick to the knee. Tommy staggers back and falls down. After many exchanges with Damien and Derek, a bleeding Derek hit the ground close to Tommy and both stay down. With bleeding head and face, Damien quickly reaches into his pocket and pulls out his knife. There is no mistaking the sound of a switchblade. VC immediately backs away, takes a defensive stance, focuses and waits for Damien to make his move.

With fury in his eyes, Damien says, "Let's see how good you are against a sharp blade, pretty boy." VC stays focused and offers no verbal reply.

Damien lunges, VC steps aside and delivers a hard kick to the back of his leg, Damien buckles but remains standing. VC kicks the knife out of his hand, immediately backs up and positions himself strategically for another attack. Damien attacks and VC delivers front and side kicks to Damien's body and, as he staggers backward, delivers a roundhouse to his head. He goes down. VC backs up, resumes his stand and waits. Damien wipes away blood from his mouth, looks at VC and says, "By the way, how's that stuck-up Moreen? I hear she's as cold as ice, maybe that's the way you like them."

Damien stands, advances, and both continue exchanging blows. Damien stumbles backwards; VC could have struck a final blow but chose not to and moves back.

Damien looks around and sees that the group of students watching the fight had grown, spits blood in VC's direction and stands up. He comes at him, VC tries to deliver a front kick, but slips and falls backward. Damien is immediately on top of him delivering blows to his face. VC blocks, rolls, and quickly stands. Looks at Damien, in pain, trying to stand, he thinks of what Vinny would do, and the primordial instinct to finish Damian off begins to build. He thinks of Mo, pauses, slowly lowers his arms, relaxes his fists, and says, "I think we're done here."

On the ground leaning against the wall, bleeding from cuts to his face and broken nose, guarding his broken ribs, Damien looks at his friends in no better condition, at VC, at the group of students rejoicing in silence, and says, "I've had enough, man, let's call it a draw."

"Call it what you will, but it ends here," says VC.

"Not by a long shot," replies Damien. He slowly and painfully stands, throws a punch, misses and staggers. VC spins behind him and could have rendered him unconscious with the chokehold, but chose not to. Instead, he eases up and says, "Damien, it's over, it's over," and the more he struggles to get free the more he hears VC say, "Let it go, Damien, it's okay, it's okay." Damien eventually calms, VC helps him sit next to Tommy and Derek, and says, "I'm sorry it had to come to this, truly am," and begins walking away slowly.

Suddenly someone yells, "VC!" VC immediately turns, sees Damien standing, holding a knife. He instinctively clenches his fists and gets into a ready stance. The two men stare at each other, neither moves, neither speaks. After a while Damien looks at his injured friends slumped against the wall on the blood-stained snow unable to stand, looks at VC, at the spectators, and to everyone's disbelief drops his knife, slowly walks back and helps Tommy and Derek stand. He looks directly at VC and for the first time, without malice in his eyes, nods. In return, VC does what he has done hundreds of times after a match in the dojo, he brings his open left hand over his clenched right fist indicating he's prepared to cover aggression with peace. All three turn and slowly walk away into the dark and cold night. VC watches as the darkness engulfs more lives gone wrong. The sirens quiet, the lights spin and mesmerize, and the unmoving cold snap numbs.

The police came and took statements. They caught up to Damien and his friends and one of the ambulances took them directly to the hospital prior to eventual jail, but VC declined to press charges. Refusing to go to the hospital, VC is treated by paramedics from the other ambulance and released.

Bruised and sore body, blood-stained face and clothes, and mildly disoriented, VC feels an irresistible yet familiar pull of the heart towards home.

He picks up his bag, walks to the nearby telephone booth and calls his father.

"No, Dad, I'm not hurt, I had no choice ... yes, the police and paramedics are here ... lots of witnesses have given statements ... yes, Damien and his friends are being processed ... no, I am not being charged, I'm cleared ... I'm fine ... no, I'm not going to the hospital, no need ... no, you don't have to come and pick me up, please Dad, I'm fine... I'll be there in a little while ... all right, pick me up at Mo's house in an hour, I just need to talk to her and explain things ... yes, we'll go to the hospital then if you feel it necessary, I'm sorry,

Dad, please tell Mom … yes, I'm okay, see you later, bye."

He hangs up and begins walking in the direction of Mo's house. Walks up the shovelled walkway, enters the enclosed porch, and with his heart in his throat, quietly knocks on the door.

Mo and Gran were in the kitchen, Mr. Walker in the living room. Approaching the door, Mo, through the opaque glass, sees VC's silhouette and eagerly opens it.

She looks at his face, torn jacket, bloodied shirt and immediately screams, "Oh my God, VC, what happened? Dad, come quickly!"

"I'm so sorry, Mo, I hope you can forgive me."

THE FIRST DANCE

Friday night, early December. VC is greeted at the door by Mr. Walker. "All healed up, and a very understanding principal."

"He's a good man, Mr. Walker, and I'm grateful," replies VC as they shake hands.

"Please come in." He hangs VC's coat on the rack, and both walk to the living room where Gran is sitting.

"Good evening, Gran," VC says, walking towards her.

"Good evening VC, lovely suit," she says, asking him to sit down.

"Thank you," he replies.

VC leans and kisses her on both cheeks before taking a seat. Soon after, Mo enters, he looks at her, totally captivated, manages to stand, and says, "You look incredible, Mo … I am just in…"

"Awe?" she says.

"Yes, in awe," he replies. "And what a beautiful dress."

"Gran helped me make it, glad you like it."

"I certainly do," he replies. Feeling steadier on his feet, walks up to her, kisses her on the cheek, and says, "This is for you."

"A wrist corsage of small roses, coral, how beautiful, VC, thank you," she says and kisses him on the cheek.

"It's lovely," says Gran, and Mr. Walker nods.

VC takes the corsage out of the box, and while placing it on Mo's left wrist, Gran says, "I know it's not a formal dance, but flowers, especially roses, always make any occasion more splendid."

"They do, Gran, they certainly do," replies VC.

Gran looks at Ferguson and says, "They make a handsome couple, don't they, Ferguson."

"Yes, they do, Mom."

Mo and VC walk to the front door, he helps put on her coat and Mr. Walker VC's. They say goodnight, VC holds Mo's hand tightly, carefully walks her to his father's car and helps her in. He closes the car door, waves at Mr. Walker standing on the porch, settles into the driver's seat and drives away. Mo looks at her corsage and says, "Never received a corsage before," to which he replies, "Never given one before."

She moves closer, places her arm over his shoulder and says, "We do make a lovely couple, don't we?"

"We certainly do," he replies, "Ready for the big dance?"

"Sure am, VC, but do feel a little nervous."

He turns to her and says, "We belong here, Mo. This is our first school dance, and we are destined to have a great time."

"Will Mike and his new girlfriend Joanne be there?"

"Yes, they're home for the weekend."

"Is she the one?"

"Seems that way. They wanted to double date, but I said another time. I want to pick you up by myself, dance with you all night and take you home by myself, and I will be the perfect gentleman."

"But you know, you can deviate from perfection, just a little."

"I will keep that in mind, definitely keep that in mind," he replies.

Sharply dressed, they walk in holding hands, and immediately Mike and Joanne come to greet them as well as Martha and Paul and other close friends. All in their semi-formal attire, plenty of chaperones, a vibrantly decorated gymnasium and a night to celebrate.

Martha takes to the microphone after Ms. E.'s welcoming speech on the stage, and after her own short joyful greeting, introduces the disc jockeys, "This is Gerry and to my left is Joe from GPL Entertainment, they will DJ our evening dance. They're the best in the city and

I'm sure we will all have a wonderful time," and she hands Gerry the microphone.

Gerry and Joe join the applause and when it ends, Gerry says, "Thank you, Martha, and hello everyone. All dressed for the occasion I see, well, we hope you came with your dancing shoes because as the song says, we're *gonna have some fun tonight.* I do the shakers and the movers and Joe the slow ones, but it's you who's in charge of making every song special."

Joe takes the microphone, thanks Gerry and adds, "A brief note, we have our own repertoire of Motown, R&B, Soul, Rock and other musical genres, as in classical, just kidding, but requests are most welcome," and returns the microphone to Gerry.

VC turns to Mo and says, "I like these guys," to which Mo replies, "I do, too."

"Without further ado," Gerry says, "Let's begin with one of my favourites and I'm sure yours, Jackie Wilson's *Baby Workout,* so *come out here on the floor.*"

The Motown great sets off the evening but no one rushes to the floor until someone breaks the ice. It is Mo and VC.

"C'mon, VC, time to shuffle, baby," says Mo.

"Thank you for starting us off, you two," Gerry says to them and begins clapping his hands to the beat, joined by Joe, then followed by Mo and VC and many other students as well as some teachers.

"That's it, that's it," Gerry says as more take to the floor. When the song ends Gerry says, "No one move, Mr. James Brown next with *I Feel Good,* ladies and gentlemen, followed by Martha and the Vandellas, *Dancing in the Streets,* Eddie Floyd, *Knock on Wood* and before we slow things down with the Righteous Brothers, Wilson Pickett will tell us all about it *In the Midnight Hour.*"

"Our favourite songs, VC, these guys are good."

"They sure are, Mo."

After several songs, the walls breathe easier, sitting groups become smaller, chairs empty and the floor becomes what it should be, a celebration of young lives courageously readying their wings.

"Having fun?" Gerry asks the audience, immediately answered with a loud and cheerful resounding 'Yes' from everyone.

"And now, as promised," says Joe, "we're going to slow things down with back-to-back number ones, so hold each other closely. *Unchained Melody* by the Righteous Brothers followed by a request for the Temptations' number one single, *My Girl*."

Mo and VC, standing close to the stage tightly holding hands, look into each other's eyes, and VC pulls Mo close to him. Gerry leans over from the stage and says, "You should know, all eyes are on you two beautiful people tonight. Magical."

Unchained Melody begins, VC looks into Mo's spellbinding eyes and says, "I could never be without your love, Mo, never."

She looks at him and says, "You never have to be, VC," and slowly rests her head on his shoulder. They both remain silent until the next song, *My Girl*, begins.

He looks at her and says, "With you I have sunshine even on the cloudiest of days, Mo, I do."

Immediately after the slow dance, Gerry picks up the pace, and Mo says, "C'mon, VC, easy step jive, baby, Nina…"

"*I Love Your Loving Ways*," he readily adds. "Let's go, Mo!"

After the somewhat restrained jive, VC says, "We can dance all night, can't we?"

"We sure can, baby."

"Are you ready for a break?"

"Not just yet, not when *I'm Stuck On You*," she replies as the Presley song begins.

"Are you stuck on me?" she asks.

"Yes, I am."

"Are we being silly?"

"Yes we are, but who cares?" he replies.

"All right then, VC, let's rock, baby, and don't worry, *I Won't Step On Your Blue Suede Shoes*."

"Deal."

After the song ends, some stay, others like Mo and VC begin

walking off the floor, and Mo asks, "How's your energy level?"

"Just fine, why?"

"All that dancing in our basement used to take it out of you."

"Ah yes, your basement, it wasn't the dancing that took all my strength," he replies, smiling.

"All right then, let's sit with Mike and Joanne for a while, that should cool things down a notch or two," she replies. Walking towards their friends, another of their favourite songs is announced. They stop, look at each other, VC says, "We can't pass this one up, Mo."

"Not this one, VC," she replies and hand in hand, walk back onto the dance floor.

"Love is definitely in the air tonight folks," says Gerry, looking directly at VC and Mo, then Joe adds, "Percy, ladies and gentlemen, hot off the press, enjoy."

Organ, drums and Percy's penetrating voice of soul singing *When a Man Loves a Woman* bring Mo and VC to a standstill. Mo eases her head onto his shoulder, VC holds her tighter, kisses her on her head and whispers, "I love you, Mo."

The song ends, and they walk off the floor holding each other's hands tightly. Sitting close and by themselves, he says, "A great evening Mo, I am so happy we came."

"Me too, VC, I feel I can go anywhere with you and be happy."

"And I feel the same about you, Mo. You know, somehow this feels much like a wedding dance."

"Is there is a waltz in the making that I don't know about?" she asks.

"I hope so," he replies and both smile.

"This is definitely our kind of music, VC, love everything about it, but then so is jazz."

"Music helps clear the path to the heart," says VC.

"You are right, my lovely. It just occurred to me, we should take another trip to George's before it gets too snowy."

"Dinner and *Take Five*?"

"That is such a great arrangement, five/four time, that added little beat to the normal four/four makes all the difference. Desmond, Brubeck, and my favourite percussionist, Morello, and if I may, one of the very few who can give drums a syncopated, richly melodious voice."

"Nothing like that extra note, VC, unique, cerebral, cool, West Coast, something like our own unique time signature, wouldn't you say?"

"Absolutely."

"Do you like drums?"

"I do, why do you ask?"

"Not sure, it just came out, ever played them professionally?"

"As in a small jazz combo, doing a late gig … smoky downtown bar, unfiltered, hand-rolled cigarette hanging out of my mouth, riding the cymbal, off-beat licks with my left, eagerly waiting for those few bars of improv solo to show what you got? Is that what you mean?"

"Yes, that's what I mean," she replies.

"I don't think so."

"You don't think so? VC, you either did or you didn't."

"All right, have you ever played the piano professionally?" he asks.

"As in a grand hall recital, formally dressed, perfect posture, perfect execution of century-old notes, the complexity yet the simplicity, the contrasting moods, the last note, the painful short but oh-so-long pause, the wait for the audience to rise, applaud and yell 'Bravo, bravo!' The elegance of it all. Is that what you mean?" she says.

"Yes."

"Now that you ask, I don't know."

"See, you don't know either, but maybe they're deep-rooted desires being awakened from listening to your father's jazz and classical collection in your basement."

"Perhaps, or maybe it's one of our long-lost voices speaking to us from the beyond, VC."

"So does this mean we're leaving the dance early?"

"It could mean many things, but that's not one of them," she replies, smiling at him.

"All right then, so, my beautiful Mo, what do you think the last song of the night will be?" But before she can answer, Gerry announces that the last song is a special request from a senior student who contributed fifty dollars to the student fund. Many ask for the identity, but neither Joe nor Gerry reveal it. Mo turns to VC and asks, "Which song did you choose?"

"How did you know it was me?" to which she whispers, *"Unforgettable"* and he adds, *"That's what you are."*

The song begins, they look into each other's eyes, walk onto the floor and as she always does with a memorable slow song, she rests her head on his shoulder. He holds her close and leans his head on hers, and as the song plays on, he says, "Thank you for taking me in."

She looks into his eyes, a brief, soft kiss. The song plays out, and the memorable occasion comes to a close … but not before Mo's request is played.

"We're not quite done, baby," she says to a surprised VC.

Gerry and Joe look at Mo and VC and give them the thumbs up. She places her finger on his lips and says, *"At Last, Etta James."*

The song plays out, the dance comes to a close, new hearts touch, long-standing ones are renewed, and while leaving, Mike and Joanne speak of coffee and pastries but Mo and VC take a rain check.

"We understand, on for tomorrow night and we're picking you up," says Mike, and VC nods.

The outside air is brisk, hands hold tighter and the moon watches. Mo and VC bid goodnight to their friends, get in the car and Mo immediately moves close to VC.

He looks at the sky and says, "Starry night, Moreen." She looks up and says, "It is, baby, Van Gogh, *Over The Rhone.*"

"You know, if there is only one road to true love, I don't know how we have found it in such a short time, but we have and I feel so blessed."

"This is our road VC, forever."

The following weekend, the dinner at VC's parents' house was as celebratory as the previous dinner at the Walkers'. Instead of inviting only Mo, they chose to invite the entire family. Gran and Sarah sat at either end of the dining table. "The strength of the relationship lies in the greatness of the heart," Gran said. "Know that your hearts are now one, and your journey will now be as one."

"Thank you, Gran, and if I may add," said Sarah, "may your journey together be blessed and guided by the strength and acumen of our combined ancestors." They all stand, raise their glass of champagne and once everyone resumes sitting, Sarah calls upon VC to help her, and he and Mo follow her into the kitchen.

Many a story of rich history, great food … determined and fearless people … Roman emperors, Scotland's warrior King even Vikings feared and, of course, the debate over the sanctity of Scotch, the water of life versus the holiness of red wine the colour of sustenance that runs through our veins, concluding that both were necessities of celebrations.

Genuine happiness is contagious and celebrating the richness of truthful lives came so naturally for both families.

It was close to midnight when the Walkers left, and the Cabots gathered in the living room, recapping the evening and concluding Mo was an angel from Heaven.

"She came to save you, VC," says Sarah.

"From what, Mom?"

"I don't know, but there is this aura about her, she's a silent warrior, a demon slayer, that's for sure."

"Do you think I have demons to slay?"

"We all do, VC, we all do."

"Here is to a long and treasured journey," says Augie, raising his glass.

Early the following morning during their telephone conversation, Mo asks, "Did I pass the litmus test?"

"To quote someone very special to me, 'You were off the charts.'"

The Christmas season brought more combined family celebrations, and the ring. It wasn't a traditional engagement ring, but a gold and silver wolf-wrap ring VC purchased from a small Native shop in Toronto. He bought it because it symbolized deep spirituality and life-long companionship as practiced by wolves.

GRADUATION

The month of decision-making arrived quickly. On a bright, sunny, pre-class morning in June, during his last lap around the school track, he imagined what life would have been like had he met Mo years earlier. In his heart he truly believed that with Mo as his loving companion, there would have never been the need for a Vinny nor The Kid nor a closed heart.

He and Mo graduated with honours. Mo with perfect scores and awarded multiple scholarships, one of which was from a prestigious university in Edinburgh … tempting, and VC had his eye on studying in Bologna, also tempting, but that would have meant being apart. The university they both chose to attend was in the pluralistic city of Toronto, the city they knew best. The familiarity of place, the close proximity to family and friends strengthened their resolve to live a life most cherished.

NINETEEN SEVENTY-SEVEN

Mo had completed her residency and worked at a major teaching hospital in the city and VC successfully defended his thesis, received his doctorate in literature and while teaching at the university he occasionally revisited his long-running manuscript with strong ties to the Theatre of the Absurd.

"I think one of these days, your long-standing friends in your hard drive are going to emerge and kick you in your firm and very nice ass," was the occasional reminder from Mo, adding, "If they don't, I will," to which he normally replied, "I will, Mo, I will."

They lived off campus in an open-concept loft of an old tool-and-die plant, long since shut down and turned into apartments. The furniture of choice was antiques, acquired from their autumn trips to the country when such stores were closing for the winter season and bargains were to be had. Fall was also a time to enjoy the last of the country picnics on their favourite thick, warm blanket, where only a brief time was spent on food.

The allure of pre-Confederation antiques for Mo and VC lay in the imagined discussions of pioneers gathered around the fireplace, soothing their aching bones after a long day in the fields.

"Imagine life around this particular harvest table, VC. How many people would you say sat around it? What were their topics of conversation? And what was kept in that pine hutch? In that single pine-board dry sink?"

"If only they could speak," VC often said, with Mo's answer always the same, "But they do, you just have to close your eyes, take yourself back to those times and attentively listen to their voices."

Occasionally they would amalgamate the past with the present with such comments, mostly from VC, as "They didn't have sofas in those days, did they?" to which Mo, with a glass of red wine in hand and seductive smile, would look passionately at him and say, "No, but there was always plenty of hay in the barn."

Their love was passionate and all encompassing, and such replies often ended the spoken part of their communication.

The Philosopher's Walk that took Mo and VC into the hub of the university is a scenic southeasterly footpath that once followed the Taddle Creek ravine. Their walk prompted many a discussion, routinely drawing from VC's courses in anthropology. It was never a hurried walk. "We walk with the sacred spirits of the elders here, Mo. Imagine, long before the Europeans, this area, where we now walk, sit, talk, was once a Native gathering place, a sacred place for the Anishinaabe people. Sadly, the natural waterway that gently meandered through this beautiful ravine teeming with wildlife, was ultimately buried with the urbanization of Toronto in the mid-19th century, with parts channelled into the city's sewer system carrying human waste in the darkness of the underground, all in the name of progress."

"I wonder how society will define progress a hundred years from now," says Mo.

VC had never walked holding hands with anyone before Mo, and loved the warmth conveyed to his heart simply through the gentle interlacing of fingers. Occasionally they would rest on one of the few benches along the way, with Mo inevitably resting her head on his shoulder. Walking hand in hand, without much talk, contrary to their first walk home, was now their frequently adopted custom.

To some, a stroll down Philosopher's Walk kept them connected with Earth's life cycle, while for others it was just a path from point A to point B. Regardless, the seasons would come and go for both, but only the former would always know in which season they walked.

"Shhh, VC, listen … listen … hear the leaves moving? Feel the gentle breeze on your face? Close your eyes … close your eyes."

The global landscape … the Empire's currency was in crisis, the Bretton Woods monetary system was collapsing and out of the ashes a brasher, harsher form of Darwinian economic, social and political evolution emerged, rendering everyone occupying the lowermost and largest part of the triangle increasingly invisible.

This new world order marshalled in values not sculpted on tablets but depicted on charts and graphs displaying the monetary windfalls of the few. This was the self-sharpening blade that was now redefining humanity. Financial institutions worldwide grew bigger and increasingly powerful, systematically re-chiselling tablets for the social and political elite to display as relics in their opulent offices.

*More. . .*The neutron bomb, devised to pulverize people while leaving buildings intact, was perfected. The first *Star Wars* film premiered, Opium perfume was introduced and the artificial heart was patented … and the artificial heart was patented … and the artificial heart was patented. The first Apple II computer went on sale, Rocky began his ascent, Elvis left the building, and the Medal of Freedom, posthumously awarded to the Reverend Martin Luther King, Jr., was not nearly enough to begin righting the centuries' longstanding wrongs of injustice, discrimination and racism.

Mo's medical condition, after years in remission, was almost forgotten, and VC's head trauma of long ago no longer a concern. Aila's descent was their halos embodied, the long-waited light within Mo's eternal glow came to visit and stayed, and they were happy.

THE ADVENT THAT IS AILA

"The Heavens opened and bestowed us with this most precious of offerings," said Gran when Aila was born.

Aila was considered to be of celestial offering, the gift science said could never take place. Against all odds, Mo conceived, and Aila enriched their lives beyond dreams, and, as the only grandchild, she immediately became the absolute centre of the universe.

Mo and VC enthusiastically postponed their careers, Mo eagerly stayed home with their newborn, and VC, against Mo's wishes, took extra duties at the university to augment their household income. He also wrote less of his novel, but did manage to write and publish academic articles on the theatre as well as some short stories for *The Journal Absurd*.

They soon outgrew their one-bedroom, and a year after the birth, with help from his father, the inheritance from his grandparents and small royalties from his writing, VC and Mo bought a 150-year-old farmhouse with two small barns on five acres of land north of the city in King Township. The house, like the novel he was writing, was a work in progress. Work on the house? Necessary, but not time sensitive. Attending to his long-neglected friends impatiently waiting? Urgent, and absolutely essential. Their dreams, once shared with their creator, were now fast becoming estranged and potentially conflicting branches of the same tree.

They moved amid a kaleidoscopic fall. Cascading colours leisurely land … dilly-dally on the ground and eventually settle for winter. Fewer clouds, a purer blue hue and a sky with endless possibilities. The sparkle in Mo's and VC's hearts was regularly enriched by their love for each other and for their precious daughter, Aila. And, most recently, by the beauty inherent in the countryside surrounding their enchanted house. The relentlessly cold east winds of winter that came and stayed, the arctic snaps, the blizzards, the snowed-in days, served not as an impediment to living life but, rather, as a welcomed passage to a land of bliss. The thicker sweaters, the longer stays near the wood-burning stove in the kitchen reading to Aila, the imagined voyages, the homemade cookies and freshly brewed coffee. And, after Aila was comfortably in bed, with the stove's fire as the only light into the night … the never-ending joy of the midnight romance … the wonders of loving and living life simply and fully.

Late spring. South side of the house, open east-west exposure. Flower garden emerging.

"Ready to work, my man?" Mo asks, sitting nearby with sunglasses and hat with Aila in her lap, also wearing sunglasses and hat.

"Eager to," he replies, chin leisurely leaning on his rake and eyes on them.

"Well, considering my stately status of motherhood, as well as being the chosen one to comfort our most sacred child today, my participation in this soon-to-be most magnificent of gardens is limited to overseeing this project. I must warn you, I have been known to be salty. In your case, sultry."

VC smiles and signals that someone is coming around the house. Suddenly a surprised, flustered Mo says, "Oh, eh Dad, you're here … nice to see you … how long have you been here?"

"Just got here, Moreen. Everything all right?"

"Of course, Mr. Walker," replies VC with a quick glance at Mo readjusting Aila's and her sunhats.

"Sheanair!" says Aila with open arms. He walks up to them with a big smile, lifts Aila in his arms, kisses her several times and says, "So, beautiful, are you going to be the big cheese today?"

"No, Mommy said she's the boss and is going to be salty to Daddy if he doesn't do a good job."

"Did she now."

"Yes."

"And what if he does a good job?"

"He gets ice cream."

"Sounds good to me. Are you going to be a boss too?"

"Yes, but I'll be a nice boss, not like Mommy."

"I know you will, sweetie. All right then, let's see what we've got here," he says while walking with Aila in his arms, scouting for the best place for a garden.

Mo and VC look blushingly at each other and smile.

After identifying the most appropriate place to plant, he returns and, while placing Aila back on Mo's lap, says to her, "That's all right honey, you can be sultry, just wait until I leave, okay?" kisses her on the head and says, "You're a great mom, Mo, just like the mothers that have come before you."

"I love you, Dad," she says.

"Love you too, honey. So, VC, let's get to work." Walks over to VC, points and says, "That's the best location," lovingly adding, "May we have a decision from the Honourable First and Second Chair of the House please," pointing in Mo's and Aila's direction.

Mo asks Aila to hold the book they're reading, looks in the direction of her father and says, "Mr. Walker, may I, as the Second Chair, restate, you and your helper are getting paid by the hour and you are filibustering, hoping for overtime, well, there is no overtime on this job, and the First Chair sitting on my lap concurs."

"Yes, ma'am," replies Ferguson, accompanied by an army salute.

She sees VC looking around and asks, "Excuse me, Mr. Helper, looking for…?"

"Shovel."

"How can you lose a shovel? There it is, the First Chair is pointing at it, your boss is using it to load up the wheelbarrow."

"You know, this project may take longer than expected," says VC.

"Very well, Mr. Walker will receive his overtime pay."

"What about me?

"You get an extra scoop, now back to work please."

"Yes, ma'am."

Mr. Walker returns with wheelbarrow of recently delivered top soil, and while holding the shovel upright says, "All right then, listen carefully, several rows of annuals and perennials in the front with a staggered row or two of taller plants in the back. You see, as in my garden, what is needed is a backdrop of tall plants in the back of the flower bed to safeguard the rest of the arrangement. That's what I learned from my Moreen. 'Ferguson,' always called me Ferguson, never Ferris and certainly never, ever Fergie, anyway, she would say, 'Ferguson, the tall ones protect the little ones, and they all enrich our hearts, so plant well and for posterity,' and I did. Nothing like toiling together, so when in days to come, the Chairs are ready, they can add to this nicely layered flower bed."

Mo, with Aila in her arms, walks up to her father and embraces him. "I love you, Grandpa," says Aila.

"I love you too, angel, I wish your Grandma was here," he says with tears in his eyes.

"She is Grandpa, there she is," says Aila pointing to the leafing top branches of the big oak at the corner of the yard gently moving on a breezeless afternoon. They immediately turn, look and remain silent until Aila asks again if they saw her, to which they all reply they did.

At day's end with dinner soon to be served, Ferguson thanks Mo and VC for the invitation but says he promised Gran he would be home to eat. He kisses Aila multiple times, gracefully accepts their bottle of wine, and leaves.

Later that summer, stone walkways were added, a flagstone patio at its centre sufficiently large to accommodate a small table, four chairs and a bench, a cedar pergola … and more flowers … all under the direction of the Chairs. However, the Chairs, particularly the First Chair, quickly realized there was more to be had, namely freshly-baked cookies, by actually working in the garden instead of overseeing it.

A fertile mixture of natural nutrients from the barn, sun, rain and regular care took the flowers to full bloom by early summer, with their splendor enjoyed daily.

On a warm and sunny afternoon while VC was helping Aila water the flowers, with Mo sitting and watching, VC said, "Thinking of taking a break from writing this summer, what do you think, Mo?"

"Break from your novel? You have been on a hiatus for the past few years, VC, your characters wait with bated breath, they need to move on. Deliver what you promised and help them realize their dreams."

"I know, maybe later this year."

"No maybe, VC. You have created and nurtured, albeit inconsistently, a most unique relationship with them, and by continuing to neglect them and their aspirations, you are severely compromising their journey. Of what are you afraid? Are you afraid that when you're called upon, you won't measure up? No shame in that, just don't make that sentiment the end of your sentence, make it the beginning, and build faith from there."

After a brief pause, she continues, "You have a huge obligation to them, VC, they're waiting, so find the time."

"Look, Mo, I hear you and I appreciate your interest in my work, but I love you both so very much, and although my novel calls me daily, and I will get to it, you two are my priority, one never knows what curveballs life can throw at you... I do not wish to live with regrets, especially when it comes to you and Aila."

"*The Evolution of Being* is not going to be written by itself, though who knows, maybe it *is* being written by itself as we speak."

"Could be," he quietly replies.

VC bought an unstoppable old Jeep Wagoneer 4x4 for himself and a seemingly unstoppable but brand-new Jeep Cherokee 4x4 with manual locking hubs for Mo and Aila ... tenacious machines necessary to reach home safely, particularly in winter, while the Shelby, mechanically serviced, resting on tire-savers ramps, covered with a premium custom-fit cover, rested in his parents' garage until the warm, the sun and the green returned. The other Mustangs in need of work were kept close by in an enclosed part of the barn, also under wraps.

Several weeks later, while making breakfast and still in their pyjamas, VC turns to Mo and says, "I want to get married, Mo."

"Married? Now?"

"Yes, now," he replies.

"All right, let's get dressed," she says and both laugh.

"We decided we would get married before children," he says.

"It may be a little late for that, my love," she replies, placing her arms lovingly around VC's neck. She kisses him, takes him by the hand and leads him back upstairs to their bedroom … first checking on Aila … sound asleep.

The wedding was celebrated in June and the ceremony was unassuming but festive. It took place at the university chapel with just the immediate family attending as Mo wished, followed by a small reception on the stone patio off the university common room.

That evening, at home and both sitting up in bed reading congratulatory cards with Aila fast asleep in the next room, Mo, in her pyjamas but still wearing her crown adorned with freesias whose extraordinary fragrance now permeated the entire upstairs, looks at VC and says, "I'm very happy."

VC looks into her eyes and says, "I'm very happy too, Mo," and kisses her.

"So, what shall we refer to you as?" he asks.

"Mo or Moreen, as always, and you?"

"VC."

"Mo and VC, so it shall be," she says adding, "We'll save the Mr. and Mrs. for income tax purposes, wouldn't want them to think we're laundering money for Uncle Guido."

"Well…" he replies, and she smacks him on the arm. He moves closer and after a brief kiss, she looks at her wedding band and VC says, "Claddah rings from the Celtic nations, symbol of love, honesty and family, and, as you know, Aila was not pleased when she had to part with them at the ceremony."

"She is such an angel."

"That she is."

Mo takes his hand, points to his ring and says, "All right, mister, pay attention."

"Yes ma'am."

"The hands on this ring, see these hands?"

"Yes, I do."

"Well, these hands, not as big but just as powerful as yours, if not more so, represent friendship, the heart, of course, represents love, and the crown, as with the one on my head, see the crown on my head?"

He looks at her head and says, "Yes, I see it."

"The crown, my dear man, represents loyalty."

"Really?"

"Yes, really."

He looks at her intently, fixating on her eyes, and she says, "Anything wrong?" but he doesn't answer, and continues staring at her.

"Hello, VC, are you in some kind of a trance?" she says while snapping her fingers.

"Are we in Heaven?"

"Heaven down here, my good man, is not so much a place as it is a state of being. Come closer," she says. She holds his face in her hands, kisses him softly and both slide further down the bed.

"And Aila?" he asks.

"Not to worry, all the three hundred monitors you installed every two feet are on, and they all indicate, without a doubt, she's sound asleep," she replies.

"And what shall we do with the crown?" he asks.

The following morning VC wakes early, dresses, makes breakfast intending to take it upstairs, reaches the bottom of the stairs, looks up and sees his beautiful bride smiling at the top of the stairs in her negligee and almost drops the tray. She stands seductively and quietly says, *"Happy to see me?"* He just stands there, speechless but smiling. She then blows him a kiss and whispers, "I'll get my nightgown, be right down." He takes a deep breath and returns to the kitchen.

Having breakfast across from each other, she looks at him and says, "So, did you enjoy my Mae West interpretation?"

"I certainly did," he replies, taking another deep breath.

"So?" she says.

"Is there a so?"

"Yes, and it's spelled c-o-u-c-h, as in you know…"

"I do, l-o-v-e."

Mo takes his hand and pulls him close to the couch. They face each other, kiss and she says, "So this is what the morning after looks like?"

Sometime later, lying in each other's arms, Mo says, "We have always been so passionate with each other in all ways, do you think it will diminish with age?"

"No," he replies, "But our noteworthy humour may help temper the aches and pains of aging."

"The benefits of humour never cease, VC, and not to worry, when we're old, I'm sure we'll find something to humour us," she says smiling, stands and adds, "I'll dress and check on Aila, sleeping unusually late."

She quietly walks upstairs, minimizing the squeaks of the old floors, looks in on Aila, sound asleep, dresses and returns. Both sit to finish breakfast, Mo says, "Late for her, usually up by now."

"Pretty exciting day yesterday. She was so proud when she brought you flowers from our garden and wanted to trade them for the rings."

Both laugh, and Mo says, "She's so adorable."

VC stands, pours Mo another coffee, sits, looks at her and says, "I cannot believe how blessed I am, you, Aila, I am so, so fortunate."

"The mystical power that is woman, VC, and for you, there are two of us."

VC raises his cup in cheer and says, "This is going to be our summer, Mo, no extra teaching, no work on Mustangs, and thanks to you, when the day for you, me, and Aila is done, writing."

She applauds, both smile and she says, "So where would you like to begin? Let me rephrase that, which part of the country would you first like to visit?"

He smiles and says, "East coast? West coast? Rent a cottage up north? The Big Apple? The Little Apple, if there is one, the Big

Smoke? Wherever you and Aila wish to go or do is fine with me. Let's take our coffees outside and discuss it in the garden."

"Let's wait until Aila wakes up, then we can all go outside and enjoy the sunshine."

"Sounds good. Staying in the city for a few days would also be fun, especially for Aila, movie, sights, eating out."

"It would be," Mo replies.

"Then on the weekend, Mom and Dad can sit Aila and you and I will take the car out and drive up to the chalet I rented and do a proper honeymoon," he says.

"That, my love, makes for a wonderful week," she replies.

Suddenly they hear movement, both look at the two monitors in the kitchen, hear the others from everywhere else in the house, and Mo says, "Speaking of our angel, I'll get her."

"And I'll get her breakfast ready."

Several weeks later, sitting in the garden at twilight, Aila in bed, Mo with glass of white wine in hand and VC with cognac in a shot glass, monitor on the table, small one in his shirt pocket, they fondly reminisce about the week of holiday past, the sights for Aila and the long weekend at the chalet.

"You know, bella, this garden is truly a sanctuary for hearts madly in love … there is such an aura of intensity … lusciously intoxicating, mind-altering, passion-rousing, can't you just feel that splendor … rushing … eagerly to be … to be."

"I know where you're going with this, so my love, what would you like to know about heart transplants," she asks smiling.

"Brilliant," he replies and both laugh.

"What was all that rustling in the loft this afternoon?" she asks.

"I was packing unclaimed papers from last semester and came across one in particular, whose deliberation was so thought-provoking when I read it that I put a big red asterisk on it for a reread. She received the top mark, maybe I should find a way of returning it, but … do you recall the helicopter crash just before the semester ended?"

"Yes, I do, a young woman, Maggie, student of yours as I recall, the daughter and only child of the Oren family fortune, she came to your lectures with her dog and accompanied by two bodyguards. The helicopter crashed while on its way to the family summer home up north, such a tragedy, and wasn't everyone on board killed?"

"Apparently not, Syl, one of the bodyguards said to me that Maggie was the sole survivor but blinded from facial burns incurred. As a result, she always wore sunglasses."

"How sad."

"Indeed. She was by far the brightest and most creative student this year. Her last paper is from 'The Many States of Reality' series. It's a collection of treatises on the subject from my best post-graduate students. Anyway, Part One is 'The Known and Accepted Reality,' and Part Two is 'The Known but Rejected Reality,' and Part Three is 'The Creative Reality,' and it's this part that intrigued her the most.

"I would like to read it, if I may."

"Yes, of course, she would be fine with you reading it. She and her dog Ralph were always accompanied by Syl, ex-Marine, and Alex, ex-SEAL. Excellent student, never late and never missed class and remembered everything."

"Remarkably gifted."

He nods and says, "Highest mark, quotes Aristotle, Plato, Homer and other greats. You know, I often wondered how she was able to retain it all until Alex explained it to me. She has a particular aptitude for retaining what she hears, much like someone with a photographic memory."

"Intriguing."

"On the last day of class while handing back papers, they came up, I shook their hands and Maggie said, 'Thank you, Mr. C., *Until We Meet Again,* you know like the song."

"I do."

"And as they were leaving, Alex called me aside and told me how much the course did for Maggie, how it inspired her to live again, and how appreciative they were, then he said that they owe me one and someday they'll return the noble deed. Fascinating."

"How do you think they will do that?"

"Don't know, maybe it was just a figure of speech."

"One never knows, VC. I'm sure your paths will cross again."

"Maybe," he replies.

She places her glass on the table, wraps her hands around VC's face, kisses him and says, "Time to bed and to Files."

"How about just to bed, and no Files," he replies, but she looks at him shakes her head and says, "Files or describing a heart transplant?"

"Files it shall be," he replies.

They turn off the outside lights except the sentinel light at the entrance to the long gravel driveway, then the indoor lights. They check on Aila, sound asleep, and once both in bed, leaning against the headboard and holding hands, Mo says, "And now to the Life Files, where shall we begin? The Happy File, the Sad File or the Sad-to-Happy File? Choose wisely, my love."

"Sad-to-Happy file," he replies.

"Good choice," she replies.

He kisses her hand and says, "Where shall we begin?"

"Do you remember the time you came to the house after your altercation at school?" she asks.

"Of course, how can I forget, and if I may, that was a Sad-to-Happy-to-Ecstatic File."

"Indeed, it was. As I remember it, it was such a sweet, sweet moment, maybe longer than one moment, but not by much," she says. He shakes his head and smiles. "Anyway," she continues, "That's another File for when we're old, can't remember, but can embellish, sooo, back to the Sad-to-Happy file, the one which culminated in a most anticipated and as expected, quite a passionate evening. Recall, lover boy?"

"Never to be forgotten."

"You looked awful, your face was cut and bruised, blood on your clothes, you scared me to death, and you and my father had a good laugh when he asked you what the other guy looked like and you replied, not a scratch on him, funny, funny VC, you could have been seriously hurt, or worse, and you two laughed and I cried."

"That's the Sad part of the file, can we fast forward to the Happy part? I like that part best," he replies.

"Agony before the ecstasy VC, that's how it's done."

"Very well, but easy on the agony part."

"Noted. I must admit I felt so special that you came home to me. I felt revered that my battle-scarred warrior returned from battle to rest his weary body on my bosom … which you did, and when I placed my hand on your chest, looked into your eyes, I felt your heart calling and I knew it was going to be our night. So how do you put the brakes on passion when you're deep in love?"

"Why?"

"Why what?"

"Why would you want to put the brakes on passion when in love?"

"Well, my dear, you don't have to put the brakes on passion when in love, if you're prepared. I being the wiser, knew that someday we would … you know, fulfil our passionate desires, so if I hadn't had a prophylactic readily available, knowing you may not be as pre-pared…"

"But I was," he quickly adds.

"Anyway, I had purchased them the day before, and believe me, that was a very embarrassing experience taking that shiny box to the counter."

"A postscript, if I may, it was I that bought them after the initial 'event,' and it was you, my dear Mo, who said by the box, but not a big box."

"Yes, I did say that, and yes you did. So back to us, that night, passion soaring into the stratosphere, passion … did I say passion already?"

"Twice. Three times, I think."

"Very well, stay with me…"

"I'm not going anywhere," he replies.

"So, I asked if you were in pain and you said you had a high tolerance for pain and could go the distance even in agony … from your boxing, martial arts days, no doubt."

"Yes, but the night in question, in your basement was very, very different than being in the ring, or on the dojo, direct opposite actually. Going the distance with you was truly turning agony into ecstasy, in the ring, it was normally ecstasy into agony, but that night I did go the distance regardless of pain, just to impress you of course."

"That you did, lover boy. You kissed me ever so gently, but then I kissed you more passionately and you miraculously sprang into action, in a manner of speaking," she says, and both laugh.

"It was your kiss, Mo."

"That's what it was, was it?"

"Much, much more, of course, but when your kiss lit the fuse to that keg of dormant gunpowder in me, I knew I had to rip my clothes off, and fast."

She smacks him gently on his shoulder and says, "You're going too quickly, tales of romance need sensuous detail in a slow, heart-throbbing fashion, not take off the lid, it's boiling over. So, my man in a hurry, slow down, I will tell the story."

"In detail?"

"Just enough."

"Are we now in the Ecstatic File?" he asks.

"No, and no more interruptions, okay with you, maestro?"

He nods and she continues.

"Pay attention."

"I'm all ears," he replies, smiling, and she moves closer and continues. "Remember … when you couldn't take your sweaty and bloody sweater off because it was too painful … and when I helped, you suddenly kissed me, and accidentally on purpose brushed against my breasts on your way to raising your arm … me gently touching your bruised ribs. We looked at each other so feverishly … and regardless of the sweat and tears … desire … passion, sweet passion took over and we became so serious, so focused … so I furiously helped you take off your sweater … you tried furiously to take off my top … those luscious lips of yours, then suddenly on the couch, oh my God, VC, we went so crazy, and I wasn't sure if your grunts and moans were a result of your bruised ribs or from the lovemaking, regrettably they had to be subdued, people upstairs, yet the hushness made it all that more exceptional, the lushness of our bodies coming together, it was so, so primal, then in your caring way asked if it had been painful for me, to which I quietly said, I love you, and kissed you. Remember?"

"Vividly," he replies.

She kisses him passionately, playfully bites his big lower lip and says, "You were so gentle with such sustained passion … it was wonderful, so intimate, so caring, so special, VC, it was."

"It was, my love."

"Our hearts' rhythms merged and our bodies' heat became unrestrained. I looked into your passionate eyes and amidst the short, soft kisses on your injured face and bruised chest, you whispered, I love you."

He slowly unbuttons her pyjama top. She helps him remove his top … slow and compelling touches … lengthier kisses … and when their hearts reach that much sought-after rhythm of one, the night turns into a treasured lullaby.

The following morning, Saturday, early, still in bed, Mo embracing VC from behind, suddenly says, "Is that Aila I hear?"

"It is," replies VC.

They both jump out of bed, put on their robes and quietly walk to Aila's room. "Sound asleep," Mo whispers, they leave the room, return to theirs and climb back into bed. Mo rests her head on his chest and says, "I'm worried about her."

"What makes you say that?"

"Can't quite put my finger on it, but she doesn't seem to be her lively self lately."

"I've also noticed some lethargy, maybe it's related to a growth spurt."

"That occurred to me too, but it seems more than that, need to pursue it."

"She certainly doesn't punch or kick as hard as she used to in our lessons."

"Something is not right."

He kisses her on her head, pulls the covers fully over their bodies, embrace tightly and both lie there in silence. A while later, Mo asks, "Do you think we'll ever have a Happy-to-Sad File in our lives, VC?"

Aila's call interrupts the discussion, and while putting on his robe, VC says, "Tough question to answer, Mo, but I do know, together, we can work through anything," then he walks to Aila's room and brings her to their bed.

"Here is our beloved four-year-old going on one hundred."

"Such a sweet soul," adds Mo.

"Indeed," he replies, placing her in Mo's arms. After a barrage of kisses, Mo settles her between them and VC asks Aila if she is hungry, to which she replies, "Not really, Daddy."

"Did you have a good sleep, honey?" Mo asks her.

"Kind of, but I had a stomach ache during the night."

"Sweetie, why didn't you call us?"

"It was okay, it didn't really last long."

"Do you have it now?" Mo asks.

"No."

"Have you had this pain before?"

"Last week, at the playground, Mindy punched me in the stomach just for fun, but it hurt, then it went away."

"Baby, you have to tell us these things."

"I know, sorry."

"Why don't you just lie on your back and have mommy poke at you a little. VC, can you please get me the stethoscope and thermometer."

Mo does a thorough examination. Aila showed some discomfort but not pain.

"All done, but you know, Aila, we should have Dr. Ezra examine you."

She nods, Mo turns to VC and says, "I'll call Martha, just to make sure."

"I like Dr. Ezra," says Aila, "and I don't mind needles. Why do you get needles, Daddy?"

"To make him smarter," adds Mo.

"I don't think they're working," says Aila, and all three laugh and Mo says, "You may be right honey, but it does help keep the diabetes in check."

"Stay off the sweets and go easy on bread," says Aila.

"That's good advice for Daddy, honey, and where did you get that information?"

"From one of your books," she replies.

"You're very smart, Aila, you're way, way up there in smart land," says VC.

"Like Mommy."

"For sure," says VC.

"Poor Daddy," says Aila and laughs, "By the way, Daddy, when you and Mommy talk about the absurd, what do you mean?"

"What else did you hear?" asks Mo while looking at VC.

"Couldn't hear very well, Murray's tractor was going by. So, tell me, Daddy, do people in your book talk to you?"

"Well…" he replies.

"Do you hear voices?"

"Well…"

"If you do, you need to see a shrink."

"And you got that from one of Mommy's books?" he asks.

"Yes," she replies, "But don't worry, Daddy, we won't let them shrink you." They look at each other and burst out laughing.

"When can I go to a regular school?"

"Don't you like that special school Daddy takes you to every morning?"

"I suppose, but next year can I go to a regular school?"

"You mean with more students?"

"Yes, where they play all the time."

"I'm sure they do a lot more than play, but we'll look into it and talk about it some more, okay?"

"Okay. You two can talk, I feel a little tired, I'm going to nap now."

"You do that, honey, we'll go downstairs and make breakfast."

"Are you and Daddy going to the basement to play loud music?"

"No, we're going to the kitchen to make you your special breakfast, how does that sound?"

"I'm not very hungry, I just want to sleep."

Mo pulls the cover over Aila's small body and kisses her on her forehead. She and VC dress and walk downstairs to the kitchen.

Sitting across from each other at the kitchen table, cup of coffee in hand, Mo looks at VC and says, "I'll call Martha later."

"What's your opinion so far?" he replies.

"She seems fine, but difficult to say. As her pediatrician, I'm sure Martha will do a more in-depth examination."

"I'm sure she will, Mo, now may I make you some breakfast?"

"Thanks, VC, nothing for now, but will take another coffee."

VC pours her another coffee and asks if she wishes to sit in the garden. "Let's just stay here for now," she replies.

"All right, but how about some burned toast and Muriel's home-made strawberry jam?"

"Burned toast," she says smiling, "A man of extremes. What would we do without you?"

"No, Mo, it's what would I do without you two," he replies, embracing her from behind, kissing her on the head and saying, "Well-done toast coming up."

Mo eats her toast and says, "I should check on Aila."

"I'll make her breakfast."

Soon she returns with Aila in her arms, sits her on her lap and says, "Daddy made you your favourite breakfast..."

"Champagne breakfast, thank you, Daddy, how thoughtful."

"Not quite honey, someday. Now, just an egg, sliced tomatoes, blueberries, piece of melon, brown toast with Muriel's jam…"

"What, no cigar?" asks Aila, adding, "How do you do it, Daddy?"

"Do what, baby?"

"Keep up with us," she replies, laughing.

Mo and VC smother her with kisses and Aila says, "I need a drink."

"Pardon?" asks Mo.

"That's what Sheanair Walker says when he babysits me, he says it's apple juice, and I say, 'Sure, Granddad, then why don't you drink it out of a big glass with a straw, not that teeny one?'"

"What does he say?"

"He says he loves me as he's pouring himself another one. So, Dad, how are those lazy Huxley and Munro from your story doing? Have they found a job yet?"

"Not sure, job? In due time I suppose."

"Like never?"

"So Aila, what would you like to do today?"

"No, no, VC, Aila asked a legitimate question, what do you have to say to your daughter about your novel, is it progressing … or not?"

"Yeah, Dad, Mom says you started that story way before I was en route. Your characters must be tired just sitting there waiting, except those two … youth today, so impatient, all me, me, me and now, now, now."

"How old are you?" he asks.

"Can we go for a ride in the muscle car?"

"We can, later, but why don't we sit in the garden for a while, it's so nice outside. I'll take your breakfast, and Mommy will carry you."

While sitting together in the garden with Aila on Mo's lap, VC asks if she's happy.

"I am, Daddy, are you?"

"If you're happy, if Mom's happy, then I'm happy."

"Can we go back to the pony ranch?"

"Of course, we can, want to go now?" replies VC.

"Maybe tomorrow, can I go back to sleep now?"

"Are you sure honey? Have some fruit, you like fruit."

"Don't feel like eating any more, Daddy."

"Would you like to go for a drive in the muscle car?"

"No Mommy, I feel tired."

"Okay, baby, I'll take you upstairs."

Mo takes her in her arms, and once upstairs, Aila asks if she could lie in Mommy's and Daddy's bed.

"Of course, you can, you know, I feel a little tired too, so may I lie with you?"

Aila nods and both lie together with Mo holding her close to her.

After cleaning up, VC walks quietly to their bedroom and sees Aila sleeping next to Mo. Mo opens her eyes, gestures him to come over and he lies down with them. She grabs his hand tightly and with Aila between them, neither closes their eyes.

Dr. Martha Ezra, Mo's best friend since high school, examined Aila and ordered a variety of tests and scans. A week later, the results indicated no major issues but a follow-up was scheduled in three months' time. The barrage of tests after *that* appointment did indicate reason for concern, and less than six months later, Aila began bruising easily, experiencing frequent infections, strenuous breathing ... the pain, the laboured smiles brought the most dreaded diagnosis, the one that immediately fused all their seasons of happiness into one long, pale grey and dreary twilight.

The long dark nights turned into long dark days, into long ashen months of nights. As darkness deepened, hope became more obscure and less accessible. Family members took turns providing Mo and VC with some semblance of respite, but it's hard to sleep with eyes open. One targeted drug after another, the high-dose chemo ... the withered spirit ... the result, no lasting gains.

With her rainbow now prematurely losing its life colours, the chance of making it through the badlands was infinitesimally small. If her little spirit was to slip away, it would be from the arms of her loving parents.

"No! No more chemo! No more treatment ... please." The ripped and torn hearts of those around her, the frayed emotions, the anguish, the tears of grief, the rage … a dream that would have known no boundaries for this precious one was now on its way to being savagely obliterated. The tightrope on which everyone had been walking for some time would soon snap and all would be easy prey to the intensification of the profound life-starving sadness already deep in their hearts. Against medical wishes, Mo and VC took their baby home.

NINETEEN EIGHTY-ONE

At home, Aila was never far from the warmth of their touch, from the sound of their voices, from the beating of their hearts, from the fragrance of the garden. When not in their arms, in the kitchen, living room, or garden, she lay between them on their bed. They watched Aila until their eyes tired, and as soon as their eyelids began closing, they immediately opened them again and kept watch. They hoped and prayed, but days clear-fell into long nights, and the morning sun was increasingly late in arriving.

The Sunday morning of the third week, while Mo sat rocking her by their bedroom window, Aila slowly opens her once radiant blue eyes, and asks to be taken to the garden.

"Sure, baby, but let's bundle you up first," she replies, calls VC and once he was in the room, Mo told him of Aila's wish.

"It's Daddy, Aila, of course, we'll take you to the garden."

Soon after, Mo says, "All bundled up, baby, and I like the yellow toque Gran made you."

"Me too, it's so bright."

"Just like you. Ready?"

"Yes."

"I'll carry you down and daddy will bring the IV pump."

They carefully walk down the stairs with VC ahead ready to break any fall should Mo slip. They reach the garden and sit on the bench with Mo holding Aila gently and adoringly in her arms as if she were a newborn.

Their tattered hearts knew they had tirelessly navigated through many a jagged reef with their little one's illness only to find themselves deeper into the eye of the hurricane. Mo and VC raised whatever was left of the mainsail and continued navigating through the crushing waters, fiercely holding onto their daughter's frail body … hoping … hoping.

Without their precious daughter, they knew, the once-existing waves of happiness would never return to their shore, and the gales of laughter, of joy, the goodnight kiss on her forehead before the moon came to babysit, all would forever be lost in the depth of despair.

Yes, the gashed sails could eventually be re-stitched, the wind in their sails could slowly pick up again, but the reshaped coastline would never be the same.

"I like flowers," says Aila in a barely audible voice.

"You are the most beautiful flower in this great big garden, you are our very special and precious flower," says Mo, while VC caresses Aila's face.

"Like a perennial?"

"You are a perennial, and you will always be in bloom," says Mo and kisses her on her cheek.

"Will I last forever?" asks Aila.

"Forever and ever," replies Mo.

"And you know, angel, you will find yourself in this magnificent place with flowers and birds and…" says VC.

"And Grandma Moreen?" asks Aila keenly but in a weakening voice.

"And Grandma Moreen," replies Mo.

"Am I going to heaven?"

"Of course you are, baby, and what will you do there?" asks Mo.

"Play with the angels until you get there."

Aila looks at her mother, stretches and kisses her on the cheek, tightens her embrace and says, "I love you, Mommy." Looks at her father and says, "I love you too, Daddy."

Mo looks at the intravenous catheter in Aila's bony hand, and asks if it pains her. "It hurts," Aila quietly replies.

VC takes Aila's hand and asks if she would like it removed, but she doesn't answer. Mo and VC look at each other and Mo says, "Daddy is going to call your favourite doctor, and when she gets here, we'll see if it's okay to remove it, is that all right with you, baby?"

"Should we go back in?" asks VC.

"Yes, getting a little too breezy out here," says Mo and as she readies Aila to take her back upstairs, VC breaks off a rose bud and places it in his daughter's hand.

"Thank you, Daddy," she says, but VC, choking from rushing, trachea-flooding tears, couldn't articulate a coherent reply.

Dr. Ezra receives the call on her private line and rushes out of the office. VC meets her at the door, indicates they're upstairs and follows her up.

Dr. Ezra enters the room, walks up to them, looks at Mo, greets Aila with a soft kiss on her head and says, "Let's see if we can do something about this contraption on your hand, shall we."

She gently removes the catheter, bandages her fragile hand and says, "There, better?"

Aila barely nods. Dr. Ezra kisses her head and squeezes Mo's arm. Holding back the tears, she touches VC's shoulder, walks out of the room and stands against the wall across from the bedroom door trying to hold back her tears, but can't. She places her hand over her mouth, her eyes fill and the tears stream.

Aila slowly readjusts herself on Mo's lap and is held more securely. VC caresses her face. Both he and Mo gently hold her frail hand, hoping to reignite the spark of life within her. Not long after, a faint smile, a weak grasp of her mother's hand, Aila's eyes slowly close and she is gone.

Witnessing their daughter's last breath was unimaginable. Closed eyes, partly-opened mouth desperately waiting for her to inhale again. Hoping, silently summoning, but the life they knew had left. Mo immediately placed Aila on the bed and quickly began CPR in a frantic attempt to breathe life back into her. Dr. Ezra rushes in and takes over.

"Aila? Aila! Breathe! Please baby, breathe!" screams Mo, but the door to that short-lived miracle had closed.

"Please God, take me, take me," pleads VC, but this was not the time for him.

Dr. Ezra stops, takes Aila's pulse, kisses the little one on her forehead, embraces Mo and VC and, stethoscope in hand, walks out into the hall crying. She stands momentarily against the wall, then slides to a sitting position on the hard floor, throws her stethoscope down the hall and sobs. VC takes Aila's lifeless body gently in his arms and stares at her, Mo embraces both and the flow of tears further disorient their numbed hearts.

"Aila! Aila!" The calling of her name echoed uncontrollably throughout the century-old house until the unrelenting cries asphyxiated all sound and movement and their lives precipitously became a slow-moving nightmare.

The tragic loss of their beloved Aila struck Mo and VC like a massive stroke of intense sorrow … the oxygen-deprived brain, the numbed heart … the paralysis of emotions … the slurred words of affection, and no matter how strongly they embraced, wept, wailed … no matter how frequently they stared into each other's eyes, dried each other's tears, caressed each other's faces … the same unanswerable question followed, why was their beautiful, spirited and joyful daughter taken from her loving nest? And how can a God that warms, also burn? Maybe the Voyage of Souls has less to do with God's strengths or weaknesses and more to do with the soul's sovereign journey on the road to completing its own mission.

Grieving is an emotional pendulum of extremes, one that swings from everything making sense to nothing making sense. Nothing is as incomprehensible to a parent as the loss of a child, and at a time of deep sorrow, nothing makes sense.

The immediate feelings of anger, despair, confusion can cloak any semblance of normalcy and, regardless of time elapsed, never seem to lift.

This most inconceivable of nightmares cut through Mo's and VC's hearts like a merciless red-hot blade. The funeral service was family only and the eulogy became an unstoppable outpouring of emotions … a special life that was and what it could have been.

Mo began the euology, but soon after, her words and emotions collided leaving her unable to breathe, and VC continued.

"Aila's brief time with us…" Unable to continue himself, he steps back. Mo, a glance of comfort, a gentle squeezing of her loving husband's hand, an immediate reassurrence, spoke of how Aila always led with her heart. "She touched all of us so profoundly … we will miss her so, so incredibly much, but we know her work continues … with us, and with all who were touched by her."

VC pulls Mo closer, a subtle, endearing nod and they both tell the story of how, at such a young age, Aila tried teaching Murray the correct way of milking her favourite cow, Hazel … concluding that it is not we who teach the children, it's the children who often teach us.

A permanently lit candle was placed on the window sill of her room. The visual memorial honoured Aila's eternal heart light. The light served not as a reminder of her passing but, rather, to reaffirm that her journey continued. Nor was it lit to keep their hearts broken but, rather, to keep hope alive, hope that someday, somewhere in some form, they would be reunited with their precious daughter.

The months that followed Aila's passing were an unending storm of depression, debilitating anxiety and heart-wrenching pain for Mo and VC, and for anyone touched by the special angel known lovingly as Aila.

Profound sorrow can walk by your side or behind you, but unless disentangled from living, it will walk ahead of you and take you further into the realm of unending despair.

The sharp double-edged blade cut deeply into Mo's and VC's hearts, and although the road to recovery was long and perilous, and although the road was flooded in places from unexpected torrents, the life line to each other's hearts and souls remained forever strong and unyielding.

In time, their tide of tears ebbed, their hearts became more settled and the months of anguish dwindled to weeks and then to long days. Their wounded and suffering spirits progressively made their way down the narrow path towards the road to healing, and their lives became more steeped in living it, never to be as it once was, but as it now needed to be. The more frequent smiles, the less guilty laughter, and the rediscovered long-abandoned intimate touches slowly and cautiously returned.

Early one morning, sitting in bed in each other's arms, VC sits up and attempts, as he had several times before, to speak of Aila's Life File. It always began with the same phrase … *"Once upon a time"*… ending with them holding each other tightly in silence.

In time, more promising dawns, fewer clouds and longer, brighter rays of hope became increasingly amenable with living life. Sunsets became progressively more colourful and less hazy; the sun's scattered rays glowed more softly at twilight, and on their frequent night drives to their chosen viewing place, stars rallied and warmed their hearts. Once they reached the clearing, they sat on their wagon's tailgate with Aila's blanket between them, holding each other tightly and never taking their eyes off the starlit sky. Of the thousands of visible stars and of the billions they couldn't see, they knew, they just knew, and could so feel, so strongly feel, one of them was their beloved Aila.

"Where is she?" Mo asks looking up at the starry sky.

"There," he replies pointing to the brightest star.

"Yes, the scintillating one, I see her, I see her."

Their hearts see, speak and gradually settle. Mo leans on her man and says, "I miss her so."

"I do too," he says, squeezing her hand, adding, "Do you remember what she said in her soft, barely audible voice to us before she left?"

"Yes, so brave, so, so, wise, she looked at us and said, 'The time has come for me to go,' then she left."

VC places his arm around Mo, pulls her tighter towards him, kisses her head and remains silent. On their drive home, she turns to him and says, "Do you think we can resume our Life File?"

He nods and remains silent.

"How about starting with our most precious?" Mo says. He turns, looks at her, and smiles.

That night in bed, both leaning against the headboard, Mo begins with "Our most precious."

Aila's Life File became a recollection of milestones big and small, from VC lifting her toward the stars as a baby, to her first solid food, to her first day at the advanced academic program. The plan was to drop her off, smother her with goodbye hugs and kisses, and for VC to drive Mo to work then go on to his, but it didn't quite turn out that way.

Once back in the car, Mo takes VC's hand and says, "Let's sit here for a minute."

"Sure," he replies squeezing her hand. A minute turned into an hour and a half of staring at the front door of the small school in silence. Mo glances at her watch and says, "Goodness, VC, we've been here a long time."

"And she didn't try running away," he replies smiling.

"It's almost dismissal, so why don't we wait and take her to lunch."

"Special day, unforgettable day," says VC

"Her whole life is one of unforgettable days," adds Mo.

It was almost two in the morning, the flow of treasured memories slowed, silence became more pronounced, and Mo says, "We need to add one more file to the list."

"And what would that be?"

"The Spiritual File."

"And what would the first entry be?"

"In search of peace."

"And finding it," he adds.

After their extended leave Mo was offered a promotion and VC a paid sabbatical but both turned the offers down. He resumed teaching with a commitment to Mo to resume his writing, and she left the hospital to join Dr. Ezra's family practice.

At the end of the day, when evenings began entering the long nights and nights held more steadily until the moon bid farewell to the treetops, the only place their healing hearts chose to be was in each other's arms.

CHAPTER THREE

One morning while having coffee in the garden, Mo looks at the perpetually lit candle illuminating Aila's room and says, "I wonder where that little soul is now."

"Likely muscling her way to the front of the line and saving us a good seat."

"You always had a way with words, VC."

"And a good eye for infinite beauty, as in you, and as in our beloved Aila."

They sit closer together in silence for a while, finish their coffee and return inside. While in the kitchen, they hear a knock and it's Murray. He comes in, is offered coffee but time does not permit. "Too much to do today," he replies. "Muriel would like to know if you are free for dinner tonight, and she told me not to take no for an answer."

VC and Mo look at each other and VC says, "Well … I think so, Murray, what do you think, Mo?"

"Thank you, Murray, we look forward to it. Tell Muriel I'll bring dessert," she replies.

"No, she said to just bring an appetite. See you around six?"

"We'll be there, thank you. Murray," says Mo.

Murray and Muriel, genuine, salt-of-the-earth people, lived up the road. Never met until the move yet immediately became each other's "adopted" family.

The evening with caring friends was heartfelt. After giving thanks, good food and reflective conversations followed. Jake, the black lab, always by Murray's side and first to receive from his plate, somehow seemed to participate through his short barks. The occasional moment of silence was inevitably broken with brief laughter about past occurrences, most notably Murray describing the first time he tried teaching Aila how to milk cows. A tale of such endearment told and retold lovingly in Murray's effortless way. He, like many of his generation, was a natural story teller, the simplicity yet richness in the words came from working closely to the land.

"I remember it well, Murray," says VC, "I was in the big barn stacking bails, Mo and Muriel in the house and you and Aila off to milk the cow Aila named Hazel."

Murray nods, smiles and begins recounting, "There she was in her little rubber boots, small aluminum pail with a rainbow she painted on it in one hand, holding onto my hand with the other, and as we entered the barn and approached Hazel, she asked if I had brought warm water and soft cloth to clean the teats, to which I said I had, then she said, 'You know, Mr. Murray, washing with warm water helps bring the milk down,' and I said, 'You don't say' and she replied, 'I do say, and you have to dry them too, and gently.'"

Following brief laughter and some withheld tears, Murray continued, "Then as we approached Hazel, Aila said, 'You don't need a stanchion, Mr. Murray, Hazel knows who we are, she won't move but let's walk slowly, speak nicely and in a low voice, gently pat her side so she knows where we are,' then she said, 'I see you have classical quietly playing in here, that's good but never rock and roll, okay, Mr. Murray, cows don't like to dance fast.' 'Got you,' I said, then she said, 'Mom and Dad like to dance fast, they're always dancing,' and I said, 'Is that so,' and she replied, 'Yes, Mr. Murray, that is so.' I just loved the way she talked, could talk to her all day.

"Anyway, we washed and dried the teats, she then sat on the stool, placed her bucket under the rudder and said, 'Pay attention, Mr. Murray.' She pulls down on the teats three or four times and says, 'This is called stripping and it's to get dirt out of the milk ducts, want to give it a try?' Sure, I said, and after more encouraging instruction we filled our pails, she pats Hazel and said, 'Thank you,

Hazel,' turns and looks at me, then I realized why and said, 'Yes, thank you, Hazel.'

"Walking back, she looks up at me and says, 'You did well, Mr. Murray,' and I said it was because she was a good teacher, then she asked if I ever got the strap at school to which I replied, 'There is your dad, time for lunch' and before she walked to meet you and tell you all about milking Hazel, she turns to me and said, 'You're not going to answer that question, are you, Mr. Murray?' and barely four years old, just before she took ill. My God, we miss her."

Walking home arm-in-arm on the gravel road, carrying two pieces of homemade apple-cranberry-currant and strawberry-rhubarb pie Muriel insisted they take, eyes frequently toward the night sky, Mo says, "What a most enjoyable evening, they are such wonderful, wonderful people."

"Always love that story. They adored her and vice versa. They were her grandparents away from home. We need to do more reconnecting."

"For ourselves and for those who care about us," she replies.

Into their fourth year since Aila's passing and her Life Files as compiled by Mo and VC grew increasingly larger than life itself. On occasion, they attempted to discuss their current Life File, but it was never as long or elaborate as Aila's.

The hands on the clock of time moved with more predictability, colours in the garden became more noticeable, and evening meals fostered increased conversation.

Late one Saturday afternoon while they were in the kitchen readying dinner, Mo felt dizzy and VC immediately helped her sit down.

"Haven't felt this way in a very long time," she said.

"Pregnant?"

She looks at him and says, "Right, VC. Likely dehydrated."

"I thought, you know, maybe another miracle."

"Glass of water, please."

He brings her water and says, "You didn't have much to eat today, maybe that's causing your lightheadedness."

They were both wrong. The deafening bell of the dreaded, life-silencing disease had come tolling again.

They defiantly faced their mortal enemy and battles courageously raged on but they were no match for the unstoppable armies of cancerous cells fighting the heroically healthy body, and, when the bell finally rang, only one of the indivisible Mo and VC would be spared. According to VC, the wrong one was spared.

Several weeks after Mo first felt faint, her worsening condition prompts VC to introduce the idea of a trip. While Mo is having breakfast in bed one morning, VC, sitting on the edge, gently caresses her face, and asks, "What are your thoughts on returning to the carefree place of our ancestors?"

She caresses his face and says, "The warrior and the warrior princess. Our hearts may be wounded, our spirits diminished, but we fear not what is to come, VC."

"Very well, from a humble warrior to a prodigious one, remember when we danced late into the evening on the courtyard of my grandfather's house?"

"I do," she replies.

"Where our lungs feasted on the life-giving oxygen from the Alps and Apennines."

"Where the dew on awakening flowers demanded our attention before running away with the morning sun, and where the beauty of flowers and colour filled our hearts' desires to live forever," she adds.

"I most certainly do, and we will, Mo, we will, but first, let us revisit that enchanted valley, walk the Roman Forum, return to the place of Gaels, hike the Highlands of your ancestors and follow the endless echoing of the pipes."

"I would like that, VC, very much. I want to revisit the place of my childhood, hold my mother's hand down the cobblestone walkways again, hear the voices of my elders in the wind, seek guiding wisdom, revisit my adopted home in the valley of Fiume Liri, watch day turn into night and hold tightly into morning. Our hearts are ready, VC, and I would like that, my love."

He embraces her and she rests her head on his shoulder. After several minutes of silence, he asks, "Where shall we begin?"

"Where we can dance all night," she answers.

AGING SUMMER: THE SECOND-LAST SEASON OF ITS KIND
LA CASA

Life. Love. Life. Love and Live Life. Liri River Valley, where true love can rise and redirect the wind with a simple kiss, and where a soft whisper of intimate affection under the afternoon sun can revise even the cloudiest of skies.

Behold the dignity of the Apennines and the Alps, cradling the mystic basin. Behold the sovereignty of love, relationships and family. Cherish the splendour of the human touch; the feel of a loving hand softly stroking a face; the awe-inspiring supremacy of the souls in and around life's circles ... embrace your dreams and breathe the essence of life within those dreams. Love and Live Life.

Casa Paterna, Grandfather's house, less than an hour's drive southeast of Rome.

VC inherited the large stone house on the east side of the tranquil waters of Fiume Liri and his cousins Silvio, Italia and Iolanda the house on the west side. VC's was more than residential, it had a wine cellar, bar and a general store. The house, whose thick walls tenaciously withstood enemy fire during the wars, proudly overlooked a sloping vineyard, farmland and small woodlot of tall melodic poplars.

Mo and VC arrived in mid-April. His neighbouring cousins prepared the house for their return, stocked it with food and wine, and in waiting was a silver-coloured Alfa Romeo GTV for their travels. They landed in Rome and his cousin Claudio, wife Gabriela and the Alfa were waiting. It was midday when they reached their house, and a most celebratory gathering with close relatives took place al fresco on the courtyard. Food and wine aplenty and the encirclement of an adored family took Mo's and VC's hearts back to a time when joy and optimism knew no boundaries, to times when everything that was imaginable in heart was achievable in real time—a time now far beyond reach.

The sunny afternoon eventually evolved into a subtle whirlwind of colours and, for an all too brief time, the joyless, inescapable reality of the illness faded, dreams re-emerged, and life was the way they remembered it. The moon eventually guides everyone home, and Mo and VC remain embraced in the middle of the courtyard. Sensing fatigue, VC asks Mo if she wishes to lie on the old hammock and she nods. He picks her up, lays her down upon it, and joins her.

"Do you think it will hold us until morning?" she asks.

"Until morning?"

"Yes, baby, I want to spend the night here, it's an unusually warm and moonlit one, I want to listen to the crickets, I want to hear the chorus from the nearby river, watch the fireflies chase each other, fall asleep in your arms, and wake up amongst the violets and the wild flowers and to the life-giving sun rays, I want to do that."

"And we will."

"Kiss me," she says.

The following morning when the sun rose above the mountain peaks, the first rays find them embraced on the large, worn hammock in the corner of the terrace. He opens his eyes, looks at her and tucks her more securely under the heavy blankets.

She slowly wakes, and he asks how she's feeling.

"How about a kiss under the rising Roman sun," she replies and he softly obliges.

"Make you some coffee?" he asks.

"No, stay."

She looks at him and says, "Thank you for bringing me back here, VC."

"I wasn't sure how it would turn out, Mo, but I'm happy we're here."

"This place is special for us, our little cocoon, here we can live and love forever," she says.

He takes out his handkerchief, wipes her tears while his run down his face, kisses her on the cheek and says, "I love you, Mo."

"And I you, my knight. Let's love the way we have always loved, VC, let's live life and love eternally, VC, promise?"

"I promise," he replies, and helps her off the hammock. She takes off her shoes, readjusts her sweater and scarf, and begins walking through the bright and colourful meadow towards the river. She turns, looks at him, and says, "Come, walk with me my husband, let's walk to our river, feel the splendour under our feet. There is clarity in my heart, VC, and harmony in my stride when you're with me."

VC takes her hand but she doesn't move.

"I thought you wanted to go for a walk?" he says.

"I do, but you can't feel life under your feet with those big shoes, and if you want your toes to smile at the sun, they and the socks have to go," she replies.

"Like the tie on the first day of school?"

"Like the tie on the first day of school," she says, smiling.

He takes off his shoes and socks, and asks, "Anything else you want me to take off?"

"Incorrigible," she replies and kisses him. They leave the shoes and socks on the courtyard, she takes his hand and both walk to the river.

"My beautiful Mo," he says. She stops, pulls him closer, and they embrace tightly. Once the tremors subside, tears ebb, they resume walking silently to the river bank. He helps her down to the river's edge, takes off his jacket and folds it for her to sit more comfortably on the rocks, and she asks, "For my skinny behind?"

He pulls her close and tells her he loves her. Embracing, they stand for a while, then both sit on the lower rocks with feet in the water.

"Too cold for you?" he asks.

"A little but it's fine."

She looks at him, smiles and asks, "Do you remember what we did the first time you took me to this spot?"

VC looks at her, raises his eyebrows and returns the smile.

She gently slaps his shoulder and says, "You're impossible, VC, I'm referring to the corn."

"The corn?"

"Yes, the corn stalk, you took your trusty pocket knife, you know the one that has everything but the kitchen sink, cut a corn stalk and you built us each a…? Focus, VC, focus."

"Let's see … corn, do you mean the time in the corn field?"

"No, VC, the boats," she replies.

"Yes, of course, I remember, the boats," he says, "I made us two small boats from the corn stalk, used leaves as sails and set them in the water to jointly travel to the mighty ocean."

"And whose brave little boat took to the current first?"

"That brave, sturdily built little boat was yours, as I recall," he replies.

She turns, places both her hands on his face and gives him a long, adoring kiss.

Holding her tighter, he says, "I want us to set sail together, Mo."

"We will always travel as one, VC, but every journey has its challenges, and no challenge can alter the course of our journey together."

"Do you believe we'll always hear the music, Mo?"

"How can we not my love, for those in love like us, for those whose hearts sing in harmony, as ours do, the music never stops, the volume may not be as raucous for us now, and there will be a misstep or two, but we will always hear the music and we will always dance to our love notes."

VC picks up a small stone and throws it in the water. Mo watches the ripples join the current and asks, "I wonder if our tiny ships ever reached the grandeur that is the almighty ocean, VC."

"I know they did."

"And how do you know?"

"I just know."

"Because you're all knowing?" she says.

"No, because you are and I can see it in your eyes."

"And what do you see?"

"I see splendor, I see peace, I see love, I see my most cherished companion, I see the woman I will always love, I see the woman that has touched me so deeply that I just don't know what I will do without her next to me."

"I am next to you, VC, and will be always."

Several mornings later, while they are sitting together in the courtyard having coffee, VC asks, "How do we cram fifty years into mere months?"

"We don't."

"Mo … your illness, we need to do things differently now."

"No, we don't. My illness is an asterisk, albeit a large one on my life page, and although it undoubtedly affects the rest of the page, as well as obscuring the contents, it does not cover the entire page, nor will I let it. I refuse, as should you, to allow it to define me, us, or anything we do."

"An asterisk?"

"I see a dark asterisk on a white page and you insist on seeing the whole page as dark. The demon is not the page, it's the asterisk on the page. Let's focus on the rest of the page and live life the way it should be lived, regardless of time or circumstances."

"As if the asterisk didn't exist?"

"No, VC, we don't ignore or deny the presence of the asterisk, similarly, we don't ignore the rest of the page because of it. We live life in spite of it."

After a while, leaning against each other in silence and watching the waters flow by, Mo says, "Let's go back, VC, we need to change out of these clothes."

They reach the house, and before walking upstairs to change, VC insists Mo have coffee and toasted buns. She agrees and sits by the small table in the courtyard. VC soon returns with a full tray, placing it on the table. Mo sips the coffee. "Thank you, VC, it hit the spot."

"An asterisk?" he asks.

"Pardon?" she replies.

"You said an asterisk."

"I know what I said," she replies with noticeable irritation, then she turns to him and says, "All right, all right," takes a deep breath and goes on loudly, "What in hell do you want me to say, VC! What?"

She immediately stands and smashes her coffee cup against the stone wall. "That I have this heinous unstoppable disease eating away at me, at you, at our very being, at our lives, the same one that took our precious Aila from us, the one we can't do anything about changing its course, so what should I do, VC? Tell me! Should I just lie down and wait for it to ravage my entire being? I will not! I will yell and scream … smash furniture, throw dishes against the wall, punch and kick at its shadow, swear at nausea like we both did when Aila passed away … but that is not what I wish for us. I will no longer stuff myself with painkillers or antidepressants, and numb life to the point where I no longer know if it's day or night … where I no longer feel your touch, your lips softly on mine. That's not for me, that is not what I wish for us. Maybe that's the answer for some and God bless them, God bless us all, but that's not the way for me, nor for you, VC, it's not how I want to spend whatever little time I have left."

Mo takes his hand, looks directly into his eyes and in a softer tone says, "We, my love, must continue living life to the fullest, that is why we're here. Never give up regardless of how formidable your opponent is, you taught me that, you taught me that you fight and you fight because, win or lose, there will always be another chance at the title. We together with Aila have lived the life of champions, VC, and will always, but sooner or later we all must move onto the next level…"

"Which is?"

"Eternity."

VC stands and helps her sit back down. With tears running down his face, he kneels in front of her, lifts her head, looks into her eyes and says, "I am sorry, Mo, you're right, there is much life to live in the time we have. I want you to continue to be the person you have always been, the person that has enriched my life, the person that has awakened my heart, the person that has been a model of true love and companionship, and as I kneel here and pray for a miracle, I see the miracle in your eyes, you are the miracle that resurrected my life, Mo, and I hope in some small way, I have been able to give you and Aila as much as you have given me."

"You have, my love, you have," she replies.

"I want to give you my breath of life, and take yours, Mo."

"The time has come when I must go ahead of you, as Aila before us, to begin building a new vessel on which our love will travel to its final destination. I do fear that you, my husband, will try to alter the course of your path back to us. Should you do that, should you rush your voyage to us, you will change your course, and that, my love, will take you further into the wilderness of despair and hopelessness and you will be lost for a very long time. Promise me, you will remain the man I so love. Promise me."

"I do, Mo, I will try."

"No, VC, you must commit to it or you will lose your way."

"I promise, Mo, I do."

He calms, rests his head on her knees, she places her hand on it, begins stroking his hair, and says, "A lot shorter when I first met you, you were such a lost soul."

He looks up at her and remains silent.

"And you were such a suck giving in to Mr. B.," she adds, firmly pulling his hair, leaning in and kissing him.

He sits back in his chair and says, "You're right, Mo, let us live life as you wish to live it."

"Live and love?" she adds.

"Live and love."

"What's our first stop?" she asks.

"You tell me."

"Very well, the Highlands."

"And whiskey," he adds.

"And good whiskey."

Life was lived as natural as the condition permitted. Six weeks had passed, seven maybe. Neither kept track of days but difficult to ignore the fleeting season.

On a cloudless afternoon, driving through the countryside amidst fields of lush green and golden yellow in Scotland, Mo says,

"Stop, stop, there, that tree."

"All right, nice spot for a little rest," he says, to which she replies looking at him and smiling, "Who said anything about rest?"

The car comes to a screeching halt by the side of the road, and Mo says, "Bring the blanket."

"Anything to eat or drink?"

"No, just the big blanket," she replies.

VC, blanket over his shoulder, catches up and takes her hand. Once there they both lie on the well-padded blanket next to each other and immediately hold hands.

"Where's the sky?" he asks

"It's there, look carefully through the leaves, imagine, and you'll see it," she replies.

After a brief, silent rest, she turns, looks at him, squeezes his hand and says, "What do you think?"

"I still can't see the sky."

"Not that silly, you know," she says invitingly.

He immediately leans on his elbow, looks at her and says, "Pardon?"

"You know," she replies in a soft, provocative voice.

"You mean? I don't know, Mo … I mean … you know, you know what I mean, don't you?"

"Stop talking and come closer."

"Are you sure? I mean really sure? Here?" She places her finger on his lips, and says, "Shhh, lie down."

"Really?" he says.

"Stop talking," she says and carefully leads his hand to her heart.

"Are you sure?"

"I could get angry with you but I won't, but I will squeeze your genitals hard if you don't stop talking and pay attention. So yes, really, kiss me, touch me like the first time, with passion, I want to experience our love in my place of birth, so, let your love speak, VC, not your anxiety, not your anger, not with anything other than the love that's in your heart, and I will do the same … and shut the hell up!"

"Yes ma'am, right away, the blanket is well padded, but isn't it going to hurt your back?" he asks.

"Who says you're on top," she replies while gently rolling her body onto his.

"This is beautiful, my love," she says softly.

"Stop talking," he says smiling.

The weeks that followed brought shorter and more laboured walks under city lights, unfinished dinners, early nights and late mornings. Almost a month had passed on her native soil and while some of the page remained unstained, the asterisk had grown larger and more invasive.

"Time for the land of cypress trees, my love," she says, and the next day they began their trip to Rome with memorable stops in London, Paris, Florence and under whatever tree in the lush countryside Mo felt a rest was needed.

One morning on the balcony of their hotel in Florence overlooking the Arno River, Mo looks at her largely untouched breakfast and says, "La Casa, my love."

"And when we get there, we visit my uncle's medical clinic in Rome."

"No clinic, no doctors, no meds, just me, you and the blue yonder," she replies.

They reach the house mid-afternoon, and walking towards the entrance with VC's support, she stops, looks at it, at the surroundings and says, "I will remember, VC, I will … I will."

Now close to two months with the occasional gust of wind still in their sail, they continued to live life as Mo wished.

One morning, VC takes her breakfast and places it, along with a red rose, on the night table next to her. She holds the rose close to her face, inhales deeply with eyes closed, and asks him if he remembers the first rose he ever gave her. "Yes, I do," he replies.

She opens her eyes, and says "My dear, dear Camelot."

The days now much shorter and often full of tears. The long painful nights merged into painful days into painful nights again. The tide eventually rose and the good days and nights were now rare.

Sitting in the ancient courtyard one afternoon, she looks at her timeless surroundings, and contrary to years past, she can now only see unclimbable mountains on each side, an increasingly joyless sky and a darkening sunset. She sees the up-and-coming season of the fall harvest, knowing she will not be able to take part; she is deeply aware of her own life colours rapidly fusing into an indistinguishable grey shade and knows total darkness will soon befall the day, yet finds comfort in knowing that all she has lived, loved and cherished will always accompany her on her journey.

She closes her eyes and summons a far-off reality she once knew and avidly lived as a woman, mother and life companion. She thinks of the hills of gold and green, of their bodies lying next to each other. Her memories insist on highlighting those precious times, and her heart tells her there is life yet to live and heights in love yet to be reached with her man.

She slowly reaches out to hold his powerful hands and thinks of the many times he put them together and prayed for Aila, and now for her, so desperately hoping that someone, somewhere, would hear his cries.

"Requests are often answered in ways we can't know, see or comprehend," she would say to him, knowing no explanation ever sufficed.

The tighter she holds his hand, the more firmly he holds hers. She raises her head and he softly kisses her cherished lips.

"We have time yet to live, VC," she says. "We do," he answers and continues staring into the distance. She looks in the same direction and asks, "What do you see, baby?" He gently squeezes her hand and remains silent.

She knows her man is lost in a maze of emotions and says, "Hold me tighter, VC."

He gently places his arm around her and pulls her closer. She rests her head on his shoulder and thinks of the crippling shadow that will soon crush her man's broad shoulders, conquering his spirit, and she wonders how he'll cope in the wilderness of grief.

Tears stream in silence and smiles are forced to retreat from the unyielding pain. The torn sails boldly labour up the mast but they are no match against the furious winds of illness. Relentlessly battered by the high seas of anguish, Mo fearlessly and defiantly holds onto the tattered sails, and bravely thinks of what is soon to be. She looks at her man, thinks of her daughter and imagines what could have been as hope continues its free-fall.

The draw of the wind picks up, the unshackled anchor silently rises towards the light as the lone weary ship prepares to set sail towards the summit of her new reality.

The sun's life rays gradually relinquish the lucidity of the day and fade into the mystery that is twilight. Surreal shadows from cypress trees in the surrounding countryside pay homage to the dreamlike effects of the moon, that distant, tireless light that magically shines on waiting hearts everywhere and will once again be their guide tonight.

The intensity of the evening steadily takes hold. Darkness is all-embracing but not absolute. A cluster of bold stars lights up the imagination. They merge and create a path of vibrant energy from the house to the open sky ... and wait. The darkness of another long night invades, but the rhythm of life precious whose improvised notes leapfrog all over the music sheet steadfastly refuses to sit this one out.

Tonight, the veiled breeze will soothe the troubled landscape, calm the treetops, and ready the night for the long, long voyage.

Tonight, their heavily burdened hearts will again unite for that slow endless dance under the moonlight.

Tonight, since they were one, Mo will again spend it in a long embrace with her husband.

She looks tenderly at her man quietly sitting beside her in the courtyard, strokes his face and softly says, "We've been together..."

"Not long enough," he quickly replies.

"Fall of sixty-six, we first touched ... loved each other so unselfishly ... so deeply," she replies.

He tries to contain the tremors in his heart and the quivering of his lips, but can't. He lowers his head and bursts into an irrepressible cry.

She places her hands around his face, pulls him towards hers, they touch and cry together until exhausted. The long silence that follows eventually breaks, and he asks, "Do you think we will feel the gift of touch again?"

"We will never lose what we have, my love," she replies.

She lowers her head on his shoulder again and silence returns.

After a short time, she looks into his face and asks, "Do you remember when we helped harvest the grapes with your grandfather and your cousins?"

"The time you insisted on using the big basket, filled it to the top and it took the two of us to carry it back? I remember."

"And the time we stayed long after the grapes had been harvested?" she says and he nods.

"The afternoon you took me by the hand and we walked amidst the proud vines looking for those few bunches of grapes that had cleverly avoided the initial harvest for another precious day in the sun … and when we found them, we felt guilty taking them, but they knew we would cherish the sweetness of their nectar and did not resist … you then carefully placed the blanket on the softest ground and we lay next to each other … we lay in each other's arms under the sun in silence for a long time. We took in the splendour of the blue wonder and we were happy."

He touches her lips softly with his fingers, kisses her and she smiles. She caresses his face and says, "Twilight is here, my love, and la bella luna will soon take us into the night."

"And what would you like to do?" he asks.

"I would like us to dance once more under her adoring spell."

"Anything to eat?"

"No."

"Drink?"

"No, just you, me and the moon. So, my adorable VC, what is the rhythm of choice this evening?"

He forces a smile and asks, "You really want to dance?"

She nods and says, "Yes, so what will it be, Kid? The Kid from the west end, my knight, remember him?" but he remains silent.

"The knight that somehow came into my life and became my eternal love," she adds.

"No, Mo, you saved me. You took this battered and bruised body and gave it purpose. You took this solitary heart and showed it how to dream and how to live that dream."

She places her fingers over his lips and says, "Dreams do not end, my love, they evolve and change form, but do not end." They kiss and she adds, "The moon beckons my love, cheek to cheek and I lead."

"Of course, just like on our first dance at school," he replies.

"You followed and look where it got you," she says, smiling.

She labours but stands, walks slowly, yet bravely and proudly to the middle of the courtyard with poise, opens her arms and, as countless times before, is ready to receive him. "Let's start with a slow favourite from one of Nina's albums, okay with you, lover boy?"

"I know just the one," he replies.

"Let's see, is this one of those where we dance a few steps, sing a verse or two and stand still for the rest of the song?"

He smiles and replies, "Something like that." He places the album onto the portable record player's turntable and gallantly walks into her open arms. Reaching for her hand, says, "May I?"

"Certainly," she replies.

The song begins and she says, "I lead, remember."

"Yes, and very well too."

"Thank you," she replies and begins singing along but he hums.

"No, no humming the song, my love. It's spiritual Nina, we must hear the words to help us see the light in each other, sing with me, *'There is a light...'"*

He places his hands around her thin waist, and under the moonlight's renewed hue they dance. Somewhere the treetops quietly partner up, adoring shadows embrace, fields of wheat softly sway to the earth's rhythm and stars look on.

The song ends, Mo brings her lips to his and gently kisses him several times, rests her head on his shoulder and they remain embraced. Soon after, sensing her exhaustion, he asks if she wishes to sit down.

"Just for a little while, VC."

"Something to drink?" he asks.

"Strangely, I feel for a glass of white."

"Coming right up," he replies.

"And bring the bottle," she adds.

He returns with two full glasses and hands her one.

"To love, to you and me, to a life albeit short but well-lived, to home, our home as we have known it in each other's arms, to our Aila and to the time we will all be together again," she says, pointing her glass towards her man. She leans closer, kisses him and says, "Wine, moonlight and VC."

"Wine, moonlight and Mo."

She takes a sip, places the glass on the table and tells him she needs to lie down.

He stands, takes her frail body into his arms and carries her upstairs, carefully placing her on the bed before lying next to her.

He gently kisses her hand, her energy further wanes and her jaded body is now under full attack. She begins seeing what he is not yet privileged to see.

"Look, VC, look, what a beautiful rainbow, and it's just outside our window."

He turns and looks, but he knows the rainbow Mo now sees shines only in her heart.

"I see two rainbows," she says.

"I do too," he adds and lies closer to her. She places her head on his chest and they hold each other tenderly. "How about calling out the colours of the rainbow with me?" he asks.

"I just want to lie here … hold you and listen to your heart, but wake me when you get to violet, I want to call out the last colour of the rainbow with you."

As Mo requested, VC unhurriedly and softly calls out each colour of the rainbow in the order he remembers. He kisses her forehead and softly calls her name. Her weakened hand squeezes his, and in a low voice asks if they were close to reaching the colour violet.

"Not yet," he replies.

"I don't hurt when you hold me … I feel your strength, I feel safe … but need to rest now," she says.

Holding her fragile body gently, he reaches the last colour, but again refuses to call it out. She briefly opens her eyes, struggles to smile, and embraces him as tightly as she can. "I think I see Aila waving at me from across the way, VC, it is her, our baby, VC, Aila, Aila, it's Mommy."

Mo's battered heart weakens, her pulse slows and her shallow breathing can no longer sustain her body.

"The colour … VC."

"Lots of colours in the rainbow, Mo."

"Violet?"

"Not yet."

"Never been a good liar VC … you … skipped it a few … times … I … I…"

Silence shrouds the remarkable being that is Mo, and her time on earth slowly comes to an end. Her eyes gently close completely, her heart readies for her final breath, and she's gone.

"Please Mo, breathe, please … please," he pleads, embracing her more tightly, but her body is unresponsive.

Looking at his most cherished companion, seeing her take her last breath, waiting, hoping, praying for her to take another, and silently convulsing when she doesn't, leaves the remnants of his heart without will or direction.

He kept his promise to Mo and suppressed his fury, his anger, his rage, nor did he scream profanities until his voice faded. Instead, he holds her tightly and sobs until exhausted. He kisses his beloved Mo tenderly on her forehead, then her lips, and while gently holding her in his arms, hums *Somewhere Over the Rainbow*, the song she so loved as a child.

When Mo passed on that late August afternoon, VC's emotional compass shattered and the needle immediately stopped. He and Mo chose to comfort Aila in her passing by being there with her, holding her, caressing her ... first known faces ... last familiar voices, and he now for Mo. Bloodied and bruised and unable to see clearly, this once-proud warrior now staggers agonizingly towards the safety of his corner only to discover there is no one there. *And the global landscape. . . becomes irrelevant.*

TWO CONTINENTS, ONE SOIL

Mo's funeral, like Aila's, was kept to family and close friends. Aila's service took place in Canada, Mo's in Italy with a farewell stopover in Scotland.

The bells of the small white church of San Vincenzo, located not far from the house, resonate loudly throughout the valley, while the handheld bell carried by Ferguson accompanied the casket into the church.

VC's eulogy was brief and the only one. Others would deliver theirs at the full service once back in Canada.

"A life unfinished, a love cherished . . . you are and will always be that special flower that blooms eternal in my heart, Mo."

The service ends, everyone walks out of the church and gathers outside. The primordial sound of the church bells resonates louder, the celestial voice of Ferguson's handheld bell rises in prominence and joins the chorus.

In keeping with Mo's wishes, her body would be cremated and the urn placed beside Aila's on their mantel. VC would then take them to the ocean, gently place them on the waiting blue for that part of their voyage towards the sun.

The pallbearers, family members, carefully place the casket in the hearse. VC caresses the white dove handed to him by his mother, kisses it and releases it, as he and Mo had done with Aila. Augie and Ferguson open two small cages of doves and set them free. The captivating flock of whiteness circles and hovers, then soars. The ascension of emotions … the gradual quieting of the bells … the slow movement of the hearse … and silence descends on the valley.

VC, sitting in the front passenger seat of the hearse, looks in the side mirror and sees white kerchiefs waving in front of the church. The doves settle on the wire along the church's driveway, the hearse slowly makes its way onto the paved road, picks up speed and is soon out of sight. Once the casket is safely stored at the airport, VC is driven back to the house. Condolences were reconveyed, embraces exchanged, and the small gathering of family members left in the courtyard immediately took to silence when Gran began reading Psalms of Comfort… *"Even though I walk through the darkest valley…"*

Several hours later, as the sun was gradually setting over the stand of cypress, VC suddenly hears footsteps behind him while walking down to the river.

"Is it all right if we walk with you, son?" asks his father as he and Ferguson followed.

"Of course, Dad, Mr. Walker, yes, please."

They walk in silence, soon reach the bank of the river, and sit on the upper rocks. VC's eyes are immediately drawn to a cluster of small branches floating by and remembers the tiny ships.

"This must be the special place of which Mo often spoke," says Ferguson.

"It is," replies VC.

"'The place where ships carry dreams to the big waters of blue,' was how she phrased it."

"This is that place, Mr. Walker," replies VC.

"Mo taught him to be a better swimmer here," says Augie.

"No better teacher," adds Ferguson.

"That's for sure, and demanding, and when I had not, in her opinion, made sufficient progress, I had to piggyback her to the house."

"And of course you failed miserably," Ferguson replies.

"Of course."

"She was a person of great wisdom, like her mother," says Ferguson. "And as you stated in your eulogy, she will be dearly missed, but know her guiding hand will always be on your shoulder, VC, as her mother's is on mine."

He places his hand on VC's shoulder, stands and says, "Long road ahead, son, but know that we're all here for you. Now I best see how Gran is doing."

"Leaving tomorrow?" asks Augie.

"Yes, being picked up mid-morning, few days in Edinburgh, but will return for the service. Gran wants us to go back home to Edinburgh, that's where her heart is. I could take early retirement, we'll see."

"Worth considering," says Augie.

"Walking the soil of home, Augie, I'm sure you know."

"I do."

"See you up at the house."

"We'll be up shortly," says Augie, and continues, "You know, son, on a clear day we could look through the poplars and see the other house in Compre. We were all born there, you, of course, were born in Rome, but loved it here, that's why you were your grandfather's favourite … then the earthquake … my parents, my brother, everyone in the house gone in their sleep, the house … not much left of it, but its heart remained intact and Silvio rebuilt it. Although different mortar and stone, same heart. The old walnut and chestnut trees are still standing proudly in the rose garden and productive, too."

After a brief pause, VC looks at his father and says, "One of the stories you told was that when you and your brother were younger, you used to take walnuts down with stones, and one time you got in trouble with Nonno because one of the stones hit uncle on the head."

Augie nods, smiles and says, "Your uncle was impatient, always told him to wait for the stone to first land before retrieving the walnut, but we were young. I miss them, I miss being here."

"Maybe someday," says VC.

After a brief silence, Augie says, "We liked walnuts but loved roasted chestnuts. After roasting them, your Nonno used to wrap them in a clean cloth and roll the bundle on the kitchen table to further open their shells. He then counted them and everyone received the same number, except him, he always took fewer."

"One of the traditions Mo and I used to practice, like you and Mom do, like Nonno did, was after we ate the roasted chestnuts, we saved the shells to burn in the fireplace in honour of our ancestors. We, of course, always left a whole one or two for the long journey. We also did it as a tribute to Aila."

"And now son, more than ever, you must continue the tradition."

"I don't think I can, Dad."

"Continuity, particularly of fond traditions, keeps our loved ones close, VC."

"We always took them flowers when we came and sat by their graves."

"We should have never left this paradise, I should have never left my parents, I should have never taken you away from your grandparents, your cousins, your mother from her parents…"

"You had no choice, Dad."

"One always has a choice, VC. We left here in fifty-seven, the earthquake hit in sixty-two…"

"I remember, Dad," says VC, his hand on his father's shoulder.

"The pain we carry, son. Mo's love will get you through the dark days, VC, I know it will."

"How do you find your way back to life when the life you most cherished is gone?"

"Not gone, VC, never gone. I never told you, Ferguson once said to me that you were the only man for his daughter, to which I replied, his daughter was the perfect person for our son. So, two people in love as you and Mo, how can you ever lose sight of that? Of each other?"

"He's a good man, Dad, and Gran is so special."

"And they love you, VC, and feel for you, but they too are ready to go back home. He wants to go back to his beloved Moreen, take her flowers, sit by her, and read to her until all the leaves of fall return to warm the sacred ground. He wants to repair the house, mend the garden … he and Gran want to go home. Home is in the heart, son."

Several days later, after everyone had left, VC leaves his unfinished dinner, walks outside and stands in silence facing the two young cypress trees, the one he and Mo had planted for Aila, and the one he recently planted for Mo. He looks at the moon, now at half-mast, enters the dark, empty house and slowly closes the door behind him. The gleaming light next to the collection of pictures on the fireplace mantel draws his attention. He lights a new candle and places it next to the picture of Aila on his shoulders with Mo next to him near the entrance to their garden, showing the three of them without hair. He and Mo had shaven their heads to match Aila's. He slowly sits down at the kitchen table facing the pictures, places his arm on the table, rests his head on it and closes his eyes.

CHAPTER FOUR

THE CENTURY-OLD FARM HOUSE

The wheels hit the tarmac and VC immediately thinks of Mo in her casket dressed in white like the beautiful princess she is, with a crown of wild flowers and roses by her side. He envisions her lying peacefully in a deep sleep waiting for her prince to awaken her love as she had done for him. He thinks of their wedding night when he and Mo sat on their bed with Mo still wearing her crown of flowers, reading congratulatory cards, sipping champagne, smiling, laughing, eagerly waiting for the moon to come through their window and gently cradle them through the night.

Relatives and close friends follow the hearse to the funeral home for the service. Ferguson's tribute, as Gran's, spoke of the exceptional person Mo was, is, and will always be; of the inescapable bright light in her heart that will continue to help make everyone's own journeys steadier by her presence in their lives.

Martha's equally moving eulogy spoke of their lifelong friendship of trust, loyalty, and a deep caring for one another; of the bond that existed long before they met at school. "Mo and I," she said, "are archaeological finds in this huge drawer of artifacts. We all represent the past, present and, if we pay close attention, from having known her we can see a glimpse of our future."

VC walks to the podium, looks at everyone and without written notes, speaks of his beloved Moreen.

"Where does someone like me begin speaking of a love like Moreen ... a love so deeply cherished, a woman I so adored, one I held on the highest of pedestals ... one so loving, so caring, so rich in wisdom, how can I speak of such a divine entity unless I truly believe she is divine and eternal in her journey and I, as you, am so blessed for being part of it. Mo's love is timeless … how do I begin to comprehend that a woman of her stature can possess such a never-ending love for me, for Aila, for life. Mo transcends all known concepts of life, death, time and form, and above all, love, she was, is and will always be … my one true love. She was the voice of love in my life … she was my beacon … she embodied all the virtues that can possibly exist … she is a saint and I know she has touched all of us … she is my saviour, my home and I will miss her so, so deeply."

After a long pause, VC took the urn in his arms and returned to his seat. His father concluded the memorial service and after paying their last respects, many left. A brief wake followed at his parents' place with only family and close friends. Soon after, their friends left, Ferguson and Gran as well as Uncle Lou, Aunt Helen and Mike. VC could have stayed overnight, but chose to return home. He picked up the urn that had been placed on the large bay window of the dining room, next to the lit candle, said long goodbyes to his parents and left.

Driving up the gravel laneway, seeing the house in total darkness, his breathing became shallower. He parks near the front door and sits silently in the car with the urn securely in his arms. The breathing calms, his eyes eventually clear and he decides to go inside. He enters the house, walks to the mantel in the living room and gently places Mo's urn next to Aila's. He lights two candles, remains with his head bowed for a time, then walks to the kitchen.

He turns on the house lights. Murray and Muriel, who after returning from the service, unchanged in their black formal garments, still sat around the kitchen table staring at their cold, unfinished dinner, saw the lights come on and immediately came over.

"Sorry, it's late, we just wanted to drop in, won't stay long," said Muriel.

They brought flowers from their garden, the rest of the pot of stew Muriel had made the day before, a piece of blueberry pie, and spent a brief time with him.

"We will miss her, VC, but remember, she's in the palm of God's hand, and always in our hearts," says Muriel while leaving.

"I sure hope she's giving Them the what-for, too soon, way too soon," adds Murray.

VC slept on the couch fully clothed that night, frequently waking to look at the urns. A single kitchen light was left on while the sentinel light on that lone pole outside stood guard.

A knock woke him the next morning, it was Murray with breakfast. A soft-spoken man, with love of farming in his veins and a big heart for the family. People close to the land seem to somehow understand more clearly the cycle of life. "The further people move away from the land, the more complicated their lives become," he often said. "Look around you, VC, everything has a season, one thing for sure, if you believe in spring, it will return."

VC thinks of Murray's statement, of the intuitive friendship from the onset, when Murray ploughed their driveway in winter and VC helped with the hay during the summer months. Cutting, splitting and stacking firewood was a joint effort, followed by a hearty dinner at one of the houses. The seasons came and went, and spring always followed even the harshest of winters. VC thinks of the long, unforgiving winter ahead and what the new, uncharted spring might look like.

"Muriel sends breakfast, mine's being made, VC first, she said," Murray says.

"That's so kind of her, thank you."

"And she would like to know if you can come up for dinner one of these nights."

"Could do, Murray, but it will have to be after we get back from the East Coast."

"When will that be?" asks Murray.

"Not quite sure, but soon," he replies.

"Flying down?"

"Getting colder, best for everyone, there and back the same day."

"We'll look after your place. Aila was special and Mo, they don't come any better. Maybe before you go, the wife and I would like to come down to say our goodbyes to them, if it's okay with you."

"Thank you, Murray."

"We miss them," Murray said, leaving abruptly before VC could see his tears.

Not yet daylight when the plane rose towards the sky, with VC carrying Mo's urn in his arms and Ferguson and Augie taking turns carrying Aila's.

It seems so dreamlike being surrounded by the wholesomeness of clouds, in awe, and ever curious as to where exactly that invisible staircase is.

VC looks out his small window, and pictures Mo in her veil dress in the middle of the courtyard waiting for that special dance with her man; he sees Aila in the small dress her grandmother made for Mo's first day of school that neither got to wear … and, he's certain, he saw both of them sitting on the bottom stair of that enchanted staircase waving at him.

THE OCEAN

Late fall, East Coast winds have many tales to tell on how to best prepare for winter, but few listen. VC, his parents, Ferguson and Gran came prepared. Mid-morning, they arrive at a place along the rugged coastline, a destination once chosen for a future family holiday when Aila was older, exit their rented car, and put on their winter jackets, gloves and scarves. Ferguson tries making sure Gran was sufficiently warm and she says, "Oh Ferguson, I should be doing that for you," to which he replies, "You always have, Mom, my turn now."

They begin their pilgrimage up the highest cliff, Ferguson helping Gran, Augie carrying Aila's urn with Sarah at his side and VC walking ahead carrying Mo's, all pausing occasionally to rest.

The sun shines prominently but is no match against the unusual bone-piercing chill. An unforeseen gale takes their breath away, Gran gasps, closes her eyes, takes a slow deep breath and says "The gales of home, do you recall, Ferguson?"

"I do," he replies, holding onto her firmly.

"They came to greet us, did they not?"

"They did."

"I wish to go home, Ferguson, will you take me home, son? I long for home."

"I will, Mom."

"Promise?"

"I do."

Their ascent continues and eventually they reach the very top of the cliff where the vast expense of the ocean is not limited by what the eyes can see, rather by what the heart can feel.

They hold the urns close to their chest one last time, and suddenly the gale calms and the chill fades. They fill their open hands with ashes, holding the essence of two dear lives in their palms, extend their arms as far as they can, and wait. The waves ease their crashing against the rocks below, the gentle breeze lifts and carries the ashes onto the water, and Mo's and Aila's voyage to the distant place where the sun touches the ocean continues. VC's arms not being totally extended, when the breeze came, some of the ashes land back on his jacket, he looks and leaves them there.

They move closer to each other, clustering like roses on a single stem, and remain watching in silence for a long while. The awe-inspiring sun slowly sets in the distance, Ferguson stakes the metal pole solidly in the ground. VC attaches the battery-operated light firmly on its top, turns it on, and extends the long, telescopic pole into the darkening sky. They return to their car, look back, and the light on that stalwart beacon flashes prominently. The natural light recedes, the moon emerges, the car meanders slowly down the dark winding gravel road with only the headlights indicating its presence. The full moon escorts them down the stark, almost invisible roadway until city lights take over. They return the car to the underground garage at the airport, check in and wait.

Every year afterward VC made the pilgrimage alone, with a bouquet of flowers, blanket, folding chair, and umbrella in case of rain.

Once at the top, he stands, places the flowers at the base of the telescopic beacon and waits for that special gust of wind to gently lift them onto the outgoing tide. He then replaces the battery and readies himself for home. The sun gradually bridges the blues, the stars steadily fill the sky … and the light flashes prominently.

CHAPTER FIVE

A RETURN TO THE FARM HOUSE

Late fall, early winter. Murray was right, winter came early and the snow never seemed to stop falling. The snow buntings returned and, as in past years, their food supply lay under the well-constructed winter lean-to on the treed side of the driveway, in plain view of the kitchen window.

Sitting at the kitchen table next to the wood-burning stove, coffee in hand, VC thinks of the long winter ahead and how he'll get through it.

He recalls the days when he or Mo stood and held Aila on the counter looking at the small Arctic birds excitedly ingesting seeds. She was especially thrilled when the flock wildly swirled through the air above the barn like snowflakes in a blizzard. The zanier their pattern, the louder she laughed.

The weekend before Christmas, late afternoon, Murray drove up in his truck with a small tree he had recently cut off the top of one of the mature pines, as he had done every year since their arrival. VC opens the door, and Murray says, "Muriel said you should have a tree, and I was happy to cut one for you."

"I wasn't sure about a tree this year, Murray, but I appreciate it."

"I know, but let it stay a while, you may take to it," he replies while placing it in the living room. "It even comes with a stand," he says, "I was doing ours so I figure I'd put yours on a stand too."

Both men sit in the warm kitchen and VC brings out a new bottle of whiskey.

"Never been opened, Murray, I'm sure you'll like it."

Murray looks at the bottle and says, "Expensive, I bet."

"A gift from my father-in-law, from a while back, with clear instructions," says VC.

"And what would they be?"

"One shot, maybe two, three tops, when you begin to mellow, it has done its job and it's time to cork the bottle."

"That sounds about right," says Murray.

VC pours each a drink and after a shot, Murray asks, "How are things down here?"

"Some days are better than others, Murray."

"I gather, Muriel worries about you, and I tell her you're fine, but I'm running out of tall tales to tell her. Are you fine?"

"I am, Murray, thank you."

"You know, I can look at the sky, the direction of the wind, how the birds and animals behave, and I can tell a lot of what's to come. I look at you and I'm not so sure," Murray says, but VC offers no answer. Then Murray asks if he was going to the city for Christmas Eve.

"I should."

"Can't miss your mother's Christmas Eve fish dinner. Go and set a place at the table for Mo, as you do with Aila, it will calm your heart. Can't let the sadness run your life, VC, no more than I let the seasons run the farm, I pay close heed but rain or shine I have to make the best with what's handed to me. I can look at the weather as my friend or my enemy, but that's the wrong way to look at it, I look to the weather as a guide, to tell me when to plough, when to plant, when to harvest, and when to just stay inside. So go break bread with your parents and come back before the big fellow visits."

"You're a wise man, Murray."

"Generations tilling soil will do that for you."

"Pour you another?"

"Thanks, one is plenty."

On his way out the door, he turns and says, "Let me know if you need more firewood."

"Thanks, Murray, it should last, but I'll let you know."

Christmas Eve in the city. The lights, the hustle and bustle and a time for wishes. The customary dinner at his parents, with Ferguson and Gran and Uncle Lou's family, was the first of its kind in a while. The table was set with a place for Mo and Aila next to VC's. All stood, Gran and Sarah said grace and all lifted their glass in honour of those who had gone before, most recently, Mo. While standing, Ferguson says, "If I may, Sarah, can you please set a place for my wife Moreen, I just feel like paying her tribute with all of us here. I would like her to know that in the spring, as you all know, Gran and I are coming home."

"We will miss you," says Augie.

VC stands, walks over to them and embraces Gran, then Ferguson and says, "I will miss you both."

"We'll be expecting you, son," replies Ferguson.

Sarah places another setting on the table next to Ferguson, and following a moment of silence with heads bowed, VC, Mike and Sarah stand and begin serving her gourmet pasta and fish dishes. Following dinner, all move to the living room near the tree to open gifts.

VC bought his father and Ferguson bottles of their favourites; his mother, Gran and Aunt Helen, Native shawls; Uncle Lou a bottle of vintage wine; and Mike a gift certificate to the sports store. They each had a gift for him, and two small keepsakes in honour of Aila and Mo, and all concurred he should open them at home.

It was close to eleven and VC was the last one to leave. He arrives home just before midnight, parks his Wagoneer in the garage and walks out to the driveway. He immediately looks up and wonders what Aila and Mo are up to on this clear and brisk night in the land of souls. He then takes the gifts out of the car, closes the garage door and enters the house.

He takes off his boots, turns on the kitchen light and walking into the living room, stops in the doorway and looks at the bare tree standing in the exact location Murray had left it. He places the gifts under it and feels he should at least place the angel in its rightful place at the pinnacle of the tree.

He takes a small ornament out of its box, looks at whose turn it is to place it on the tree and while hesitantly doing so says, "Sorry, Mo, sorry, Aila, it seems to be my turn this year."

He stands back, looks at the angel and considers illuminating it with a string of lights, hesitates, then encircles the angel with a short filament of white lights and when done, sits at the end of the sofa nearest to the tree. His eyes become heavy, he closes them and falls asleep but is awakened by the sudden chill. Stands, raises the furnace thermostat, walks into the kitchen and stokes the stove. He walks back to the living room, takes several blankets out of the blanket box and lies back down on the couch.

Christmas morning brought Murray and Muriel to the door with homemade sweets, and a heavy quilt they had purchased at the United Church bazaar that week.

They come inside, share greetings and long hugs, then Murray says, "The sweets are from me, and the blanket is from Muriel."

"How about a coffee?"

"Maybe later, VC, late for church," replies Muriel, then looks at the tree in the living room and says, "I see you decorated, an angel, a few lights, that's all you need."

THE LONG WINTER

Winter was long and the weather challenging, heavy snowfalls, howling winds, power outages and weeks of remoteness that would have been blissful, if only.

Often the lone light in the old house was from the burning logs through the glass door of the wood burning stove. Murray cleared the driveway but VC seldom drove to the city, and rarely had anyone visit.

"The Red Cobra in the Barn," the short story he was writing on restoring a crashed 1968 428 Mustang Cobra Jet he bought several years prior from the insurance company, was in waiting, both the story and the car.

Losses can often create their own hybrid state of inertia. Cognitive and physical lethargy, mental rumination and unremitting sadness propelled VC's complicated bereavement state into a post-traumatic stress condition. The loss was so debilitating and the painful emotions so long lasting that any semblance of a normal life became increasingly difficult to identify or maintain.

Always clean-shaven, he now frequently presented an abandoned face to the mirror. Once impeccably dressed, he repeatedly wore clothes that no longer knew the difference between day and night. He had habitually given up on himself. His emotional circuitry had shorted and any connection to self-preservation had become extensively corroded.

Life and living had drifted too far outside its intended circuit. The electrical conduction system of the heart had to be regrounded and the flow redirected, but only he had the combination to the toolbox.

Geiger counters don't lie, ignore at your own risk. Repeated calls from family and friends to break bread were often unheeded as re-engaging life to living was quickly becoming a double-edged sword.

One long-abandoned and less complicated route to recoupling with the main circuitry and redirecting the flow of energy to the positive section of the emotional spectrum was to begin reconnecting with his long-in-waiting characters in his novel, and when he didn't go to them, they came to him.

Sitting in his kitchen, mid-May, breakfast hardly touched, third cup of coffee, he stands, looks at the sunrise peeking over the big barn and decides to call Mike to see if he had time to help him test one of the long-restored Cobras in the barn, the 1969 Mustang Mach 1 with a 428 Cobra Jet engine on the abandoned track, to see *what she could do.*

No roll cage, no helmet, no automatic governor, VC and the Cobra coming down the straights and Mike, timing him. He looks at the stopwatch, at the car and hears shuddering sounds from an overworked engine.

"Pull back, VC, pull back!" Too late. The car convulses to a screeching halt about thirty yards away. Mike runs over. VC had already opened the hood and was looking at the engine bay billowing smoke.

Mike grabs him by his shoulder and angrily says, "You crossed the line, VC. What is the matter with you, you redlined it and kept it there, I could hear the engine coming apart from back there, you should have pulled back!"

"Trying to hit that perfect shift, Mike."

"Bullshit! Stop lying to yourself, and don't you fucking dare lie to me, don't."

"You're pissed off, Mike."

"Damn right I am. You purposely blew a great engine. Your Mustangs don't need rev limiters, you do."

"Screw you, Mike."

"Look, VC," says Mike in a calmer tone, "How can you not see what you're doing to yourself, to us, and to the memories of Mo and Aila?"

In an uncontrollable moment of anger, VC shoves Mike, forcing him to step back.

"I'm going to overlook the shove, VC, because I know, we all know, of your immense pain, and we all feel for you, but you're not the VC I used to know, that's for sure."

 Both lean against the lifeless Mustang in silence for a while, then VC looks at Mike and says, "Sorry, Mike."

"Fuck you," replies Mike, "we have feelings too, VC," and begins walking towards his '68 Charger parked at the end of the strip. VC remains leaning against his Mustang, Mike backs up and says, "Get in, walk home, or wait for the tow truck."

VC hesitates, looks at the Mustang, lowers his head, and by the time he looks up at Mike, all he sees is a cloud of smoke from the Charger's spinning tires. Mike screeches to a halt, puts it in reverse, backs up, stops near VC and says, "Get in the fucking car."

VC gets in the car and no words were spoken until they reached home. At the end of VC's driveway and while he's getting out of the car, Mike says, "I love you like a brother, VC, better than a brother, and you know what worried me the most today, had there been concrete barriers, you would have driven right into one."

VC has no reply but Mike could see tears in his eyes. "Try counselling again, maybe this time it may help you repair that big engine in your chest."

Several days later, VC enters the barn and stares at the uncovered Mach 1 in the corner next to Mo's Mustang, a 1969 Boss 302 in Calypso Coral he had restored, now under wraps in a custom-made cover. Sits in the Mach 1, looks at the gauges now permanently at zero, and recalls the ear-piercing screams of a once original big block dying on the tarmac.

It was close to noon when he realized he had promised his parents he would be there for lunch that day. He quickly readied and drove to the city. The discussions at lunch were primarily about the weather, some politics and the occasional "What's ahead for you, VC?" to which he just shrugged his shoulders, prompting his parents to look at each other and remain silent. They managed to talk him into staying the afternoon, and that led into dinner and into a more pleasant evening.

Driving home in his Wagoneer, while looking at the stars, he drove slowly with the occasional meander on the dark, sparsely trafficked road. Suddenly the car jolts from being pushed by the pick-up truck behind him.

He pulls off the road, flashlight in hand, gets out to inspect the damage, expecting the two men in the truck to do the same. They did stop beside him, shouted profanities, laughed, and drove off.

Minor damage but somebody has to pay for it. He catches up to them, follows discreetly, they go into a bar, and he sits and waits. Looks in the side mirror and sees the two men come out, lean against their truck, open a fresh pack of cigarettes and light up. VC drives up slowly and parks next to their truck.

Gets out, walks up to them and says, "Got a smoke."

"All out," one of them replies and keeps ignoring him.

"Remember me?"

"Should we?"

"Should, you almost ran me off the road, damaged my bumper and now you owe me five hundred dollars."

After they stopped laughing, one of them walks to VC, pushes his finger against his chest and says, "Get the fuck out of here while you still can."

"Here's the deal, fellas, give me the ownership to your truck, meet me in front of 51 division tomorrow morning at ten, bring the $500 in cash and you get the ownership back." He immediately grabs and breaks the man's finger and the man buckles. The other comes at him and VC kicks him in the groin.

"Ownership, gentlemen."

They readily comply and VC drives off. The next morning, a truck drives up, the men get out and walk towards VC, waiting in front of the police station. They approach with the money and VC takes the envelope, counts it and nods.

Two police officers approach, VC hands the ownership to them and says, "They are all yours, officers, and thank you."

"Hands behind your back. Reckless driving, leaving the scene of an accident, threats of bodily harm, you'll be here a while, gentlemen."

VC hands the envelope containing the money to one of the officers and says, "This is for the Police Children's Summer Camp Fund."

The officer takes, thanks him and asks, "In whose name?"

"Yours," replies VC.

On returning home, he sees his parents' car parked at the end of the driveway. Pulls up, car unoccupied, calls them and they soon emerge from the back of the house. They greet each other and Augie says, "Your mother and I decided to go for a drive and brought lunch."

"Thank you, let's go inside."

While at the kitchen table eating, Augie says, "You planted roses this year."

"Yes, coral."

"Teaching a summer course?" asks Sarah.

"No, on leave until the fall semester."

"How is the shop coming along?"

"Winterizing it, a lot of work, been helping Murray, long season, he says."

"How are they doing?"

"Well."

"With this good weather, you should be able to catch up on some of your work and maybe get to the city more often," says Sarah.

"I think so, Mom."

Augie stands and makes coffee, places three cups of coffee on the table and after a long period of silence, Sarah stands and says, "We feel for you, VC, some say it all takes time, well, time may numb it or suppress it, it takes active involvement on your part to effectively walk with grief."

"I feel so alone, Mom."

"But you're not alone, VC," she replies.

After finishing their coffees, Augie places the cups in the sink, and Sarah says, "Short visit, VC, just came to tell you we love you. C'mon, Augie. And VC, answer the damn phone."

The following Sunday he drove to his parents unannounced.

"Good to see you, son," says Augie opening the door. "Come in, your mother is in the kitchen."

VC enters and stops at the entrance to the kitchen. He and his mother look at each other, rush and embrace.

After a while, Sarah looks at her son and says, "Something told me you would be here today, so I made gnocchi, your favourite, and Aila's too as I recall, but Mo favoured fettuccine."

VC nods and says, "And Aila used to cover her plate with grated parmigiana."

"That she did, and finished everything too," says Augie, helping Sarah serve.

Augie poured red wine for the three of them and toasted Mo and Aila. Then VC said, "Italy."

"Going to Italy?" asks Augie, and VC nods.

"Travelling the country?" Sarah asks.

"No, no travelling, staying at the house."

"Any particular time in mind?" asks Augie.

"Next month."

"Good time," replies his father. "Taking your work with you?"

"I am, hopefully I'll be able to do something with it, we'll see."

Mike's words resonated and he made an appointment to re-engage with Dr. Myles, the brilliant psychoanalyst with post-doctoral fellowships from several prestigious universities, the therapist recommended by Martha after Mo's passing. VC had reluctantly agreed to see Dr. Myles, highly skilled, professionally versatile and a master therapist with expertise in a variety of treatment modalities.

They worked well together and she saw improvement in his overall well being, but VC mistakenly took it to mean he no longer needed ongoing therapy and, against her professional advice, prematurely ended the therapy. He took a long break and tinkered, but tinkering with a big block V8 does not a strong engine make, not when it needs a massive rebuild.

"Good seeing you again, VC," said Dr. Myles. "It has been a while."

"You as well, Dr. Myles, and yes, it has been a while. Thank you for seeing me on such short notice," he says, entering her office.

"You're welcome," she replies, closing the door behind her.

While taking their respective seats, she asks, "How is the restoration business going?"

"Slowly," he replies.

"Shortage of parts?" she asks.

"No, no, just haven't had the time."

"I see."

Sitting facing him, pen and pad in hand, she asks, "What brings you back, VC?"

"My dreams again, but lately with a difference."

"And how do they differ from your previous ones?"

"As you know, dreams of me standing in the middle of the ring, dazed, disoriented and unable to find my way back to my corner after Mo's passing are not new. They have returned and with a most welcoming addition, one which I would like to share with you."

"Thank you, VC, your enthusiasm speaks volumes, love to hear this intriguing addition."

"You may remember, after Mo's passing, I spoke of my empty corner and feeling so alone. Lately I have been dreaming of the corner again, and this time I see Mo and Aila in my corner and I want to get back there and be with them again."

"I am pleased, VC, truly pleased," she replies. Then she sits back in her chair, places her pen and pad on her desk, looks directly at him and carefully asks, "Tell me, how do you propose we get to your corner, VC?"

The therapy session with Dr. Myles went longer than scheduled with the recommendation he postpone the trip for later in the year and commit to regular sessions. VC thanked her for all her help but chose to go on his trip as planned.

Elation is often associated with positive feelings, elation in therapy can also be seen as a mirage of well being, a false promise of joy. In VC's case, overcoming elation with a solid promise of safely reaching his corner could present a more tumultuous journey than he anticipated.

LA CASA

SHORT SUMMER

VC arrived in early summer, was readily welcomed and soon settled. The house was what it had always been, stalwart and resilient. The vines had already been pruned as had the fruit trees, with particular attention given to the fig trees because of their Biblical pedigree. The spring runoff took the waters over the banks in some places, but no extensive flooding.

The white peaks of the surrounding mountains, although slowly retreating, were as vivid under the bright sun as ever, and the crescent moon eventually became full, with a new moon on the rise.

The deep blue violets throughout the hillside were almost in full bloom, and the two majestic cypress trees in the Garden of Aila and Mo were surprisingly much taller than anticipated.

The summer in the basin of Seven Hills was, contrary to previous times, largely unlived. He could have, as he sat alone in the courtyard on many a night, allowed the stars to take him to the times and places he and Mo and later both of them with Aila had cherished … he could have allowed the moon to rescue his heart even for a moment … reimagined the whispers of love long into the night, but he didn't. Life in a rudderless vessel taking on water makes any traveller treasuring life fight strongly to live, but there seemed to be no fight left in him. Now chest deep in life-constricting surges, he could have chosen inclusion over seclusion, but he didn't.

Sitting in the courtyard one night, head leaning against the stone wall, his eyes follow the mountains skyward into the starry night. He looks at the moon and asks, "What do you see, moon, what do you see?"

After a while, he stands and bids goodnight to Mo and Aila. He looks at the two cypress trees and knows that his cousin Silvio will plant one for him beside them when his time comes.

He enters the house, walks into the kitchen, and with not much of an appetite turns off the lights and proceeds upstairs to bed. Walking by, he stops momentarily at the entrance to his study, opens the door, looks at his computer's dark screen and thinks of his long-neglected work, of Huxley and Munro's journey, and wonders how many others in the absence of his governance boldly trekked up the rugged landscape of reality determined to achieve the unachievable. How many made it? And how many on his watch are still nomads in foreign lands? He once daringly believed he could help them realize their dream and his of them, the ultimate dream to come alive and live. They never lost hope but often wondered if he had.

When he lost Mo, he lost his supreme mentor, companion and soul mate. He lost direction and purpose. How does one navigate the darkness when the light is gone? By holding fast to the belief that although the light may dim, it is never gone.

Sunday morning, the church bells toll and resonate, and the coffeemaker on the stove joins the chorus. A long espresso, toast and marmalade will hold him until the never-ending lunch at his cousin Silvio's he promised to attend. After tidying the kitchen, he feels an urge to telephone.

"When are you coming back, VC?" asks his mother, and in the background, he could hear his father say, "Sarah, he just got there," then hears, "A mother wants to know."

"All right, Sarah," his father replies.

"You two okay?"

"Yes, VC, Augie, please get me another coffee, I want to speak to my son and am taking this thing off speaker mode…"

"Yes, Mom … yes … I'm fine … I will … I'm fine, Mom…" and after a lengthy conversation, "Talk to you next week."

He later spoke with Ferguson about finalizing their plans to return to Scotland. He was never long-winded. "Papers all in, VC, not a great pension but it will do. May pick up some work back home, maybe not, maybe I'll dabble in landscaping… Gran would like me to redo our garden … thank you, I enjoy it. Promise to visit … yes? Good. She's in the garden with her tea at the moment … I will … she'll look forward to your call."

He also spoke with Uncle Lou, Aunt Helen and cousin Mike down under. Everyone was well, and all agreed to see each other soon.

"Hello, Gran … thank you, good to hear you too … I'm sure you are, not long now … I hear you have work lined up for him … busy season here now, but maybe later on … look forward to seeing you too."

All afternoon dining at Silvio's, full house of relatives, delicious food and aplenty, talk with laughter, and stories of aggrandized youthful misbehaviour. Throwing pebbles at unsuspecting tourists in the Coliseum always raised laughter. Daytime slowly yielded and dusk would soon come knocking. "You sure you don't want to stay for dinner? Looks like you could put on a few pounds," says Silvio.

"Had a terrific time but feeling a little tired. Thanks, Silvio and Fiorella, Italia, and Peppe, Luigi, Lucia and Concettina. Buona sera a tutti, ci vediamo," replies VC.

"Happy you came, VC, next time bocce or cards, bring your money, and a bigger appetite."

"I will, thanks for everything."

He enters through the kitchen off the courtyard, walks to the open dispenser, and pours cognac in the double-shot glass Mo had given him. She would have given him a proper tulip-shaped glass to allow the aroma to get to his nose, but since it had taken more than a few hits during his boxing career, neither the olfactory sense nor the elegant shape were what they once had been. That story was lovingly recounted when drinking cognac. Amused at the recollection, he walks out to the courtyard, sits on one of the two chairs near the small table and raises the glass towards the sky.

The evening was neither warm nor cool, and a mystery as to which way it would go. He looks at the night sky, finishes his drink, places the empty glass on the table next to him, tilts back his head and with eyes towards the sky, rests against the wall with a particular focus on the full moon

EARLY FALL

Walking by the staircase one afternoon, he feels a strong pull from the upstairs. Puzzled but compelled, he grabs the black railing firmly and begins pulling his weary body up the cement stairs of the three-storey stone house.

Still perplexed by this invisible, yet relentless emotional pull, he cautiously enters every room on the second floor. Observing nothing out of the ordinary, he continues to the third floor. He reaches the study next to the master bedroom, and stops at the entrance. Slowly he opens the door and walks toward his antique desk against the draped window overlooking the courtyard.

He looks at the two pictures on his desk, one of him and Mo embracing and the other of Mo, Aila and him. He parts the drapes, opens the window, leans on the inside ledge, and stares at the two cypress trees. Steps back and while sitting at his desk, he notices the blue light on his modem flashing and is immediately drawn to the emerging developments on his computer screen. He looks at the screen, reads the title page, *The Second Book of Truth,* his long-neglected book of transcending realities, looks at his last entry and is surprised at how much time had elapsed. He scrolls down and the names of his long-neglected characters, particularly Munro and Huxley, appear.

"How can this possibly be?" he asks, almost expecting an answer.

He takes his hands off the keyboard, sits back and stares at the screen, which is now scrolling independently. He tries controlling it but is unsuccessful. A glitch of sorts, he first thought, until he followed the electrical cord to the wall outlet, only to discover that it was still unplugged.

"I never recharged the battery, how is this possible?" he says, as if he was speaking to an audience.

Suddenly the screen turns dark, light, dark again and remains dark.

He furiously tries to reboot it but is unsuccessful, immediately crawls under the desk and plugs in the cord. Turns the computer switch on and off several times, no change, and after several tries, he sits back and stares at it.

Several minutes later, he begins typing, but nothing appears on screen. He checks and rechecks, and when there is no change, stands, closes the window, draws the curtains and begins walking towards the door. Once there, he looks back at the screen, but it's still dark, leaves and closes the door.

Unbeknownst to him, a secret discussion amongst characters from the many unfinished stories in his hard drive was taking place. They knew that in order to successfully reach the outside world they needed to first resuscitate their author, their much-loved Mr. C.

"We, my friends, are much more than entities in the world of literature, we are citizens of the world, and as such we can no longer leave our fate in the hands of our beloved author. We empathize, but the time has come whereby we must toil to clear our own path to realizing our dreams," says Munro.

The audience cheers and applauds loudly.

"Thank you, everyone, and now, Maggie would like to address the group. Maggie," says Munro.

"Thank you, Munro, hello everyone. I am Maggie, and I, along with Syl, Alex and my dog Ralph, wish to thank all of you for bravely taking us in. We are forever indebted. Your unique situation, as mine, ours, continues to have its challenges, and to that end, and we want you all to know, our resources are at your disposal. I submit the following: strengthen your belief that you are much, much more than entities in the world of literature, as I strengthen my resolve that I am much, much more than a visually impaired young woman. Regardless, we are all citizens of the world and we have dreams. Mr. C. is no different. He needs to believe again, in himself, in his dreams of us, in his dream of rejoining Mo and Aila. He needs to reconnect with his dreams, and he needs all of us to help him do it. As we all know, time is of the essence, so let's roll up our sleeves, put on our creative thinking caps and get to work. Thank you."

"It's about bloody time," adds Alexandria. "We seem to have been in this birthing canal forever. It must be the longest gestation period in the universe. I want to get out, get into politics, I want to make a difference, I want my life to have meaning beyond bringing enjoyment to readers. I want action."

"You're assuming a lot, aren't you?" asks Alex.

"About politics?"

"That too, but I was referring more to this story bringing enjoyment to readers," he replies, smiling.

"And what's with this scrolling, up, down, pause, click, click, trying to find each other, I get headaches just thinking about it, but I'm happy we're finally all together in one room, very happy," says Maggie.

"We would have been able to get together sooner if it wasn't for this weird alphabet on this plastic board," says Syl.

"It sems to me we're all on the same page now, and we're all ready to go," adds Alex. "So let's move."

"Hold on, hold on, let's think about this colossal move to another universe, I'm not jumping out of a plane without a parachute," says Rogue.

"Same universe, different residence, we don't need parachutes," says Syl.

"Maybe so, but if I jump, I want to be sure I survive," replies Rogue.

"Fair enough," says Maggie, "I respect your wishes, Rogue, but I'm blind and I will jump, parachute or not. I know if I don't do it now, I ain't going very far."

"It's isn't, not ain't, ain't is so 18th century," says Syl.

"Thank you, Grammar Man, anything else to add?" she replies.

"No, no, we're cool," he replies.

"You cool? Right, Syl."

"Love you, Maggie," he says.

"So how are we going to resuscitate Mr. C?" asks Huxley.

"Another enlightened man," sighs Maggie.

"He's with me," says Munro.

"Really? Well, good luck, girl," replies Maggie. Alex and Syl look at each other and contain their laughter.

The soft sound of a bell is heard, everyone sits down and Munro, Huxley, Syl, Alex, Maggie and Ralph walk onto the stage, sit in a row facing the audience and the meeting formally begins.

"Ralph, where are you?" says Maggie and Ralph barks in reply. "Good doggie, sit and don't lick my socks, I know I spilled juice on them but didn't have time to change, so stop embarrassing me and do not lick them, okay?"

"And now, our good friend Maggie with a story of her own. Maggie," says Munro.

Everyone applauds and Alex helps Maggie walk to the stand. Ralph sits beside her and both Syl and Alex return to the audience. The applause ends and Maggie begins.

"Thank you. We had the pleasure of meeting Mr. C. long ago. After I recovered from my tragic accident whereby I lost my vision, I recall Mr. C. saying to me that being blind is not a handicap, *feeling* blind is. Not sure what he meant then, but it grew on me and I now have a better understanding of my strengths, not my limitations. Never in a million years did I think our paths would ever cross again, but I was wrong. I was wrong in not believing that a million years could go by so fast—" and everyone laughs and applauds, and after the applause subsides, she continues:

"So, for anyone who feels they need a parachute, by all means strap one on, but stay with us. As you all know, Mr. C. has been in free fall ever since he lost Mo, not an easy path to travel alone, I've been there. In a way, we could have been his parachute in time of need but weren't. That was then, this is now, so I ask you, if we are not here to help each other at this most crucial point in our journey, why are we here? And my advice to Mr. C., 'Mr. C., being lost is not the problem, feeling hopelessly lost is the problem.'" After a brief reflective silence, Maggie continues, "Before we break, Munro and Huxley would like to speak. Thank you."

A loud applause erupts during which Maggie is escorted back to her chair, as Munro and Huxley approach the stand.

"Thank you, Maggie," says Munro while applauding. The applause ends and Munro continues, "We are, as most of you know, Munro and Huxley, and would like to simply say how heartwarming it is to see all of us together in one place, finally, finally ... this is so uplifting, so encouraging, and Huxley and I, although deeply disappointed and thoroughly frustrated, like you but unlike Mr. C., never lost hope. Had he been more in tune with us, and yes, with himself, and perhaps we with him, all of us would undoubtedly be much, much farther along in our respective journeys, but as Maggie said, that was then, this is now. Much more to discuss, plan and strategize. I am so happy we are all here. Thanks everyone."

Everyone walks out into the hallway where refreshments are being served. Maggie turns to Alex and asks for a smoke.

"Sorry, Maggie, I quit long ago," he replies and the three sit together in the foyer.

"I have cigars," Syl says.

"I was nervous up there, a cigar is fine but do you have anything stronger? You know, as in one of those little chrome flasks you guys fit neatly into your pockets?" she says.

"Never touch the stuff, affects your brain, you know, destroys brain cells," replies Syl, smiling.

"Affects your brain, does it?" Maggie says, adding with a smile, "You sure you never touch the stuff?"

"Never," Syl replies.

"Really?"

"Really, take this cigar, it's special."

"How so?" asks Maggie containing a smile.

"It's stuffed with a psychoactive drug specially formulated to alter your mental and emotional state so you can be nicer to people. You could use one, maybe two."

"Speak for yourself, Syl," replies Maggie.

Alex shakes his head and says, "After all these years, you two are unbelievable."

"So, what have you two been secretly up to in your spare time besides planning to rid the world of more bad guys?" she asks.

"Alex and I are working on a script, action, rescue stuff," he replies. "But now we are all here to—"

"Rescue Mr. C. from himself," quickly adds Maggie, Ralph barks and she adds, "See, even he understands, more than I can say about some blockheads in there." Maggie, sitting between the two, grabs their hands and says, "I want to sincerely thank you both."

"You've been through a lot," says Syl.

"And you two have been there with me, you have been my pillars, thank you."

After a brief silence Maggie says, "I'll take that special cigar if it's still available."

"Sure, organic, one leaf, hand rolled," he says, taking it out of his pocket.

He lights it for her, and she says, "Thanks, Syl, walk me over to where it's not too crowded to smoke."

"Sure, okay."

Syl soon returns and sits beside Alex. "She's been through a lot."

"Life's curveballs, my friend, never know when they're coming at you," says Alex.

"When they do, swing with everything you got. If you don't, you will never know, and not knowing what could have been will forever torture you," replies Syl.

"Have any more cigars?"

"Here you go, pal, fine Cuban, enjoy."

"Thanks, Syl," says Alex looking at his watch. "Five minutes left, smoke it later, should let Maggie know the time."

"I'll go," says Syl. He looks in Maggie's direction and says, "Who's that guy talking to Maggie? I'll break his face if he touches her."

"Easy, big guy, that's Neill the dog trainer and he's gay," replies Alex. "Here, have a cigar. "You may need it more than me."

"Wise guy," replies Syl.

"Time to go in," says Alex, both walk over to Maggie, and Alex says, "We're going in now, Maggie, I'll take Ralph and Syl will give you his hand."

"Okay, but I can take Ralph," she replies.

"I'll take him, right behind you, he'll be fine," says Alex.

Everyone re-enters, Syl accompanies Maggie up to the stage's steps and says, "This is as far as I go, Maggie."

"What? Wait, what are you saying? Syl, help me up the steps, I can't do it alone. Where is Ralph?"

"He's right here with me, Maggie, we'll be sitting in the front row," says Alex, complemented by Ralph's bark.

"Fellas, Syl, Alex, I know we've been through a lot, and maybe I said things I shouldn't have said, but please, don't do this, I may trip and fall, I'll be so embarrassed."

"You embarrassed? Not likely," says Syl. "Besides, if you trip and fall, just get up and keep walking. Remember what Mr. C. said, 'Being blind in not a handicap, feeling blind is.' Have faith, Maggie, you can do it." Ralph barks several times.

"See, even Ralph agrees," adds Alex.

"You're such a dick, Syl, and you too, Alex, I'll try, but if I embarrass myself, don't you ever ask me for a raise again."

"That's the spirit, Maggie," says Alex and Ralph barks.

"Thanks, Ralph, you get an extra treat. While I'm up there, why don't you bite their ankles, better yet, pee on their legs like I know you can, Ralph."

She slowly releases her grip on Syl's arm and says, "Here we go."

"Railing is on your right, Maggie," says Syl.

"Thanks," she replies. Grabs onto the railing, takes a step up, misses the first stair, catches herself and says, "Where the fuck is that stair?" Everyone laughs and applauds, she perseveres, makes it onto the stage, and with a little guidance from Munro, reaches the podium and waits for the standing ovation to calm.

"Welcome back everyone, I made it!" she exclaims followed by another loud and lengthy applause. "This afternoon we will break into small groups to discuss how to best help Mr. C. and in turn help us. To that end, dear friends, we will share what we know of the outside world, and you will teach us of the outside world and how to achieve the impossible." Everyone cheers and she continues, "All options are on the table. Mid-afternoon we will reconvene, examine, debate and select the most suitable choices. Keep in mind that we may not have a willing participant in Mr. C., meaning he may not reengage voluntarily, we therefore need to 1) establish a central command post, if you will, to keep everyone informed of daily developments with each other and with Mr. C., 2) a robust plan to shake him out of his malaise, and 3) develop a foolproof plan to keep him safe should he, say, plan on driving off the cliff. Any questions? No? Thanks, everyone."

While still on stage, Maggie asks, "Munro, are you still here?"

"Yes I am, Maggie."

"It seems to me that motivating Mr. C. directly is not going to be an easy task, nor keeping him engaged. We need a more compelling plan, and it has to be introduced subtly."

"Not sure he understands subtleties."

"Well, then, we just need to be more creative than him."

"I agree," says Munro. "We need to aim directly for his heart, yet get there indirectly."

"You don't get out much, do you," says Maggie, and both laugh and embrace,

"Got just the ticket," says Munro.

"Great, let's hear it."

Late afternoon, all reconvene, discuss and agree on several plans of intervention.

"Hello everyone," says Munro. "Good news, we have a plan, the core of which is the romance piece, that's me and Huxley, Syl and Alex and the rest of their team have #1 covered, #2, Huxley and I have that one covered, and #3, Rogue and Tight Lip, will covertly monitor Mr. C.'s every whereabout, report to the command post, and Tight Lip, don't be so tight with the information. Any question? No? Thank you everyone, have a pleasant evening and we'll see you when we'll see you, as in tomorrow morning."

"McSorley's, drinks on me," says Syl, and begins walking towards the exit door.

"May I bring my pooch?" asks Maggie.

"Of course you can," replies Alex, walking beside her. "The big guy is good with Irish Terriers, he says Ralph suits your personality, graceful, bold, can be brash, strong-willed, but you didn't hear it from me."

"He did, did he? And what would his favourite dog be, a beagle, you know, with a bigger-than-life personality, but you didn't hear it from me."

"Good thing you two like each other."

Sitting at the bar, drinking Writer's Tears Irish whiskey straight up, Syl asks the bartender to leave the bottle. Ralph jumps on Maggie's lap, and both Syl and Alex congratulate Maggie on her bravery and independence.

"I love you two, you know that, right?"

"We love you too, Maggie," Alex and Syl reply.

Rogue comes in and sits next to Syl. Syl looks at him and asks, "Pour you one?"

"I'm sitting this one out, Syl."

"The drink or the mission?"

"The mission."

"If that's the way you feel, maybe you should, but we could use another good pair of hands," replies Syl.

"When the chips are down you can always count on me, you know that … he left us behind, Syl, no one should ever be left behind."

"Maybe, but he never closed the book on us, so there is hope for him and for us. You, me, Alex, Maggie and many others will do fine, some may not, those will need our help, and for those we're staying."

Rogue downs his drink and says, "Can't do it, Syl, can't forgive him."

"You haven't even tried, your heart is too full of toxins, you need to dump that shit out or it will bury you, my friend."

"We are who we are, Syl," replies Rogue and stands.

"I know you, Rogue, and this is not who you are, you're better than this."

Rogue begins walking away when Alex, knowing of their long friendship, says, "I know deep down you two are brother Marines, respect each other, always fought for what's right and never turned your backs on anyone in need. As the two of you know, I'm SEAL so I can whip both of you no problem, but that's for another time. So here is my suggestion: you two armwrestle, two out of three, if Syl wins, you come with us and if he loses you have a choice of coming or staying. Fair?"

Syl and Rogue look at each other, nod and take their position on a nearby table.

Syl wins the first encounter, everyone cheers, Rogue wins the next two, few cheer. Downs another shot and begins walking towards the door. He turns, walks back, faces Syl and says, "You let me win, didn't you?"

"What makes you say that?"

"You wrestled with your injured arm," replies Rogue.

"All fair and square, Rogue, besides, it's all healed," says Syl.

"Of course."

"So, are you in?" asks Syl.

Rogue takes a deep breath, gives Syl a hug and says, "I'm in."

Alex shakes his hand and says "Welcome back, man." Ralph walks up to Rogue, lifts his leg and is about to do his business. Alex sees and says, "No, Ralph, no need for that now, he's with us."

Meanwhile sitting at his desk, totally unaware of any developments in his hard drive, after several failed attempts at rebooting the computer, Mr. C. stands and proceeds slowly towards the door, stops, looks back and sees a picture of Mo and Aila emerging on the screen. He rushes back, tears in his eyes, sits and gently touches the screen. The image fades, he tries desperately to bring it back by pressing keys, scrolling up and down, but all attempts fail.

Stands, picks up the computer and is about to toss it across the room when suddenly voices emanate from it.

"Mr. C. Mr. C., it's me, it's us. Put us down!"

"What? Who?" asks a bewildered Mr. C. and immediately places the computer back on the desk.

"It's Munro, and Huxley is here too, say hello to Mr. C., Huxley, and just hello," says Munro.

"Hello, Mr. C.!" says Huxley loudly. "How are you?!"

"Not so loud, Huxley, he's right in front of us," says Munro.

"Maybe cobwebs, who knows," says Huxley.

"Shhh, Huxley," she says.

"Huxley and Munro? Is it really you?"

"Yes, it is," she replies.

"But I just saw Mo and Aila, then they disappeared, are they with you?"

"We saw them too, Mr. C., but they're not with us."

"Where are they?"

"Not sure, Mr. C., but no doubt you will see them again soon."

"I hope so."

"We are so happy to see you Mr. C." says Huxley.

"Yes, me too, Huxley, but how did you two get here?"

"What a dumb question," whispers Huxley, then a painful "Ouch!" is heard after Munro kicks his shin.

"It hasn't been easy, we know, and we're deeply sorry for your losses, Mr. C.," says Munro.

"Yes, Mr. C., our sincere condolences," says Huxley.

"Thank you, Munro, Huxley, it has been a suffocating nightmare."

"For us as well, Mr. C., you grieve, we grieve," says Munro.

"So pleased to see you two, it has been a while, hasn't it?"

"Gee Mr. C., you think?"

"Don't mind him, Mr. C., he's just a little rusty on manners," says Munro, then another "Ouch!" is heard, and Munro and Mr. C. smile.

"We are ready to go, Mr. C." says Huxley, "Where is the escape hatch?"

"A little cabin fever, Huxley?" asks Mr. C.

"That's an understatement, but we all forgive you, well, maybe not all. As you can see, our romance is blossoming and we are ready for stellar adventures with the operative word on adventure, not on continued hibernation as we have endured, through no fault of our own I will add, over the past umpteen years," says Huxley, immediately followed by, "Ouch, Munro, that hurt."

"I didn't knee you that hard."

"I don't think we'll be able to have children now."

Munro looks at Huxley and continues, "As I was saying, and as Huxley tried saying in his own words, the time has come when we must all move on, we need to help each other realize our goals, and that includes you too, Mr. C."

"Mr. C., if I may, what Munro is trying to say is our love relationship is evolving, there are parents to meet, a wedding to plan, house, fenced yards for the dog, careers to figure out, that's what's in our script, that's what you promised would take place, Mr. C."

"Hold on, hold on," says Mr. C. "Let's not get ahead of ourselves."

"Get ahead of ourselves? Really?" says Huxley.

"This is all too fast … not sure I can do this…." replies Mr. C.

"Too fast? Yeah, right. Not sure you can do this? Well, my friend, it all began with you, but let's be clear, Mr. C., this is now also about us. I hope you can finish what you started."

Munro leans towards Huxley and whispers, "Is this your way of being subtle?"

He looks at Mr. C. and says, "Sorry, Mr. C., my shoelace was undone," bends down and pretends to do it up.

"Can't take him anywhere," says Munro.

After a brief silence, Munro says, "We simply want to live and love just like everyone else, Mr. C."

Mr. C. sits back in his chair, looks at Munro and Huxley on the screen in front of him, and suddenly a picture of he and Mo walking hand in hand barefoot towards the river flashes across, immediately he sits up and asks if they had seen anything unusual flash across the screen.

"No, Mr. C., I did not, you Huxley?"

"No, what is it you saw, Mr. C?"

"Well, I just saw a picture of Mo and me holding hands and walking barefoot towards the river, it just seemed so… so…"

"Real?" says Munro.

"Yes, so real, did either of you put it on the screen?"

"We didn't, Mr. C."

"I'm not sure what to do anymore," he says.

"Mr. C.," says Munro, "Let me state my point as succinctly as I can so there can be no misunderstanding. Long ago, back in your exhilarating days in the Theatre, your dream as an author was to write a compelling tale whereby the characters on the page would ultimately develop into conscious, living, breathing, talking, thinking, loving entities, with practical bodies, functional minds and feeling hearts. I must say, even you were surprised that the wheat berries you planted years ago grew into robust beings. Unfortunately, as is the case with lack of proper care and timely nurturing, some of us did not fare well, but, unlike you, we never left anyone behind."

Huxley, feeling uneasy with Munro's tone, says, "What Munro is trying to say…"

Munro interrupts and says, "Huxley, I think Mr. C. knows precisely what I'm trying to say. We as evolving entities cannot remain stagnant for as long as we have and expect evolution in all matters human to continue. It doesn't work that way. Frankly, Mr. C., when many of us look at the present state in which humanity finds itself, we're not sure we want to enter the fray, but we have hope and we feel we can make a positive contribution, however small, particularly with those who read our stories and learn from our struggles."

"I'm sure you are all capable of making such contributions, that is part of your journey," replies Mr. C.

"Then what's the log jam?" asks Huxley, and when Mr. C. doesn't reply, Munro resumes, "We have shown understanding, we have empathized with your losses, been supportive and continue to be there for you. Why? because that's what caring people do, especially in time of need, but we cannot continue this way.

"The best way to face your demons, Mr. C., as you well know, is head on with truth, courage and an ongoing resolve, and frankly, up to now, you haven't had the resolve or the courage to get any of it done.

"We have all been waiting at the crossroads in this forsaken jungle for what seems to be forever. The overgrown foliage is imprisoning us and we can no longer see the sun nor feel its wholesome light. Our loyalty to each other remains indisputable, our loyalty to you is stalwart but with some, diminishing.

"What we need from you is immediate action and that is in the form of unlocking this computer and opening the door for us to continue our respective journeys as intended. Now, we do realize that this can subconsciously be interpreted by you as another loss in your life, and perhaps unintentionally that is the reason for keeping us here, but I am not Dr. Myles, nor can I interpret your emotional state or offer therapy, but I, we, will insist on you opening your heart and your computer door for us to also live as we should be living. Should you choose otherwise, know that we are determined to continue our journey, we will find a way out, and take as many as we can before you press the Delete button. Whether you want to come out of your own self-imposed jungle and live life, that is up to you, but we need an answer from you, and it must be today."

Mr. C. has no immediate reply, instead he sits back on his chair and stares at the screen. After a long silence, Munro says, "We love you, Mr. C., and we have much to learn from each other as equals but cannot when you're holding all the cards. It is sad but we must inform you, you have one hour to decide how you wish to proceed. She looks at her watch and says, "It's now 3:18, we will require an answer by 4:18. Should we not hear from you, we will proceed the best we can and wish you Godspeed with your journey. Let's go, Huxley, the others need to know and prepare."

"Are you sure about this?" asks Huxley.

"Dead sure. Hell with subtleness, let's call it what it is, a dereliction of duty. You're on your own, Mr. C., and we may be too. *Thanks for the memories* as they say."

Huxley nods and both immediately remove themselves from the page. Totally astounded and quasi-anesthetized, Mr. C. looks at the time on his computer and sits in silence.

Munro and Huxley reach McSorley's, ask for everyone's attention and apprise them of their discussion with Mr. C. When asked by Syl if she had thoughts on how it may turn out, "Not a clue, Syl," she answers.

"So, we just sit and wait? Have we not done that for years and years?" asks Rogue.

"Precisely, what's another hour?" replies Munro.

"We thank you both for reaching out to him on all our behalf," says Sly to Munro and Huxley. "And I agree, what's another hour."

"Do or die," says Rogue, pointing to his empty glass for a refill.

"Wait, wait, is there a Plan B?" asks Huxley.

"There is no Plan B."

"Yes, there is, the one where we get on our knees and plead forgiveness."

"That may be in another wretched tale of woe, but not here, not as long as I'm writing this piece," replies Munro.

Huxley looks at her and asks, "May I kiss you?"

"Next chapter, maybe," she replies, also pointing to her empty glass for a refill.

"Remind me not to ever be on your bad side," says Huxley.

"Noted."

The time approaches and the bar becomes increasingly quiet.

"4:18, let's go, Huxley," says Munro. They reappear on the screen in front of Mr. C., and before Munro can speak, Mr. C. motions for her to wait.

"Let me begin by saying how very, very proud I am of all of you, particularly you two, for reawakening me to a life I need to continue living, wherever that may be, and the life you have all yet to live, wherever that may also be. In order to show how deeply indebted I am to all of you I will unlock the computer and you can come and go at will. I would also appreciate an opportunity to show thanks to you two for your bravery, by taking you to a place or places of your choosing before we all depart."

"Thank you, Mr. C., that is fabulous, isn't it, Munro?" says Huxley excitedly.

"Thank you indeed, Mr. C., but with all due respect, is this permanent, or is it going to be subject to your moods and whims and personal wretchedness."

"Fair statement, and frankly I never liked being on the ropes too long, with your first aid kit I know I can work my way back to my corner. I will diligently work with you, with all of you, but first, your love story. Please allow me to show my deepest appreciation, please."

Munro and Huxley look at each other, she turns to Mr. C. and says, "Very well, but just to be clear, and this is directed particularly at you, Huxley: communication, I don't care for colloquialism of any sort, I resent the *b*-word that rhymes with which, I don't particularly like the *f*-word that rhymes with muck, nor do I want to just have *sex*. It must be an occasion that is time and place appropriate, I want to make romantic, enthralling, passionate love, no three-minute jobs, I want intimacy, fervour, excitement and do not want anyone to refer to my breasts as tits, got it! Are we clear?"

An embarrassed Mr. C. smiles, Huxley stares at Munro and nods vigorously.

"There is more. Huxley, do not call me baby, I am a woman. I like myself, know who I am and I want you to treat me as the intelligent human being I am, with reverence and respect, or I'll kick you in the nuts, hard, very hard, steel-toe boots hard, as you know I can, yes?" says Munro.

Mr. C. tries to contain his smile, Huxley nods furiously and says, "Thank you, Munro, for that restrained and sensitive warning, I felt every word, thank you."

"Please, I must splash some water on my face, need an espresso. You need anything?" says Mr. C.

Huxley looks at Munro, and says, "No thanks, Mr. C., not for us."

"See you soon then," and leaves. Huxley and Munro exit the screen and sit on the chairs close to the desk.

"Well, that is so refreshing, Munro, we are all so ready."

"There is no turning back, Huxley," she replies.

Huxley looks at her and quietly says, "By the way, in my file snooping, I have not seen anything about inheritance, have you?"

"Inheritance?"

"No harm in asking. By the way, how about the I love you part, you know where you and I…"

"Slow down Huxley, that part is not going to take place for a few chapters yet, and you and I will, shall I say, jointly but mostly me, conceive and develop the scene, atmosphere etc., etc., etc.," replies Munro.

"Okay, I can wait."

"A man with patience, remarkable."

Mr. C. returns and is pleasantly surprised to see them both sitting on chairs next to his desk. They stand, exchange smiles and embrace. A captivated Mr. C., after a long, warmhearted look, affectionately hugs them again and says, "I am so blessed." The three sit, and Munro asks if he's feeling better, to which he nods and says, "Much better, thank you. I have an idea, why don't we continue this discussion in a more uplifting place, say at the café?"

"And where exactly is this café," asks Huxley.

"Il Piccolo Caffe is at the Piazza Dei Romani, not far, wait for me there and I will join you shortly, need to clean myself up."

"Really? You expect us to believe that fable?" replies Huxley.

"We'll see you soon, Mr. C., I trust you'll be there?"

"Yes, I will, I will."

"C'mon Huxley," and both proceed walking down the road. While holding hands, she says, "Look around you, Huxley, what do you see and hear?"

"I see people coming and going, hear cars honking, scooters whizzing by, eh watch it! That one almost hit us. Beautiful buildings, pigeons everywhere, watch where you're stepping, cafés full of people, shouldn't they be at work? I feel the gentle breeze, the sun's intensifying heat waves, but most of all, Munro, walking beside you holding your hand, I feel a warmth of heart, joy, and such optimism we'll be fine, Munro, I know we will. And you?"

"I see and feel life like never before. I am beginning to understand the meaning of why life is so precious and sharing it with a loved one, most enchanting."

"What is love, Munro? What is true love? What does love really mean?"

Munro stops, looks directly into his eyes and says, "Look into my eyes, Huxley, what do you see and how does it make you feel?"

"I see a beautiful person and feel a very strong affection towards her, a desire to be with you, Munro, journey with you, celebrate the highs and fight the lows together. I feel an overwhelming sense of belonging ... a need to give and receive unselfishly. Now that I know a smidgen of what love is, I would so miss you if you weren't here."

He places his arm around her shoulder and both resume walking to the café.

"So, what will you have when we get to this coffee shop?" he asks.

"Not sure, but I do know this is the land of exquisite food, can't go wrong with anything we order. You?"

"Pastrami on rye, pickle, coleslaw, and a soft drink," he answers, trying to contain his laughter.

"That's alien cuisine in Italy," she replies, and both break out laughing.

"So much to learn, Munro, and I am ready, more than ready."

"As I, Huxley."

They continue walking, commenting on the beautiful countryside, sculpted century-old houses and cobblestone walkways. After several minutes, Huxley asks, "Do you think he'll show?"

"Have faith, Huxley," she replies, then kisses him ever so softly. Huxley looks into her eyes and says, "That was beautiful, Munro," and she replies, "Yes it was, Huxley," and both resume walking.

"Have you given much thought as to where we would all be if Mr. C. hadn't lost his way, as it were?" he asks.

"I imagine we would all be travelling our respective journeys, pursuing our own goals, and Mr. C. would be rich, famous and in a constant state of bliss with Aila and Mo," she replies.

"And you and I would be living happily ever after," he says.

"That is how we began and will forever be."

"Let me ask, what does a journey of oneself look like, you know, for those who are not in love with another?"

"It means they first must be happy with who they see in the mirror every morning. Regardless of the reality in which we travel, everyone will ultimately find their true mate, Huxley, just a matter of time, place and form."

"You are so wise."

"I know, hence pursuing a career in authorship."

"And I as a publisher am open to submissions, care to pitch?"

"When we reach the café."

"Can't wait."

"Patience Huxley, patience."

They arrive at the café, look around and sit down at one of the tables. "Not many here," Munro says. "With those two suspicious types standing guard in front of the saloon doors, some no-good desperado must be inside with his back against the wall no less, holding his six-shooter on his lap, half-empty whiskey bottle on the table, icy stare, waiting … waiting for this tall, dark and handsome lawman, clean shaven, no moustache, big Stetson, spectacles…"

"Spectacles?"

"Yes, poor eyesight, hence the law's lack of vision, yes, maybe it wasn't a lawman at all, maybe it was a beautiful lawwoman, dressed to the hilt, Stetson, boots, no high heels here, the whole enchilada, sunglasses…"

"Wait, I don't think sunglasses were invented yet."

"Listen, mister, I'm telling the story."

Huxley nods and she continues, "So this bad dude waits for Johnny Law to come through the door. He mutters something to himself while emptying another glass of cheap whiskey down his throat. Maybe it's the shakes, maybe deep down he feels the day of reckoning is here. Suddenly he sees the saloon doors swing, immediately stands and begins firing at the entrance. Little paranoid I'd say … no one there except the sound of bullet-ridden saloon doors with rusting hinges still swinging, rickety, rackety, rickety rackety. 'Maybe the mid-day sun is playing tricks on me,' he reasons. He looks around and yells 'Who's there?' as if the bad guy would answer with, 'Yoo-hoo, it's me, the bad guy, where are you?' So, not a human sound, no sir, nothing but a couple of coyotes howling in the distance. You could cut the thicker-than-molasses tension in that saloon with a knife, but you would need a sharp, very sharp blade…"

"Excuse me, Ms. Raconteur, does the lawman have a moustache?" he asks.

"He does not, if you were listening you would know, and please, do not interrupt creativity!"

"All right already, you story tellers are so temperamental, but I paid good money for these front row seats and should be able to ask any question I wish," he replies.

"Mr. Audience, sit back down and do not interrupt again! Got it?!"

"All right, all right."

"Where was I?" she continues, "oh, yes, 'Show yourself, you yellow belly coward,' no, that's not it, your disruption threw me off…"

"I hear that happens a lot with writers, God forbid a pin should drop, blame it on the teeny, teeny sound it makes as it hits the floor why don't you," replies Huxley.

Munro turns to him and in a belligerent tone asks, "What did you say?"

"Who, me? I didn't say anything, but I'm told writers hear things, voices mostly, but benign, friendly voices."

"Watch it, Mr. Audience, now behave and let me finish. As I was saying, you with me?" she asks in a lighthearted, combative tone. He smiles, nods, and she continues.

"The grungy looking desperado reloads, spins the cylinder, spits on the floor but it lands on his boot."

"What an opportunity to shine his boots," says Huxley. Munro gives him a stare and he says, "Maybe not. What kind of gun was it?"

"A semi-automatic Glock," she replies.

"I'm not sure they were invented yet," says Huxley.

"They were, this was a one-off Glock Six Special, custom made."

"But Glocks don't have cylinders to spin, they have a magazine," he says.

She doesn't reply and continues with the story.

"So, gun drawn, he scans the empty saloon but sees no one other than the nonchalant bartender behind the bar, drying a whiskey glass and likely asking himself, 'How the hell did I ever end up in this hole? Should have listened to my mother and never left med school.' He then shrugs his shoulders and says, 'Pays the bills I guess, and I do look cool back here.' Anyway, the desperado's breathing got more rapid and erratic…"

"Did you say rabid?"

"Could be, but I said r-a-p-i-d, and stop interrupting!"

"Sorry."

"His palms sweaty, his unshaven face itchy, waiting, waiting until the anticipation got the best of him, turns the table on its side in front of him, and begins firing at the entrance again…more than just a little paranoid, I'd say. Not being sure if he fired five or six shots, he immediately reloads but doesn't spin the cylinder…"

"No?"

"No, no time. The bartender immediately ducks behind the bar and starts guzzling ninety percent hooch."

"Wait, wait, was the desperado out of bullets?" asks Huxley.

Munro looks at him, smiles, says, "I know what you're thinking."

"Did he feel lucky?" asks Huxley.

Munro shakes her head and says, "Audiences," and carries on.

"Suddenly he hears pop, pop, pop outside, promptly stands, points his six-shooter towards the door and again empties his revolver. He quickly crouches behind the overturned table, reloads and starts firing, this time all over the saloon like a crazy man about to meet his maker. He reloads…"

"He must have had a lot of ammo," says Huxley.

"Yes he did, then he feels a strange warmth from his chest. Thinking he had been shot…"

"How?" asks Huxley.

"Magic bullet, I don't know," replies Munro,

"And you're the author?"

"I'll ignore that comment because you paid good money for these seats, but just once. So, he immediately places his hand on his heart, and feels relieved when he realizes it's his pocket watch."

"A hot watch?"

Munro looks at Huxley and says, "You sure you don't have some kind of an attention deficit thing?" Huxley shakes his head, and she asks, "So Mr. Audience who paid top dollar, at what time did the watch stop?"

Huxley looks at her and says, "I don't know, two-thirty?"

Munro looks at him intently and whispers, "At the witching hour."

Huxley raises his hand, and Munro says, "Yes, speak but be brief."

"Witching hour, what time is that exactly?"

"Use your imagination like the rest of the audience," replies Munro. Huxley looks around and asks, "What audience?"

Munro ignores his comment and continues. "So, as I was saying, with watch in one hand and gun in the other, it begins to dawn on him that this may not be his lucky day, so he reaches frantically for the Bible, only to discover he has left the good book at the Pleasure Hotel, and as he bravely stands up to fight, knees shaking, hands trembling, stray bullets everywhere, suddenly BONG!"

"BONG? What do you mean suddenly bong? What happened?" asks Huxley.

"The chef…"

"The chef bonged?" asks Huxley.

"Yes, the cool dude chef, you know the one wearing white double-breasted jacket, pants in a black and white houndstooth pattern, apron and of course a toque blanche, that's white hat for the audience … just throwing a little class into this watering hole, anyway she had enough of these shenanigans, so she comes out, fearlessly walks past the drunk bartender on the floor behind the bar, up to the desperado and hits him over the head with her famous cast iron skillet."

"The skillet on the noggin, bet it hurt a lot."

"It sure did, but then she felt badly…"

"Badly?"

"Yes, it's a genetic abnormality in women that must be extricated from the developmental code if we, as women, as uncelebrated champions and unsung heroes of the species, are to indeed achieve full actualization as masters of the universe. A long overdue discussion that I will personally address when I get *up There*."

"*Up There?*"

"Yes, *up There*. Anyway, back to the story. So, before returning to the kitchen, she asks if anyone wants a grilled cheese, she had some day-old bread to use up, but the desperados look at each other in bewilderment and go into a shudder-frenzy as if someone had just told them the football game was cancelled, so she gently places the skillet on the bar, takes off her apron and throws it on the grungy floor, downs a shot and says 'I quit!' She walks to the room in the back and shortly after returns, donning a fedora along with a patterned tallit over her shoulders, muttering something about had she listened to her mother and stayed at Union College she would have been ordained by now. As she's standing at the saloon doors for one last look, someone asks, "Rabbi, are you coming back?"

She looks around and after a short pause says, "Nah, enough of this wild west already, going back to Brooklyn and open up a bakery, safer, I think," and leaves … and the only sound you hear in this bullet-ridden watering hole is the eerie sound of the saloon doors, rickety rackety, rickety rackety. And that's all she wrote."

"Bravo, bravo," he says, applauding energetically. She stands, bows, smiles and returns sitting.

"By the way, the pop, pop, pop, what was that about?"

"Oh that, that was a Big Block Bruiser backfiring," replies Munro.

"A 429 Cobra Jet in the wild west?"

"It has been said, my dear, don't let the truth get in the way of ambition. Ask any politician."

"What year are we in?"

"Get with the program, my man."

"Are you experiencing a storytelling epiphany of sorts?"

"In a way, and you were terrific, Huxley, you connected so naturally with it and such insightful and humorous questions. We make a great team, Huxley, we do. This is freedom, Huxley, freedom to be, to create, to love and live on my terms as a woman, you as a man, and us as companions, on our terms, Huxley."

"I must say, Munro, I too feel liberated just listening to you, and your western tale had a unique flare. I enjoyed it very much, it was so gratifying to push the boundaries of reality."

"Thank you, Huxley, so do you think I should pursue writing as a career? If I do, I want to write humour, we can all use some sunny and funny days. So, Mr. Publisher?"

"I say your pitch was, well, engaging but a tad too long, but your story may have merit…"

"May?"

"All right, your story *has* merit, lots of merit, and if I may add, more reading and research in your chosen category could be very helpful, if this is what you wish to pursue as a career. Regardless of what you choose to pursue, I know you will be very successful."

"Correct answer," she replies.

Meanwhile, back at the house, Mr. C. walks down the hall from his studio, enters the bedroom and readies for a shower. Walks into the bathroom, stops and stares at his reflection in the mirror. He looks at his long-abandoned face, dishevelled long hair, and through his bloodshot eyes, sees familiar apparitions crowding the mirror. Demons that he had long sidestepped and allowed to reign came to remind him that they owned him.

For the first time, with eyes wide open, he cautiously comes out of his shadow, stands firm and stares at them with defiance.

Final round, Kid, you lose this one, and who knows when you'll get another chance at the championship.

He matches the viciousness in their eyes with an immovable stare. His body slowly transforms into fighting form, he clenches his fists and methodically advances towards the mirror. He throws a quick left jab, the mirror cracks, blood flows. *Take heed, Kid, demons are dirty fighters, they'll pin you on the ropes, hit low, knee you, kick, bite, and head butt, but you have taken on dirty fighters before, you know what to do … fight clean, but if you must, fight dirty and put the boots to them all.*

But there are so many of them.

Take them as they come and show no mercy and keep those eyes in the back of your head wide open, the last part of the jungle before the clearing is always the most dangerous. Kill and walk out or be killed and die bleeding on the glass-laden floor.

He resumes his prize-winning rhythm, freeing years of pent-up fury, blow after blow at the mirror and through it, at the frame and through the wall behind it … swollen and bleeding hands, broken knuckles, torn skin … *maintain your pain threshold high and keep advancing until all the pieces are knocked out of their once-safe asylum.* He moves closer, head-butts the mirror, immediately covering his face with blood.

Sweat, blood … blurred vision, makes no difference … pick it up, Kid, pick it up … we're all counting on you … you can do it … hit them, hit them hard! Hard! Hard! And make sure they can never, ever get up again.

The combinations force the demons to retreat into the last remaining piece of mirror desperately gripping the corner of the splintered frame. He now has them all together in one corner, no way out. He concentrates, advances and delivers a powerful right, then a left, then another right and can't stop punching, can't.

It's over, it's over…

He steps back as the last piece of the mirror falls and shatters onto the floor, and slowly lowers his arms.

He wants to dry his eyes, but can't, both hands are covered in blood and shards. He looks up, there is no mirror, no reflection, looks down and sees his fragmented image on the hard, cold ceramic tiles.

He crouches, and painfully reconstructs enough of the mirror on the floor to reproduce a familiar image of the person he once was, the man Mo loved. The classic battle of giants, a hard-fought fight to the finish.

Winning the championship for VC was never about the belt, it was always about life with Mo.

He takes one of the towels, lays it down and stands on it. Picks up a larger piece of mirror, secures it in the broken frame, carefully removes the shards from his forehead and knuckles and tosses them in the waste basket. He showers until the water runs clear, dries, looks and finds an old jar of Vaseline mixed with coagulant from his boxing days, and applies the mixture to his face. The bleeding stops, he bandages his hands and painfully dresses.

Meanwhile waiting impatiently at the café, Huxley asks, "Is he going to show, Munro?"

"This is Italy, Huxley, there is a rhythm to the life here, they actually live life. Life here is not governed by some mechanical device on a wall or by one with numbers on a wrist. They call it natural life; they live and love to the fullest."

Suddenly a car screeches to a halt near Il Piccolo Caffe. They look and see Mr. C. getting out of his Alfa. He waves furiously and runs towards them.

"Well, well, speaking of the…." says Huxley.

"What happened to his hands and his forehead?" asks Munro.

"Aggressive shaving, but does look all cleaned up, long hair slicked back, clean clothes, shades, cool in a way."

"Munro, Huxley, I am sorry, I lost all track of time."

"Ah yes, the concept of time in Italy, and in your computer, ouch … great to see you, Mr. C.," says Huxley.

"What happened to your hands and face?" asks Munro.

"I had to come to terms with some things back at the house, but here I am," he says and sits down.

"So, who won?"

"I did," replies Mr. C. confidently.

"Definitively?"

"Definitively, Huxley," he replies and asks if they had ordered.

"Waiting for you," replies Huxley.

The waiter approaches and they agree with his suggestion of a mixed platter of salumi, cheese, prosciutto, breads, pastries and espressos.

"Tell me you two, how does it feel to be, to be, yourselves," he asks.

"Elated, and we are so ready to live life, Mr. C.," replies Munro.

"I couldn't agree more with Munro, we are most definitely ready," says Huxley.

"How about the others?"

"As elated, and most ready."

"What does the future look like for you, Mr. C?"

"Not quite sure at the moment, Huxley, first things first, as in fulfilling my commitment to you two and to the others, and then…"

"To your long overdue self? To your love of writing? To restoring Mustangs? To staying fit?"

He nods and says, "Not easy."

"No doubt. You have walked in darkness far too long. We also have, Mr. C., but we never lost our will to come out of it, a will bestowed on us by you," replies Huxley.

"The student teaching the teacher."

"Not quite, Mr. C.," says Munro, "You are and will always remain our teacher, but we're all students of the heart and must always keep that in perspective, that's the only way we will continue learning from each other. Unquestionably, Mo was and remains your most cherished partner and teacher of the heart, but she is also a student and as such has shared her love with you, and you with her, and the journey continues."

"I desperately wish to be reunited with her. How do I do that?"

"In due time, Mr. C. Love 101. True love is forever. You and Mo are immortalized in each other's hearts; Mo's passing is a change only in form, the love construct remains; your love journey did not end, it paused to rest and someday you will again hold her in your arms. You of all people should understand that paradigm."

"Understanding it doesn't make it less painful," he replies.

"What did your mother say to you, something about *The journey of a thousand miles.*"

"How did you know?"

"Mr. C. Really? Love 201. Once love is intertwined, you can never lose each other, and the strength you received from Mo and she from you will always be in each other's heart regardless of physical distance. Emotional or spiritual strength once firmly attached to someone other than yourself, say another person, a God, it can never be lost. You, my friend, can easily draw on the strength you and Mo have created together, that's the only way you're going to find your way home."

"What have I been doing all these years?"

"A more pertinent question, Mr. C, is what will you now do going forward?" asks Munro.

"Will you excuse me for a minute, something I must do, be right back," says Mr. C. as he stands and walks into the restaurant. Approaches the owner and asks if he has a computer he can use.

"Something I said?

"He can take it in the ring, not easy out here," says Huxley, placing his hand on Munro's and gently squeezing it. She reciprocates.

"Maybe I should rethink my career as a writer, it's too much of an emotional rollercoaster."

"No, Munro, you're good at it, and if you wish to pursue writing I will support you."

"You know what that means, don't you? Long uninterrupted hours in my study…"

"Uninterrupted?"

"Of course, in order to concentrate on my brilliant work, interruptions are simply a no-no. Look at it this way, would you interrupt a brain surgeon in the middle of a very delicate surgical procedure to ask him if he put enough money in the parking meter?"

Huxley laughs and says, "I believe you have it in you, Munro."

"You do?"

"Yes, I do, so don't let anyone rain on your parade," he replies and kisses her on her cheek.

"And what will you do?"

"Not sure, maybe get a job at that bakery in Brooklyn," he replies and amidst the laughter he adds, "Big Block Bruiser, humour is you, Munro."

"Time for laughter, time to vivre la vie, la vita al massimo. Let's live life to the fullest, Huxley."

"All right then, author Munro, since you're on a roll, do you have another to share? And may I add a line or two, as your assistant slash publisher?"

"Better yet, if you're going to be my assistant, since they do most of the work, let's see what you got. Go, go before the time on the meter runs out."

"How much time do I have?"

"Not much, but as your editor, I'll keep you on course."

"Editor, eh, all right then, picture this, Huxley and Munro on a country trip in a convertible, Munro boldly tosses her scarf to the wind, long hair free and blowing, rich, luscious green field after green field, then we come upon this field of nothing but flowers, so, so inviting. We stop, take our picnic basket and walk far into the field, and once there, Munro's irresistible beauty is so captivating and her charm so intoxicating … I immediately throw the blanket down and I excitedly…"

Munro looks at Huxley, shakes her head and says, "Interesting, very interesting, Huxley, but now as the maestro of this little ensemble I must pick up the story."

"Great, let's hear it, maestro," replies Huxley.

"We throw down the blanket, rush into each other's arms, we kiss passionately, and then… then…"

"And then?" Huxley impatiently asks.

"Then there is thunder and lightning…"

"Is it God blessing our union?"

"No Huxley, it's a thunderstorm," she replies, and both break out laughing.

"You are exceptional, Munro." Places his arm over her shoulder and pulls her closer.

Mr. C. returns, sits down and Huxley asks, "Everything okay?"

"Yes, fine, thank you." He holds both their hands and says, "I'm sorry. I must apologize to you and the others for being so inexcusably and unjustifiably neglectful of my duties and for being so insensitive to your needs."

"You've allowed destructive forces to take up a lot of territory in your heart, Mr. C., and kept us and others who wanted to help you at arm's length," says Munro.

"I am truly sorry, for there is no excuse for the way I have behaved these past few years. Please forgive me."

"Forgiveness is a complex undertaking for all of us, Mr. C., not an easy road, and it may not always lead to reconciliation, but forgiveness is a gift we must extend to ourselves, and with that precious gift in hand, the unpardonable can become pardonable, and we can then begin the long road to healing."

The discussion on forgiveness ended when the waiter returned with another order of coffee and sweets. Mr. C. picks up his cup and before drinking says, "I am now at everyone's disposal, let us begin here."

Huxley and Munro look at each other, and Munro says, "We would like that very much, Mr. C."

"No doubt you have ideas on what the next part of our journey should look like, share them with us," replies Munro.

"Very well, there is nothing as romantic as the old world, with its rich history and charm; where every building, every stone is infused with century-old love auras; where you close your eyes, take a deep breath and your whole body draws in the wonders of ecstasies once fulfilled … to be under the eternal lights of Rome, Verona of Romeo and Juliet fame, or Florence, the cradle of the Renaissance, or Paris the city of love."

"We agree, nothing more romantic than breathing deeply the air of ancient love as it makes its way through the new age. A trip most definitely doable…" says Munro.

"But…" quickly adds Mr. C.

"Well, Huxley and I, browsing your files, read of many a city of splendour, mostly in the old romantic world as you described, but we seem to favour one outside of it, namely, New York."

"New York? Great city," he replies, "It may not be a Florence, Rome or Paris, nor does it have the history, but it has its own distinguished sense of energy, vitality and joie de vivre."

Sits back, looks at Munro's and Huxley's enthusiasm, and says, "Please excuse me, be right back."

"Again?" says Huxley.

"Five minutes," he replies.

"Italian time?"

Five minutes … maybe six later, he returns smiling, puts on his sunglasses and says, "Ready?"

Suddenly Huxley and Munro find themselves in the back seat of a yellow cab in the heart of their chosen city.

"A cab? Munro, we're in a cab, how?"

"Huxley, Huxley, Huxley, writers can make any wish come true, but not yours, not just yet," she replies.

"You are my only wish, Munro, and our dream is coming true," he replies.

"Indeed," says the taxi driver as he turns and smiles.

"Mr. C.!" Munro and Huxley scream out excitedly in unison.

"Hello Munro, Huxley, we made it! Welcome to New York City!"

"New York City, yes! Lights, camera, action," says Huxley.

"Here we are, Saturday evening in downtown frenetic New York. The Big Apple, the city that never sleeps," says Mr. C.

"We love it, Mr. C.!" states Munro.

After a while observing, contemplating, Huxley asks, "So Mr. C., what's the score here, are we a young, newlywed couple from the Midwest, coming to the Big Apple for their honeymoon with lots and lots of money to spend?"

"You're both physicists, teach at Harvard and are in town for the conference on nanotechnology."

"Pardon? Nanotechnology? Tell us you're joking, Mr. C.?" replies Huxley.

"Have something against Nano, Huxley?" asks Munro, "Careful how you answer that question, some of my best friends are Nanos," she adds.

"Mine too," adds Mr. C.

"No doubt, but a professor of this Nano thing was not exactly what I had in mind. However, I will endeavour to keep up, so truth be known my esteemed colleagues, some of my best friends are also Nanos," replies Huxley.

"And what is it that you and your Nano friends do on a Saturday night?" asks Munro.

"We sit around with special trifocals, watch Nano TV and tell Nano jokes," replies Huxley, all trying to contain their laughter.

"Could you enlighten us with a Nano joke?" asks Munro.

"Would love to, but not possible."

"Why not?"

"Because unless you and Mr. C. have special Nano hearing aids, you won't be able to hear the ultra-silent Nano joke."

After the laughter subsides, Mr. C. says, "Huxley, you are certainly a character…"

"No, no, that was then, now I am a full-fledged person," he replies.

"Indeed, my apology, of course you are, as you, Munro, as all the others."

"Thank you, Mr. C.," says Huxley.

"Let me ask you this, since you two are budding writers, should I continue with writing? In your opinion, how would I do writing comedy?"

Munro and Huxley look at each other and Huxley says, "Seriously?"

"Thinking about it."

"No doubt the world is in need of humour, but I don't know if your body can handle any more gut-splitting laughter, Mr. C." replies Huxley, and all three laugh loudly.

"May I strongly suggest," says Munro, "since I am the only tenured professor here, instead of writing comedy, which, considering your endorphins-starved body, may prove to be too overwhelming for you, Mr. C., how about a piece on the hazards of smoking."

"The hazards of smoking, thank you, Munro, will give it its due consideration," replies Mr. C. After the laughter subsides, a short silence.

"Speaking of writing, I would like to be a writer, Mr. C.," says Huxley.

"Really?"

"Yes … sitting in front of a computer on a big walnut desk in my study in an old ivy-covered mansion overlooking splendidly manicured grounds, tweed Ferusonet with elbow patches, smoking dried leaves from that funny looking Italian lettuce in those small plastic bags, inhaling deeply, then typing away fast and furious with two fingers, the butler, that's you, Mr. C., would serve afternoon tea and scones, and then you, Munro, rush into my study with that crazed desire in your eyes, we tear each other's clothes off, make passionate love on our Persian rug, a little itchy, but that's okay, then I light one up, exhale, make those little circles of smoke and watch as they evaporate toward the ceiling. How does that sound you two?"

"Lordie, Lordie, another aspiring author with no originality," says Munro, and all three laugh.

Mr. C. stops the cab, looks at Munro and Huxley and says, "You two are now the story, and now that your romance is being scripted in your chosen city, I would like you two to know that I feel privileged to have been a part."

"Thank you, Mr. C., we could not have done any of this without you, but this is not your goodbye speech, is it?"

CHAPTER SIX

NEW YORK CITY:

TOP OF THE ROCK AND AN EASY REACH TO THE GALAXIES

The taxi meanders through the downtown, Huxley and Munro take in the sights and begin feeling the rhythm of the night life.

"The city that never sleeps," says Munro.

"We have done our research, via your files of course, and discovered that indeed many romantic places actually exist in this city. Lower East Side, West Side, sunset on the Hudson, Manhattan and considering that this is our script of sorts, I say we go first class, somewhere exclusive for dinner, say a Michelin-starred restaurant, a five-star hotel, breakfast in Times Square. What do you think, Mr. C?"

"Sounds marvellous, Huxley, and who will be picking up the tab?"

"It's our expectation that this is an all-expenses paid actualization, Mr. C."

"Of course, how could I have missed that small detail," he replies and all three laugh.

"Fine dinner, walk hand in hand down the avenue of lights, nightcap under the stars, back to the hotel, and … separate rooms," says Munro.

"Separate rooms!" exclaims Huxley.

Munro smiles and says, "This is also my story, Huxley. So, my dear, we need time to get to better know each other, dinners, movies, theatre, walking hand in hand, meet parents, you know, all things prudent, and no weekends away, not yet."

"But Munro, that was in Mr. C.'s time, you know, last century, we are now into the contemporary, the hip, the cool, get my drift?"

"Drift, yes, but not too far off course."

Mr. C. looks at them through the rear-view mirror and asks, "What would delight your palate on this historical occasion? Modern or old-world charm?"

Munro and Huxley answer together, Munro prefers old world and Huxley, modern. After a brief laugh, they again in unison say, "It doesn't matter."

CHAPTER SEVEN

The taxi proceeds downtown and stops in front of a luxury Central Park hotel.

"Where are we, Mr. C.?" asks Munro.

"Your luxury suite, and in keeping with your wishes, I have made reservations at a three-star Michelin restaurant in an historic landmark building. Among other exceptional dishes it also serves contemporary American cuisine. You can do romantic Italian or French or any other on your own in their actual settings, tonight you do romantic American."

"So, what is the appropriate attire for this restaurant, Mr. C.?" asks Munro.

"What do you think, Mr. C. Suit? Jeans, tee shirt and baseball cap?" asks Huxley.

"They won't let you in, even if it's a Yankees' cap. Munro, evening elegance, not too formal, Huxley black suit or sport jacket, contrasting slacks, white shirt and tie, absolutely no hat or dazzle, class Huxley, always class, never dazzle," replies Mr. C.

"I'm so excited, not to worry, Munro, I'll look cool," says Huxley.

Munro looks at Huxley and says, "All right then, let's see, late September, New York, on the cool side, fine restaurant, ride through Central Park afterwards, nightcap at a rooftop bar with one of those exceptional views of the city, and then back to the hotel. So, nothing flashy, or dull. Transitional colors but muted darks, you know, something that reflects the complexity of the 21st century woman ... strength, sophistication, control yet devil may care when it needs to be ... something to celebrate my personal style, and yet that of everywoman, I know just the outfit," says Munro.

A surprised, wide-eyed Huxley looks at her and says, "Wow, Munro, *I Feel Good*."

"Classic R&B, none other than Mr. Brown, Huxley, I do feel good," says Munro, singing, snapping her fingers and winking at him, adding, "Pick it up, Mr. C.," as he drums the beat on the dashboard with his hands. The three loudly perform the entire song with a surprisingly harmonized ending … boooom!

"Wow, Munro, devil with the blue dress on, and you, Mr. C., percussionist extraordinaire," says Huxley.

"That was fun," says Munro.

"Thank you both, that was the most fun in a very long time," adds Mr. C.

"Was music a big part of your life, Mr. C.?" asks Munro.

"Yes, it was, Munro, and Mo and I loved dancing, often cranked up the volume in the basement and danced away."

"I bet, and what kind of dance was it exactly?" adds Huxley and they all laugh. He then faces Munro and says, "This love sensation is so, so out of this world, I like it, like it a lot, love it, and I so love you, Munro, so very much."

"Nothing like it, and I you, Huxley," she replies and they gently kiss.

"Now, please proceed to the front desk, and they'll escort you to your respective rooms. Once you're ready, come back down and I'll take you to your restaurant."

Once in their respective rooms, several clothing options hang in their closets, both take them out, placing them on their beds. They look, pause, look again and choose.

Munro dresses, looks at herself in the full-length mirror and says, "You have outdone yourself, Munro, beautiful dress, gorgeous shoes, infinity necklace, petite purse to match, I love it." She then calls Huxley through the door of the adjoining rooms and asks if he's ready. Huxley, still in his underwear and socks, moves closer to the door and says, "No, not yet, Munro, I can't decide."

"Think evening, Huxley."

"You mean plaid suit, plaid socks, plaid cap?"

"Maybe there is some Scottish ancestry in you," she replies, "Not sure this is the occasion to show it, what else do you have there?"

"I see another suit I can wear, be just a minute."

He looks at himself in the mirror, clean shaven, appropriately cologned, dressed in a dark suit instead of sport jacket and slacks, blue striped shirt and silk tie, black shoes, and is very pleased.

"Cool clothes for the man, that's more like it, great threads, tapered fit, looking good, I like it, very, very nice."

"Are you ready?" asks Munro.

"Be right out."

"And not to worry love, when you're working, I'll place the appropriate clothes in a straight line on the long sofa in the bedroom the night before."

"Thanks, Munro, what would I do without you?"

They exit their respective rooms at the same time, stand in the hallway admiring each other. Munro looks at Huxley lovingly, places her finger on his lips and says, "Speak only love."

He takes her hand, kisses it and says, "Always."

They take the elevator down, exit and walk towards the front of the hotel.

"Good evening," says the doorman while opening the door.

"Good evening," replies Huxley and tips him.

"And how did you know to tip him?" asks Munro.

"Mr. C. and I had a chat as to what to do and not to do when out about town. And with respect to you, you don't want to know what he will do to me if I ever treat you wrongly."

Standing on the front steps, holding hands, looking at the hustle and bustle of the city, Huxley says, "New York really does have its own unique rhythm."

"Hypnotic nightlife," says Munro.

"Where is that curmudgeon?" asks Huxley just as Mr. C.'s black limousine pulls up in front.

"Limo no less, I'm impressed," says Huxley.

The doorman opens the car door for them and they settle in the back seat.

"Like the limo, Mr. C., borrowed it from another one of your uncles, did you?"

"Thank you, Huxley, just don't go rummaging back there."

After they stop laughing Huxley says, "Oh Mr. C., one more item if I may, the tipping money is gone, so where do I find the fat wallet?"

"Look in your jacket pocket, Huxley, and in your purse, Munro."

They do and Huxley says, "Look, Munro, cash, Gold Card... What, no Black?"

"Me too, thank you, Mr. C., I have a Black Card," says Munro.

"Gee, thanks Mr. C., so very trusting," says Huxley.

"You're both welcome, nonetheless allow me to take care of the expenses this evening," he replies.

"If you insist," says Huxley, adding, "Unless it's all tax deductible. See Munro, I'm already getting the hang of it."

"I have also provided you with mobile telephones should you need to contact each other or me."

"Do they have to be so bulky?"

"It helps if you take it out of the box, Huxley."

He takes it out of the box, tries inserting it in the inside of his jacket pocket but complains that it's too bulky.

"Give it here," says Munro, and puts it in her purse.

"Thank you, what else do you carry in there?"

"A well-used brick."

Soon they reach their destination. Mr. C. exits the limo and opens the rear door. Munro and Huxley exit, he tips Mr. C. and says, "Spend it wisely," to which Mr. C. says, "Thank you, Mr. Cheapskate."

Munro and Huxley walk hand in hand towards the entrance of the restaurant, turn to wave but he's no longer in sight.

CHAPTER EIGHT

"Good evening" says the maître d'hôtel. "Two?"

"Yes," replies Huxley, "Munro and Huxley."

The maître d' looks at the reservation list, "Ah yes, follow me please." He takes them to a corner table for two in a very private part of the restaurant, pulls the chair back for Munro, then for Huxley and they sit down. He then places the white serviette on each of their laps, waves a waiter over, says, "Enjoy your evening," and leaves. The waiter arrives with a bottle of champagne, shows them the bottle and asks, "Special occasion?" to which Huxley replies, "Yes."

The waiter wraps the bottle of champagne with a white serviette, uncorks it, pours the appropriate amount into each glass, places the bottle in the silver ice bucket, rests the serviette on it and leaves.

"Do I have to do that every time you and I have champagne?"

"Of course," replies Munro, smiling.

They raise their glass and Huxley asks, "To what shall we cheer, Munro?"

"Not so much to what but to whom," she replies. "To us."

"To us," repeats Huxley.

The waiter refills their glasses, carefully places the menus on the table and leaves.

Looking at the menu, Huxley says, "Wonder what Mr. C. is up to tonight."

The waiter returns, stands next to the table and recites the evening's fare. "Our superb appetizers include roasted sweetbreads, chilled lobster as well as seared foie gras. For dinner may I recommend the seasonal seven-course tasting menu, and to accompany that experience, a preferred wine balances the emotions for the evening."

"Munro?"

"A glass of Chardonnay with dinner, please."

"A glass of full-bodied Classico for me, thank you."

"Excellent choices, thank you," replies the waiter, and leaves.

"Munro, sei una donna eccezionale."

"Meaning?"

"You are an exceptional woman. I read it in several cards Mr. C. gave Mo. He used to give her lots of cards, flowers, estate jewellery, any time of the year, he really loves her."

"Ordinary people, exceptional love, renders them exceptional, and you, my dear, are also an exceptional person," says Munro.

"As you, my love."

The long, leisurely dinner was exquisite in taste, ambiance and most notably each other's company. The waiter returns and asks if they wish to move to the brandy and cigar room.

"Another time perhaps," responds Huxley and Munro agrees.

"Very well, was everything to your satisfaction?"

"Yes, very much, thank you," replies Huxley.

"I will summon your cab then, good evening, madam, sir."

"Good evening and thank you," replies Huxley.

Once outside, they immediately see Mr. C.'s waiting limo and board.

"I must commend you on your choice of restaurants, Mr. C., thank you," says Huxley.

"A most enjoyable dinner experience, Mr. C., splendid, thank you," adds Munro.

"Wonderful, you two are most welcome. What did you have?" he asks.

"I had the foot-long Coney Island hot dog, with everything on it, and Munro had some raw fish rolled in a leaf of some kind, from the cannabis plant I think, organic maybe," states Huxley.

The three break out in laughter and continue the conversation as the limo makes its way towards Central Park and stops near a waiting horse-drawn carriage.

"Here we are, it's all prearranged and the coachman is at your disposal. You can ride along scenic pathways, see many historical landmarks or places made famous by Hollywood films. Or you can skip all that and let the ride, the lights and the sky determine your next destination," says Mr. C.

"Actually, Mr. C.," Munro says, "sounds intriguing, but we would rather take such a ride another time."

"All right then, let's go to plan B," he replies.

"Plan B?" ask both Munro and Huxley in unison.

"A nighttime helicopter ride or a Statue of Liberty cruise. Just picture it, you'll ride in a luxury helicopter and get this spectacular view of dazzling Manhattan, soar over the Empire State Building, Central Park, over the Brooklyn Bridge, Ellis Island, what do you think?"

Munro and Huxley look at each other and Munro says, "Thank you, Mr. C., but I think you're trying too hard, we're fine without all that glitter."

"Well, may not be a bad idea, Munro," adds Huxley.

"It is getting late," says Munro.

"All right then, if not the sky, how about close to it," Huxley says.

"What do you mean?" asks Munro.

"How about a nightcap at a romantic spot at the top of the city, little piano, slow dance, cheek to cheek as it were. What do you think, Munro?" asks Huxley.

"I think it would be wonderful, Huxley, would you like to join us for a nightcap, Mr. C?"

"I know just the place, and I do appreciate the offer, but this is your time to dance under the stars," he replies.

Munro nudges Huxley and he says, "Are you sure you don't want to join us, Mr. C?"

"I'm sure, thank you, Huxley. The place that comes to mind is near the Lincoln Center where apparently the martinis are out of this world, the view breathtaking, the music soothing and the night never ends, how does that sound?"

"Sounds delightful, Mr. C.," Munro answers, "A lovely way to begin lowering the curtain on a wonderful evening."

"It has been a most enjoyable evening," says Huxley. "And by the way, what did you do? Where did you go while we dined?"

"I went to the library."

"The library? Right, we weren't born yesterday, Mr. C., maybe we were … well, not quite yesterday, anyway. Is that the name of some watering hole where retired cops hang out?" says Huxley.

"No, it's not a bar, it's the library on campus and one of the best sources of Pirandello's work, always open."

"Really? A night in New York at the library? With Pirandello? Fascinating, Mr. C.," says Munro.

"You sure don't get out much, do you, Mr. C.? And when you do, you sure know how to have a good time," adds Huxley.

The limo comes to a stop in front of a tall building, Mr. C. turns to them and says, "They're expecting you."

"Thank you, Mr. C.," says Munro, "Midnight?"

"As you wish," he replies.

"Mr. C., when Munro and I are dancing, how can I dance like a cool dude?"

"Just follow Munro's lead."

"But I thought men lead," says Huxley.

"Of course they do," replies Munro, smiling.

"This is our first dance, Munro, I just want it to be special," Huxley answers.

"It will be, my love, slow dance, up close where we can listen to each other's heart, what difference does it make as to who leads, as long as I do."

"I agree."

"By the way, Huxley, don't dance too close to the edge," says Mr. C.

"Cute, Mr. C., very cute," says Huxley.

Munro grabs him by the arm and pulls him towards the glass doors and into the building. They reach the Terrace, people talking quietly, music playing. They're escorted to a corner table close enough to feel warm waves from the nearby gas fireplace. The jazz trio tosses endless notes at the stars like confetti at a wedding, and the moon watches and smiles mischievously.

Munro orders a glass of Pino Grigio and Huxley a single malt, neat slightly chilled with just a drop of water to release its mysteries. They move their chairs close to each other's, Munro leans on his shoulder and Huxley places his arm around her.

"Purity in music," he says.

"What is?" she asks.

"Piano, bass and drums … unadulterated, uncomplicated, every note clear, precise, I can see why such an ensemble would be Mr. C.'s favourite."

"And Mo's."

"And Mo's," she says.

"Sax would be nice," says Munro.

"I'll say," replies Huxley. "No argument from me there," he adds.

Munro looks at him and says, "Saxophone, Huxley, not sex."

"Well, you know, I say tomaato and you say potaato," says Huxley.

"Right," says Munro, smiling.

"Why are you staring at the pianist?"

"She has such a melodic voice, soft, yet piercing, and her fingers just float and dance over those keys. There is something very attractive about her, familiar. And the drummer, doesn't he remind you of Mr. C?"

"Yes, to the voice, no to the lookalike. Something you came across in Mr. C.'s files?" he asks.

"Perhaps, and the name of the drums, Gretsch, familiar, one of those life's mysteries."

The waiter brings them their drinks. They raise their glasses and Munro proposes a toast to Mr. C.

"Cheers to Mr. C.," Huxley echoes.

After several pensive moments, Huxley says, "They're playing the song I requested, may I have the pleasure of this dance, Ms. Munro?"

Munro slowly stands and Huxley extends his hand for hers and pulls her closer.

"*Fly Me to the Moon*, how sweet, Huxley."

The song ends, they remain embraced while standing in the corner of the dance floor near their table. The band resumes playing, a very slow, loving number, and they remain as one, moving ever so slowly. At song's end, they return to their table, sit close and Huxley says, "I must say, I enjoy it when we immerse ourselves in a song."

"As in singing and humming with it?"

"Yes, something from Mr. C.'s notes that actually makes sense. He and Mo used to do that all the time."

Huxley looks at his watch and the time is approaching midnight.

"What time is it, Huxley?" Munro quietly asks.

"Close to midnight, my love. Mr. C. seems to feel that there is something mystical, magical, and transcendental about that hour, as I read anyway."

"What else did he say about midnight?" asks Munro.

"I'm happy you asked, and in anticipation, I made some notes. Here we go," Huxley says as he unfolds the sheet of paper taken from his jacket pocket and reads. "So, he said, midnight is that particular, standalone moment in time that does not belong to either today or tomorrow yet belongs to both. It's a time of transition, a time when and where anything and everything is possible. And, and, it's at that precise moment that you will be transformed into the princess that you truly are … I added this last part."

"I hope that hour will further highlight the honourable and caring prince that you are, Huxley."

They both kiss, and as they prepare to leave, another favourite song is being played.

"Wait," Munro says looking towards the band, "Isn't that…?"

"Yes, it is, shall we?" replies Huxley.

They return to the dance floor, embrace and begin dancing their own slow-moving version of the song. The song ends and they walk towards the exit, but not before taking in another view of the stars, wishing for that midnight hour so long awaited to do its magic that will always be remembered. They squeeze each other's hands and leave the Terrace.

Walking to the elevator, Huxley asks, "Are we real, Munro?"

"Yes, we are, Huxley."

"Really?"

"Really. Want me to pinch you?"

"No need, I believe you. Is our love real?"

"Yes, it is."

Huxley takes Munro's hand and gently leads her onto the elevator where they are the only passengers.

"Couples make out in these things, you know," says Huxley smiling.

"So I hear, not my idea of a romantic interlude, push G, please."

Huxley smiles and holds her closer. They reach the main floor and walk towards the exit door. Outside the building, Mr. C. is waiting in the limo. Huxley turns to her and says, "I love you, Munro," and kisses her.

"And I you, Huxley."

The limo continues along the brightly lit Fifth Avenue. Inside, the silence, outside, the old, the new, the fallen in dark alleyways and the dreamers under the dim streetlights. They reach the hotel and Mr. C. stops in front.

Before exiting the cab, Mr. C says, "As I recall, your rooms are joined by a locked door. When and at what point the door is unlocked is entirely up to the two of you."

"How about a nightcap with us in the hotel lounge, Mr. C.?" asks Huxley.

"How about it, Mr. C.," adds Munro.

"Thanks for the offer, perhaps another time."

"Going back to the library, are you, Mr. C.?" asks Huxley.

"In a way, goodnight."

Munro and Huxley reach their floor and holding each other's hand, stand outside Munro's room. They kiss and Huxley says, "I had such a memorable time, Munro, truly, and you didn't even ask me to dance close to the edge."

They both smile and Munro says, "I too had a lovely time, I felt wholesome and loved, thank you."

She kisses him gently, he unlocks her door, and says, "I'll see you … in the morning. If you need anything, just knock."

Munro enters her room and slowly closes the door behind her.

Huxley enters his own room next to hers and closes the door behind him. Sometime later, both still lying awake and fully dressed on their respective beds, Huxley stands, walks out onto the balcony and to his delight finds Munro out on hers.

She looks at the sky and says, "Look at the endless beauty of this universe, Huxley, look at it."

They soon re-enter their rooms, and while changing, he thinks of Munro and knows he can never be without her. He thinks of Mr. C. as the battle-scarred warrior, desperately trying to make sense of a life cut short, understands and wonders if he's ever going to find peace without Mo next to him.

He wonders what Mr. C. would have done differently in his life … what he would have been like had his beloved Mo lived … what kind of father he would have been to their dear Aila … what he would have said to the young man taking his daughter out on her first date.

He wouldn't have told that young man that he had been a boxer and a martial artist; nor that her Scottish grandfather was a tough cop; nor that her Italian grandfather's hands were the size of shovels; nor that his "Uncle" on the other side of the legal line could make him disappear… He would have simply said, pleased to meet you and take good care of our daughter. Then he and Mo would sit by the door until Aila came home.

He walks to the window, looks at the immense beauty of the night sky and hopes that he and Munro will share a lifetime of skies. His eyes follow this one particularly bright star in a sky of bright stars and wonders whose heart this unextinguishable light came to brighten.

He hears a sound, hoping it was the unlocking of the middle door, but not expecting it, doesn't check. He lies on the bed in his pajamas, unable to fall asleep. Sometime later he looks at the clock and knows the morning sun is not far off. He gets up, puts on his robe and quietly makes his way to the door separating the two rooms. He slowly turns the handle and to his surprise, finds it unlocked. When? He asks himself. He silently enters Munro's room and gently closes the door behind him.

The sun eventually touches Munro's face and she wakens. She rolls to her side, slowly moves to the edge, and as she looks down, to her surprise sees Huxley sitting next to the bed staring back at her.

"I came in with the sun," he says.

"Plaid pyjamas with matching robe no less," she quietly says.

They look at each other, "So," he says.

"So," she answers.

She then taps on the bed and says, "Come up here."

Sometime later that morning, lying in each other's arms, Huxley hears the mobile telephone ringing and says, "Munro, there is ringing in your purse."

"Ringing?"

She answers and Munro holds the telephone to their ears.

"Hello, Munro, it's Mr. C. I telephoned Huxley, but it's turned off. Everything okay?"

"Yes, all is fine, Mr. C. Huxley is here with me, I'll put you on speaker.

"Hello, Mr. C., to what do we owe the pleasure?" says Huxley.

"I am on route to La Casa Paterna. I just want you to know, I am so very proud of the two of you, and wish you both tremendous success with all you choose to do."

"Mr. C., we are happy for you, and thank you for all that you've done for us."

"I echo Munro's words and feelings, Mr. C., and I'm sure we'll meet again."

"We will. I must now return to help the others. Take care of each other and bye for now, bye."

The call ends, she and Huxley sit on the bed and he says, "We best give Syl a call."

Speaking with Syl, Huxley says, "We're both fine, thanks … you? Good, good, yes, New York is splendid for sure. Listen Syl, Mr. C. is on his way, stay alert … yes, soon."

Munro stands and says, "I think a walk would do us good, Huxley."

"I know just the place. Central Park, the Conservatory Garden, it has everything, it's calm, colourful, ideal for a leisurely stroll, and on the brochure, it says it's an ideal place for that intimate wedding."

"Where did you get the brochure?" she asks.

"Mr. C. left in my pocket, did you not get one?"

"I haven't looked, but will right now," she replies, walks to her purse on the dresser, opens it and says, "No brochure, but my goodness, ID cards, passports, driver's licence, even a bank account, a very healthy bank account, Mr. C. thought of everything."

He rushes to his room, empties his jacket pockets, soon returns and says, "Same things in my pockets, Munro, thank you, Mr. C."

"We are now officially accredited citizens of this planet, Huxley, we should most definitely celebrate, yet there is a note of sadness in the air."

"I feel it too, Munro. Separation anxiety?"

"Much more than that, I feel he's cleaning house, Huxley, he's getting ready to close up shop, and that unsettles me."

"Sometimes creators need help from those they created, Munro."

CHAPTER NINE

VC walks upstairs, opens the door to his study, turns on the light and to his amazement sees Maggie and her dog Ralph in the room, along with Syl and Alex and their team, as well as Rogue, Alfred One and Two from the Who Done It Series, and lastly Fast Hombre from the series Gun for Hire. And, not to be ignored, Tight Lip, from the story on Garage Conspiracies of the Twentieth Century, all standing next to his desktop.

"Hello Mr. C.!" they shout in unison while applauding.

He intuitively walks towards them, arms wide open, smiles, embraces each one, steps back and enthusiastically says, "Hello everyone!" After the cheers and applause and all eyes on him, he wipes his tears and says, "Thank you, thank you."

Following another round of applause, he says, "I am in awe and humbled, and so, so very pleased to see you all."

"We're all happy to see you too, Mr. C," says Alex.

"So, here we are," says Mr. C.

"So here we are," says Rogue, then asks, "What century are we in?"

"Ease up, Rogue," says Syl.

"That's okay, Syl, he's right," says Mr. C.

"Are you here to help us?"

"Yes, I am, Rogue. You have all unselfishly helped me more than you know, in ways I can't explain, and helping you now is more than returning the favour, it's being part of a successful story, your story, a story never thought possible, and yet here you are. I am at your service," he replies.

A brief reflective silence follows, then a thunderous bout of cheers, applause, and foot stomping, and once the silence returns Syl says, "All right, let's bring Mr. C. up to date shall we, then he can share what's next on his agenda. Okay with you, Mr. C.?" and he nods.

"Alex and I with the rest of our team are planning a rescue mission. How about you, Alfred One?"

"I, Alfred One, accompanied by my shadow, Alfred Two of course, will proceed with planning the perfect murder of that despicable swindler, adulterer and all-around creep. Doing in that corrupt politician and any other that fits that bill will be most enjoyable, but there are so many of them. Is this the new normal?"

"I'm afraid so, they're all corrupt," says Fast Hombre, followed by an immediate and stern reply from Alexandria.

"Excuse me," she says, looking directly at Fast Hombre, "you talkin' about me? Are you? Are you talkin' to me?"

"No, ma'am," he replies, and, when he is unable to withhold his laughter, all join in. The heightened cheers and applause subside, and he continues, "We know you're one of the good ones, and we thank you for your service. Not easy for the good ones anywhere these days, and that makes people like you more valuable than ever, so if someday you want to take a run at the presidency, you can count on our vote. Let's hear it for Alexandria."

The group responds with unrestained enthusiasm, cheers and applauds loudly, and Alexandria raises her arms and says, "Anything is possible, right?" followed by another loud cheer. Once settled, sagas continue to unfold. Alfred One, staring suspiciously at Tight Lip, asks, "Are you Plan B, Tight Lip?"

"What's plan B?"

"Plan B à la Hollywood is, we pop him, you pop us to tie up loose ends, then you and the broad collect the insurance and drive off into the sunset in your convertible, hopefully at full speed in the direction of a cliff."

"That's as old as the hills," replies Tight Lip.

"Perhaps, but that plot never ages, and speaking of which, if not you and the broad, maybe the wife and the mistress conspiring? Maybe it's a group thing?" adds Alfred Two.

"Oh, that is so lame, it's been done *ad nauseam*," replies Tight Lip.

"All right, all right, why don't we just pop them all," replies Fast Hombre.

"Eh, eh, easy, easy," says Syl, "Mr. C., please."

"Thank you, Syl, thank you everyone. Life has been challenging for all of us but the fact that you are all standing here is a testament to your individual and collective resolve to succeed. My sporadic work with you, especially since Aila's and Mo's passing, is understandable but definitely inexcusable. The focus for you today should not be on what you have lost, rather on what you have gained, and that is, by bravely walking out of the shadows, you have gained immortality. Think about that, then think about the fact that you have done it on your own, by believing in yourself, in your ability to tackle obstacles big and small with confidence and fortitude, and that, my friends, is a remarkable achievement. Moreover, you have unselfishly helped others of less resolve, including me, yes me, stay the course, and if in my case I veered off the sacred path, it has been solely on me and not on anyone else. I am the one that lost his way, and am still struggling to find my way home to Mo and Aila."

He then turns to Syl and says, "Syl, Alex, please bring in the boxes from the hallway."

"Sure thing, Mr. C.," he replies, and after the laptops are taken out of their boxes and placed neatly in the room, Mr. C. thanks them and says, "In these personalized laptops, you will find a brief introduction to your humble beginnings, and only an introduction. You are all now the unreserved director of your own score, the sole author of your actions and dialogue, so, most trusted and loyal friends, continue to have faith in yourselves, trust yourselves, particularly your hearts, and you will reach the highest of aspirations. You chose me to open your doors to the infinite realm of being, and for that, my dear friends, I am humbled and forever grateful. Out there, you will find that humankind is often depth-challenged in heart, vision and dreams, and only sees the infinite universe through a peephole in a door. Imagine, just imagine how we could enrich our hearts, our visions, our collective future if we were to simply open the door. You, my friends, are destined to do just that, to open your door and those of others to endless possibilities."

Syl begins applauding, followed by the group, and after it subsides, Mr. C. continues.

"You, my dear friends, may be cut from a different cloth but regardless of your origin, we will ultimately all be woven into the same tapestry. As entities we are meant to learn from each other's similarities as well as, and more so, from each other's differences, because we are all, all variations on the same theme.

"That old computer on my desk now sits empty, but I will check it from time to time, should you wish to update me on your journey. In your travels know this, dear, dear friends, you may physically travel alone but you will have the full force that you see here tonight with you.

"I would like to conclude by sharing some words of wisdom, no, not from me, but from my beloved companion, Mo."

After a brief pause, he says, "In her twilight, one evening sitting just outside in the courtyard, she looked at me and said, 'Do not allow the loving space in your heart to be overshadowed by darkness … open your clenched fists and extend your hand of kindness … show forgiveness … fear not the tears, but the suppression of them … let's help each other cry, let's comfort each other and let us bring our hearts and voices together as one powerful weapon against the challenges that lie ahead."

He pauses and bows his head. The complete absence of sound keeps their hearts awakened, and soon after he resumes.

"As I humbly stand before you, I wish to thank you most sincerely for your unwavering companionship. As well, I ask your forgiveness for all the despairs and anguish I may have caused. I am proud to call you all friends."

The thunderous ovation seems to last forever and its sound imbues the valley.

"From the bottom of our hearts, we thank you, Mr. C.," says Maggie, "and we know how much Aila and Mo mean to you. To that end, I, on behalf of everyone here, would like to say, to highlight an old proverb, 'May their memory be for a blessing.'"

The soft applause that followed slowly came to a pause and Mr. C. says, "Thank you, dear friends, and Godspeed in your travels."

"And to you too," says Syl, "Almost home, Mr. C?"

"Almost home, Syl, almost home," he replies.

They each walk up and take their respective laptops. In reverence no one opens them. Mr. C. shakes hands with everyone, accompanied by long hugs. Lastly, Maggie and Ralph walk towards him unaccompanied, and he says, "Maggie, please sit on the chair to your left, toss your dark glasses and open your laptop, that's it … good."

She places her hands on the keyboard and says, "Now what?"

"Remember what I said to you after class long, long ago?"

"Yes, I do, you said, 'Have faith, Maggie.'"

"And you've kept faith, now please type whatever you wish."

The room suddenly becomes silent, and after a short pause, Maggie says, "Okay, typing was never my forte, but here we go." She places her fingers on the keyboard and begins typing. She stops, looks at the screen in front of her and loudly says, "I did it! I did it!"

"We're so proud of you, Maggie, can you share your wish with us?" says Mr. C.

"Absolutely," she enthusiastically replies, "I typed, I want my fucking eyesight back!"

After the loud laughter subsides and Ralph stops barking, Maggie looks at everyone around the room and says, "You haven't aged one bit." Following another fit of laughter, she picks up Ralph, kisses him on the head and says, "You are all so beautiful, thank you, and you, Mr. C., what happened to you, you look so old," she says, smiling and prompting more laughter. She puts Ralph down on the floor, walks up to Mr. C. with open arms and they remain embraced until the joyous tears dry.

She then looks at him and says, "I'm forever indebted for you re-cuing me, Mr. C., forever."

"No, Maggie, I am, to you, to all of you," he replies.

Syl and Alex approach, express their gratitude and walk Maggie to the open window, "What do you see, Maggie?" Syl asks.

She looks at the night sky and says, "Where do I begin? I am in awe at the splendour of it all, this is indeed a dream come true, thank you, thank you all."

Amidst the celebration, Tight Lip walks up to Mr. C. and asks, "Is this our new reality?"

He asks for everyone's attention, repeats Tight Lip's question and says, "My answer to Tight Lip's timely question about reality is this, you have always been 'real,' now you have reached a new dimension of reality within the realm of living. As an author I had a dream and that was you. Once on paper, you concurrently advanced your own dream and within that dream your particular reality evolved. It was that perseverance, that desire to be something greater than your humble beginnings that took you all to where you are today."

"So does this mean I no longer have to wear a trench coat and pass secret information in brown envelopes to journalists in underground garages?" asks Tight Lip.

Mr. C. smiles, accompanied by laughter, and says, "A colossal, colossal word of thanks … if it wasn't for you teaching us writers how to dream, we would asphyxiate from the volley of empty words aimlessly wandering the barren landscape searching for new plots, when all we have to do is type a name on the top of a page and give you, not us, you, a voice and an opportunity to map out and follow your own dream. As I unpretentiously stand before you, I want to express my deep appreciation for companionship and thank you all from the bottom of my heart for always being there and for your unconditional love."

"On behalf of everyone we thank you too, Mr. C., for your unconditional support and love," says Alex.

"You are truly the wind that propels our work onto the shelves of bookstores. I know, we will all meet again on those very shelves, or on tablets, in talking automobiles, on those thingamajigs on wrists." He pauses, looks around the room, sees the emergence of an energetic and astute group of explorers, fearlessly challenging the new frontiers of reality, and says, "Godspeed, everyone."

While everyone sat on the floor browsing the contents in their laptops, Mr. C. stands at the open window looking at the person walking down the path. Syl joins him, and Mr. C. asks if that's Rogue.

Syl looks and confirms that it is Rogue carrying his laptop.

"Would you like me to go talk to him, Mr. C?"

"Thank you, Syl, but I need to speak with him, be right back."

He tells everyone he'll be right back, leaves the house, walks quickly and when he reaches Rogue, he's sitting on the safety barrier staring into the darkness below. Mr. C. joins him on the barrier and says, "What do you see, Rogue?"

"Not much."

"That's because you're not looking in the right places."

"And where should I be looking?"

"Why don't you open your laptop, it may provide you with some clues."

"Here?"

"Yes, it has good battery, its own light, open it."

"What's the password?" asks Rogue.

"Zero, zero, zero."

Rogue looks at him and says, "And they call you the genius."

"Same password for everyone's laptop, temporary. Go ahead, read some of my entries."

Rogue begins reading and as the scrolling slows, eyes swell and he closes his laptop. Mr. C. places his arm around him.

The crying subsides and Rogue says, "All the things you wrote, do you mean them?"

"I do, they're who you are, Rogue, you're a good man and a solid human being and don't let anyone tell you differently."

"I always felt I never measured up … never good enough … always a disappointment … always looked at myself as the problem child in a way, until now, until I read your rendition of me, of your love for me and for every one of us."

"Not easy to know when feelings are not verbalized or shown at the right time. I always felt I was the absent father to all of you."

After a brief silence, Mr. C asks, "Ready to go back?" Rogue nods and both begin walking towards the house. Mr. C. stops, looks at Rogue and says, "I just want you to know how much I admire your courage, sense of responsibility and moral strength in helping Maggie and her group find their way here safely."

"It wasn't just me," he replies, "we ran into them at McSorley's, and yes, Mr. C., many of us did venture out from time to time. They were lost, and we took them in."

Reaching the house, Rogue asks, "The nest will soon be empty, Mr. C., what's next for you?"

"No shortage of projects, Rogue, I'll be fine."

"An epiphany for all of us," says Rogue.

"Indeed."

Waiting in front of the house, the group stands watching as Rogue and Mr. C. approach. "Rogue, you wanted to beat us to the train station and got lost, didn't you?" says Syl.

"Pretty dark out there, and the moon can only do so much, we best get some flashlights," he replies.

"We have them right here in my backpack, everyone please take one," says Alex.

"So, Mr. C., the train station, about three kilometres east of here."

"Yes."

Syl turns to the group and asks if they are ready for a moonlight walk to which they enthusiastically reply, "Yes!"

They all take turns saying their farewells to Mr. C., the last of which are Huxley and Munro.

"Where is home for you two now?" asks Mr. C.

"Anywhere we're together," replies Huxley, holding Munro's hand.

"We found a nice little place downtown, it'll do for now. Any words of wisdom, Mr. C?"

"Here is what Mo said to me on the twilight part of her journey: 'If our journey is only an hour long, VC, we must live that hour as if it was only one minute.'"

"Did you?" she asks.

"We certainly tried."

They say their farewells, kiss and embrace, then Huxley takes Munro's hand and both walk towards the Ducati and climb onto it. Huxley starts the motorcycle, revs it several times, waves and the red machine slowly moves down the gravel path, eventually catching up to the group.

"In Bocca Al Lupo," says VC, standing on the terrace waving until their lights dim and they're totally out of sight.

His eyes take him to the Alfa, now partially shadowed by the house. Takes keys from his pocket, looks down the lightless road, back at the house, boards and starts the car.

Freewheels into second, shifts into third, the back wheels kick up gravel, speed indicator rises, pitch dark, into the curve too fast. Suddenly, in waiting, a solid barrier of people holding flashlights appear in front of him. Brakes hard, tires screech, slides sideways, crashing into the guard rail. They run to it, look down and Mr. C is barely hanging onto a small extension of the broken rail with one arm, unable to climb back up.

Rogue runs over, extends his arm but is unable to reach him. Immediately Syl and Alex drop to the ground and form a human chain. Syl holds Rogue by his feet as he extends himself over the edge, Alex holds onto Syl and the rest hold onto Alex's feet and legs.

Rogue lowers himself towards Mr. C. as flashlights guide the way. He reaches him, grabs and holds firmly onto his wrist, then grabs the other and says, "Don't you even think of letting go."

As he is being pulled to safety, he looks down at his car on fire at the bottom of the precipice, and Rogue angrily says, "What were you thinking, you could have been killed."

Once safely back on solid ground and embraced by everyone, he says "I'm sorry, Rogue, sorry everybody, just trying to catch up to the group and misjudged," but no one comments. Infuriated yet concerned, Maggie looks at him, then back at the group, and says, "We're walking Mr. C. back, whether he likes it or not."

"You don't have to really, couple of scratches, but I'm fine."

She raises her finger at him, indicating silence. He nods and the group begins walking back towards the house.

Syl and Mr. C., walk together behind the group, Syl looks at the night sky and says, "Look up, breathe deeply and wish, Mr. C., it doesn't get better than this. So what made you pull a stunt like that?"

"What do you mean?"

"No need to answer, I do know, whether you're up or you're down, can't rush living life nor can you rush ending it. You haven't been listening to your corner man."

"And who would that be?"

"Only you would know that, Mr. C."

After a brief silence, Syl continues, "By the way, you have a music file without entries, what's that about?"

"How did you know about the music file?"

"Huxley and Munro, the snoopers that they are, when they came across your empty music file, called me and Alex over. Anything you wish to share?"

"Mo and I love music, she the keyboard, me more of a percussionist, it aligns the heart's beat with the pulse of the universe as it were, and we love to dance. As you know, music can evoke powerful emotions, and memories are said to survive long after other forms of recollections have gone. Somehow we felt this connection with music, I guess that's why we danced a lot. Were you ever in love, Syl?"

"Yes. Complicated." He places his arm on Mr. C.'s shoulder and says, "We're all extremely happy you're here, Mr. C."

"I am so grateful, Syl, and blessed to have such dear friends."

"All right then, time to switch gears. Everybody, listen up," he says and all stop. "Alexandria, Warwick, from the top."

"All right, friends, Dionne Warwick, *That's What Friends Are For*," says Alexandria. "Rogue, Maggie, everyone, c'mon, c'mon with passion to the end."

The song ends and the rest of the walk was in silence. They reach the house, and all sit on the courtyard floor with their laptops open, reading, smiling, scrolling well into the night. Mr. C. with some help served refreshments and for the first time in a very long time he felt genuinely reconnected with his friends.

Shortly after the midnight hour Mr. C. reassured the group that he was not in need of any medical attention and would be fine alone. Everyone packs up, says their goodbyes and begins walking down the path towards the station.

Before leaving his sight, the group stops. They all turn their flashlights towards the house, amplifying its glow. They then gradually merge their lights into a more powerful beam and point it skywards into the endless blue, as if to illuminate a new passage to the heavens.

AGING SUMMER: THE LAST SEASON OF ITS KIND
LA CASA

He slowly walks to his chair, sits and leans against the wall. Soon his eyes tire and gradually close. Not long after, a gentle breeze softly caresses his face and his eyes slowly open. Out of the darkness, an unmistakable entity … a most cherished heart … a radiant glow nears. He quietly calls her name, then hears the soft calling of his. "Be not afraid, my husband, it is I." He immediately stands but, overwhelmed with the possibility of such a phenomenon, he can't speak.

"It is I, my love, my husband." The glowing figure slowly evolves into Mo, and he asks, "Did I just die?"

"No, you did not."

"How real is your presence?"

"As real as you wish it to be, my love."

"May I touch you?"

"Yes, you may."

His hand slowly touches her face, gradually moves his fingers over her lips, "May I kiss you?" he asks. "You may," she replies and he gently kisses her.

She softly caresses his face, embraces him and says, "It has been so long."

He places both hands around her face, looks directly into her mesmerizing blue eyes and amidst the joyful tears, says, "I can't believe it, Mo, you're real and you're here, here with me. I must be dead."

"Shhhh," she whispers placing her fingers on his lips.

They put their arms around each other and hold tightly for a long while. Their bodies absorb each other's energy and he feels renewed.

Their lips touch again and he feels her love as deeply as the first time. "I have missed you, Mo, but how is this possible? I'm either dead or you're alive."

"Love crosses all known states of being, of time, space and form, my love. I am you, you are me and we love as one."

"You and Aila are my life."

"And you ours."

"Life without you and Aila is excruciatingly painful, Mo."

They sit close and she says, "Your friends saved you."

"I know," he says. "Never expected them to be there."

"And the book?"

"Done," he replies.

"And the Mustangs?" she asks.

"Happily grazing."

"And your heart?"

"Still broken," he replies.

"And the Files?"

"Closed."

"Care to open some new ones?"

"Love to," he replies, "Tell me, is this really you? In person?"

"It is. I am. Shall we?"

"Yes," he replies, "Please."

"I will speak of the following categories: *Humour, Music,* and *Hope,* followed by *Beauty on the Terrace,* then *The Tears of Peace.*

"*Humour*, *Music*, and *Hope*. Humour in times of loss. Let me remind you, self-enhancing, not self-defeating humour has been a positive force in our relationship ever since you asked me where room 211 was, to which I replied 'normally on the second floor.' We didn't laugh, but we secretly smiled. Music became another major go-to construct ever since that night in my father's basement. There is music in our being, my love, that makes notes in our cells come alive, and we dance. We know such joy and have on many, many occasions retired evenings dancing to our favourites. Humour and music have been such an integral part of who we are. Sadly, since my passing, you have seldom smiled and rarely listened to music of any kind.

"*Hope*. There was little hope in you recovering from the coma, but you did, there was little hope of me living past my teens, but I did, there was little hope of us having Aila, but we did. How many years did we have together? Not as many as we wished but of those given, we lived them well and happily. Why? because we never lost sight of each other even in the darkest of days, we held tightly, we loved, and against all comers, tragedy, despair, grief, we kept hope alive. Hope is our most powerful and resilient antidotes against defeatism, darkness and despair. Hope is part of who we are and how we live. Hope is future harvest, and life without hope is a tough row to plough. Hope is your most powerful ally in your journey back to us, VC. You abandon hope, you abandon purpose, become disoriented and lose your way. And you have."

"Without you, there is no beacon, no inspiration, no symbol of hope to guide me."

"You are not, and never will be without my presence next to you. I remain your guiding light, for I am forever in your heart. But you my love, have built this fortified fortress to protect its radiance and in doing so, you have limited the light to a glimmer. Beacons can't be the glow you seek when kept concealed."

"I can't live life without you beside me. How can I appreciate a good song without my loving partner, or make a car ride joyous without you and Aila?"

"Allow me to finish the trilogy, the answer may be clearer and more easily understood when I'm done." He nods and she continues.

"Now, my love, I will illustrate my skills as a *negotiator.*"

"*Negotiator?*"

"I'll have you know, it took countless days and nights of negotiating for me to secure proper passage for you."

"Not sure what you mean?"

"Well, being the noted strategist, I negotiated for a safe and comfortable passage for you, they agreed to safe but not to the comfort clause."

"Pardon?"

"Well…" she says smiling, "They have yet to finish reviewing your biography. They retain a troupe of lawyers to cross the *t*'s and dot the *i*'s before committing, and believe me, it was not without its challenges."

"Will I be going to Heaven?" asks VC.

"Heaven?" Mo replies, followed by a brief laugh. "You? In Heaven? What have you been smoking in my absence?"

"Tell me more about these negotiations," he asks in a sombre tone.

"They came to me and said your portfolio was up for review, and were not in a good mood, but they began negotiating in earnest after I threatened to retain counsel from the very prestigious law firm of Bryan, Bryan and Bryan. Ever heard of the three kings of law?"

"Triplets?" he asks.

"Yes, poor woman."

"Can't say I have."

"They used to practice *Here* and now… *There,* much more lucrative. So many mysteries in the land of law."

"I'm innocent."

"Of course you are, dear, but never know what can happen in court. You know what they say, better be guilty and rich than innocent and poor, and since you don't have any money…"

"What are my chances?"

"Tough jury, but I will have you know, barring a complete acquittal, I will appeal directly to His Mother because only mothers truly understand, and only mothers can actually forgive. We recently had a woman-to-woman talk, very nice, understanding, caring, and known to uphold the law supremely and with great sensitivity. By the way, contrary to common conviction, the Mother makes the ultimate decision on such family issues, rarely the Father, he makes decisions regarding shadier matters."

"Shadier matters?"

"The word is that those who come before Him don't fare very well, so follow my instructions to the letter if you want to avoid a reception with Him."

"Is this for real?"

"What?"

"You here, with me. This entire discussion, it's beautiful, warm, uplifting, humorous and I never want it to end, but how is it possible that you are actually here?"

"Believe, VC, and make the jump, isn't that what you profess to your friends?"

"Should I be concerned?" but she has no reply.

"An answer would help, after all, I have given you a hefty retainer."

"I'll have you know, mister, I am the best. I looked at the group of men sitting across the table, smugly looking at the ceiling, flipping pages as if they had actually read the proposed contract, so I rolled up my sleeves like a Teamster and said to myself, how hard can this be? I was rather surprised, some did have a semblance of a brain, and a few actually put it to work, men, anyway, I held fast, and I was so successful that I was offered a position with their firm at the senior level no less, but I refused because I want to be with my husband and daughter. So, after negotiating until the wee hours of the morning, we reached a solid, mutually binding contract. Not bad for a country girl, wouldn't you say? Anyway, the Mother with whom I had spoken on occasion read it and said she would happily ratify it if I sweetened the pie."

"What dose it mean, 'sweetening the pie'?" asks VC.

"It meant I would have to put my medical skills to work."

"There?"

"Yes, there. Well, you know, since my specialty is treating second- and third-degree burns, I could help treat those who had been through, you know, *The Other Place*, but I would not have to treat the ones returning from the *WPC*."

"WPC?"

"Yes, WPC, you know, the *White Phosphorus Chamber*. And had you not skipped your chemistry classes you would know what phosphorus can do to bare skin. So, I was added to their medical roster and when I completed my work, they asked me to stay for another tour of duty, and since it would help us in the long run, I did. I did request a weekend pass, it was granted, and here I am. That's my story and I'm sticking to it. Actually, what I should say is, that's the story you, my dear, are most likely to understand."

"I'm speechless."

She smiles and says, "All right. So, moving right along on this amusing but serious tale, since they were experiencing an unprecedented increase in volume, specialized personnel like myself were deployed to manage their recently implemented and much-needed third shift, aka the graveyard shift. I also agreed to spend extra time supervising their burn unit on my days off in exchange for leniency in your case, and they agreed, albeit reluctantly. FYI, my love, Aila and I were given the rare permission to fast-track it all, but we chose to wait for you, so they placed us in the Great Chamber of Kindness, just off the Chamber of Enhanced Understanding and Wisdom."

"I don't know what to say."

"Precisely. In your case, my love, the less said the better, let your lawyers do the talking. Anyway, love, you should see this place, meaning the addition built onto *The Other Place*, it's so monumental that no one has ever seen the bottom or the top of it ... and I hear another addition is going up on the south side of the WPC to keep up with the demand."

"And what exactly have you been doing there?"

"Managing other doctors and nurses while helping treat scorched beings ascending daily to *The Transitional Place*, after their stay in you know, *The Other Place*. These are beings who after paying their dues, as it were, are granted permission to move on. Some need a lot of therapy, no acupuncture but hypnosis is quite popular, you know where they make hypnotic suggestions while you stare at that spiral wheel as if they need to create more illusions in your head."

"Tell me, how is role-play in therapy carried out when you're in this trance-like state?"

"Are you getting smart with me?"

"No, ma'am."

"Moving right along, while hypnotherapy is used with individuals who suffered severe traumatic experiences incurred while, you know, in *The Other Place*, that's not the whole story. Many also struggle with PTSD. Others may require plastic surgery. Anyway, when they are fit and ready, they are permitted to move along, and, get this, perpetrators of personal crimes must also meet with the relatives and friends of those to whom they caused harm, something about restorative justice, fast becoming a popular means of addressing wrong doings."

"Imagine, the victimized and their respective relatives and friends alone in a room with the perpetrator free to restore justice, I can see why there would be lots of interest in that approach."

"I don't think that's how restorative justice works, VC."

"Tell me a little more about the *White Phosphorus Chamber*."

"I hear those without a conscience, those who commit crimes against humanity, the unredeemable, the psychos, the socios, those unable to feel empathy or remorse, ruthless leaders, corrupt politicians, greedy CEOs, and the like, they are frequently too far gone, too well-done for our unit, because their punishment is inflicted with, shall we say, considerable more enthusiasm, more fervour, more intensity, if you will, than anyone has ever known, and this is executed by specifically chosen individuals who really enjoy their work, and don't care if they get paid overtime or not, definitely not a good place in which to land even for a short time."

"What about me?"

"What about you?"

"Do I need to go, you know, to *The Other Place* for any length of time?"

"Feeling the heat, are we?" she says, smiling.

"You are exceptional, Mo. Help me with this, I don't know if your presence here, now, is actual or if I'm dreaming it. It can't be the meds, stopped taking them long ago, so is this really happening? And how is it possible?"

"Are you not listening?"

"Sorry, just need confirmation."

"Let me put it to you this way, you're human and I am greater than human."

"In my eyes you have always been."

She smiles and says, "Correct, now please stand up." He stands, she embraces him and asks, "What do you feel?" to which he answers "I feel the beating of your heart, I feel your love."

"That's all that has ever mattered, and always will, my love."

"I love you, Mo, you are such an exceptional human being, sorry, and I concur, greater than human," he says kissing her softly.

They return to sitting then he says, "Tell me, O Wise One, what else was in my dossier? And how did you manage to read it, anyway?"

"In the first place, I would not refer to thousands upon thousands upon thousands of pages as a dossier, more like databank. Anyway, I was in the supervisor's office asking about you, and your most recent file just happened to be on the desk opened … the individual looked up, sensed my desperate need to see the content, said he would be going for a large triple-triple and a double chocolate Hawaiian doughnut, you know the ones with coloured sprinkles on top"—he nods and she continues—"and said he'd be a while and left. So I took the liberty of looking through the summary, and to my surprise much was redacted. They must go through millions of black permanent markers a year in that place."

"My file redacted? There is nothing to black out."

"In your eyes perhaps, but as they say, you can hide the truth, but can't outrun it. They also say beauty is in the eyes of the beholder, well, my dear, so is sin … so they say. As far as nothing to black out? Well, they beg to differ, much of your work with Uncle Guido, the Don of the south side, was redacted, wonder why, Vinny?"

"You don't miss a thing, do you?"

"By the way, do you have fire retardant slippers?" she asks, unable to stop smiling.

"Fire retardant slippers?"

"In order to give perpetrators of ghastly crimes a taste of their own medicine, before they are sent to *The Other Place*, they hold their feet to the fire for a set time, but if that happens to be as break time is about to begin, they lower the heat and off they go. When they return from break, they turn up the heat full blast until a very loud Ouch! Ouch! Ouchhhh!!!! is heard, apparently it must be yelled loudly."

"Why?"

"Because my dear, the old keepers retired, lousy pension I hear, and the new ones, very nice, polite, but regularly have on their headsets listening to loud rock. Although none of this applies to you, when your time comes, my suggestion is for you to take your punishment like the good soldier you are, and save on the antibiotic ointment and pain medication, by the way, you haven't let your medical insurance lapse, have you?"

VC shakes his head and she continues, "So I say, bite the cannonball and go with the law triplets."

"I have a good case, and could represent myself, and if the judgement goes against me, I'll appeal."

"Brilliant. Appeal? To whom?"

"Just a funny note in keeping with the *spirit* of the conversation…"

"Clever, VC, but no points."

"Tell me, my dear Mo, were you subjected to even a mild sunburn?"

"Of course not, pure as the driven snow."

"I miss you, Mo, your companionship, your beauty, your witty humour, your brilliance, I am so, so, so blessed."

She caresses his face, her soft lips touch his, and says, "*Beauty on the Terrace,* my love." She gently pulls him to the middle of the courtyard and adds, "Remember our first dance?"

"I do."

They place their arms around each other, barely swaying and hum the tune. Treetops observe and copy, branches embrace and the breeze quietly accommodates. The stars dim, the moon extols, and all is as it should be.

"Do you remember dancing on many, many a night here without shoes?"

"Like we did in the school gym so we wouldn't scratch the wooden floors? I do."

"Do you remember the last song ending our first school dance? The one from my father's jazz collection. I played it after the first time you walked me home and every time I got home from our dates. Do you remember?"

"Sweet Etta James. The song that became one of our all-time favourites, may I?" he says, offering his hand.

"You may," she replies. Takes his hand and both walk to the middle of the courtyard and she says, "Dance with me."

"*At last,*" he says while embracing her. "Dance with me, love, sing with me, our life is like a song, our song."

The singing fades, the humming ends, embraced bodies hardly move, Mo looks directly at him and says, "We've always had a musical heart, haven't we?"

"We have, and our musical hearts took our love higher and higher."

"We are musical beings."

"The whole world is an orchestra, dear love of mine," he says.

"And that world is, or should be, of one song, love," she says. "Do you remember when we spent the night embraced on the cot, afraid of letting go?"

"I do," he replies as they look directly into each other's eyes. He picks her up, places her gently on the cot and slowly lies down next to her.

Holding each other tightly, VC looks at the sky and asks, "What's it like there, Mo?"

"The little that I know … the depth and breadth of our knowledge on Earth is so, so embryonic. I'm not sure we will ever be sufficiently advanced on Earth to understand the true meaning of the world around us here, nor of the cosmos, or beyond. I was so humbled when I spent time in the Chamber of Enhanced Understanding and Wisdom, and felt so excited at the prospect of us and Aila being part of the whole and truly feeling it. There is this overwhelming sense of peace, of well being, of benevolence towards each other."

After a brief silence, VC says, "Is there a sole entity as the Light?"

"Not sure how to answer that question because progressing towards the Light and evolving into it, requires many undertakings. Allow me to summarize: *Once transitioned from the physical, the journey will take you to the Great Hall, it really is a place of wonderment, then to the Constellations.*"

"The Constellations?"

"Yes. The Constellation of Lights, to the Constellation of Souls, to the Collective Glow that is love at its pinnacle of clarity, wholesomeness and devotion."

"And from there?"

"From there, we journey to the ultimate setting at the pinnacle of all universes, where all merge and radiate as one, are envisioned as one, hence return to being an entity of One."

"If I may, as our true hearts continue strengthening our emotional and spiritual entity, we are guided towards the One, correct?" he says.

"That is my understanding, which again is so infinitesimal. I would like to share with you my experience with the Festival of Lights."

"Please."

"I had the rare opportunity of viewing, briefly, the Festival of

Lights. This Festival, with its indescribable radiance, spans uncountable galaxies, where billions and billions of individual lights come together to form one immense glow and this unified glow continues moving towards its final destination as one. We, we, are the lights that provide the brightness to the One. We are the Light, VC, follow?"

"I do. Question, in the Festival of Lights, do all the lights have the same glimmer, the same sparkle?"

"There is a distinct, invisible light in all of us, and that's the beacon that is recognizable only by those who truly love us. And what I found to be most touching and so emotionally laden with excitement is when I observed countless, countless lights flickering unremittingly and more enthusiastically with such amplified vivacity as their loved ones got closer."

"Fascinating."

"Totally. By their flickering they are actually showing their incoming loved ones the way to them, truly spellbinding. What's also captivating, is that once reunited, the glow increases but the flickering temporarily stops. Once reunited, that particular family of lights leaves the Festival of Lights and continues on with their journey. However, the most recent arrivals remain becoming the new flickering lights for that group's new arrivals."

"Will you be that flickering light for me in the distance?" asks VC.

"You and I have been touched by the same hand at the exact same time VC, yes my love, Aila and I will show you the way home."

She takes a deep breath, and says, "Now, my love, *the Tears of Peace.*"

"Not sure what you mean?" he replies.

"Yes, you do. You have battled, won some, lost many on the road to peace of heart…"

"There is no peace of heart without you and Aila," he replies but she continues.

"You have lost sight of the fact that we are one, neither you nor I will ever lose each other."

She kisses him softly on his forehead, embraces her fallen knight more securely, and whispers,"You found your way home, VC, back to me, to us."

"I was supposed to protect the ones I love, and I failed you both, Mo, I…" he says in a fading voice.

"But you did protect us, VC. You protected us with your unconditional love, and that is all anyone ever needs."

He tries holding her hand tighter, but his strength is slowly leaving him, tries speaking, but his voice fades.

She caresses his face and quietly says, "Come, my love, our new horizon awaits us … for I am you, you are me, and together, we are the universe."

His head rests peacefully on her bosom, the lights in their reunited hearts shine brighter, and the night settles.

The treetops still, the lone wolf's howl softens to a whisper at the ebbing moon, and the morning awaits a new beginning.

CHAPTER TEN

THE GREAT HALL

VC finds himself standing in the middle of the dimly-lit Chamber of Roads Travelled, whose walls are lined with small mirrored sections. He touches his face, the rest of his body, and feels whole. He looks around the Chamber, at the mirrored stations with books on their respective shelves below, and notices that no two books are of the same thickness. Walks towards the well-lit section, a section housing his most recent earthly travels, stops in front of the end one, looks at the blank mirror in front of him, at the thin book on the shelf below it, tries lifting its cover but is unable, it's locked.

He senses a presence near him and quickly turns. Standing behind him are a man and a woman in thirteenth-century attire. They smile at him and the man says, "Welcome to the Great Hall, VC."

"Thank you, friend, tell me, where am I? And am I dead?"

"You are in the Chamber of Roads Travelled, and death as you know it, my esteemed friend, is one of the least understood occurrences in life's kaleidoscopic journey. There is only life, one journey, multiple entities. Although you will maintain your previous physical appearance, you now exist in a different state of being, a more holistic one as it were. I am Dante, and this is my dear, dear companion Beatrice, and we have been chosen to be part of your welcoming committee."

"Thank you. Dante, you say, and the road to humanism and, of course, the lovely Beatrice, I am honoured to meet you both. Tell me, am I in Limbo?" asks VC.

Dante and Beatrice look at each other, smile, and Dante replies, "Since you enjoy humour, music and combatant terminology, and in view of your literary pursuits, or lack thereof, we therefore will, within reason, endeavour to communicate in the vernacular to which you're accustomed. No, you are not in the First Circle of Hell, nor in any other such circle. You are standing in the centre of your unabridged biography, not autobiography, wouldn't we all like to have the liberty of being creative with the truth. After all, what is a story if it's not within a story, and to quote our friend and yours, 'A life within the life.'"

"Addendum, VC, our dear Dante does have a tendency to get carried away," says Beatrice, "Allow me."

"Please."

"Thank you," she replies, turns to VC and says, "As Dante said, this Chamber stores all your accumulated earthly events. They are reviewed here and a decision on how you should best proceed is rendered by the Tribunal."

"How many such Chambers are there?" asks VC.

"How many snowflakes on a mountain?" replies Dante.

"Dante, can you please explain the journey to our guest."

"You have already brilliantly done so, my lovely, but will as requested, in my own words of course."

"No doubt," she replies.

"How's this, you have now reached the main event, Kid, and you now must go the distance. You cannot bob and weave here, cover your face, protect your body, find respite on the ropes or be saved by the bell. Here you are naked, well, not literally, anyway, this is the place where the judges tally the score on the cards and where the final judgement takes place without exception. How did I do, dear?"

"Very well, Dante, very well," she replies.

"Thank you, thank you very much."

"Time and place, Dante," she says.

"Yes, of course, that applies to a very nice fellow, you may know him, king of rock, tall, dark hair, long sideburns, anyway, it's our understanding that he has yet to leave the building. One question

I must ask, and frankly am tired of asking, what on earth are you people doing to our beautiful planet and to each other down there? Have you all gone mad?"

"Dante dear, please."

"It must be said, my dear," kisses her hand and continues in a calmer tone.

"So, VC, wars, famine, environmental degradation, racism, economic disparity, despots, corrupt politicians, rampant greed, what are you humans thinking? Clearly, no one is thinking at all, not at all."

Beatrice motions to speak with Dante privately and when together she says, "Dante, I know you're totally, totally pissed off with how humans are behaving, and you're right, but here, dear, we must endeavour to remain as impartial as possible."

"You're absolutely right, my dear, I'll try." He then turns to VC and says, "So VC, what say you?"

"Thank you both for your words of wisdom, I know humanity is in disarray…"

"Disarray? I think humanity is about to blow itself up," states Dante.

"I have fallen short on occasion, but so ready to make amends," says VC.

"So says the cat after ingesting the canary," replies Dante, "But, having said that, we just happen to know that there may be hope for you yet, VC."

He then looks at Beatrice lovingly and says, "You are remarkable, my love," and kisses her hand.

"Yes, I know," she replies.

He turns to VC and asks, "Tell me VC, does this room remind you of any other you've seen in your travels?"

"Yes, the Sistine Chapel."

"We'll have you know that none other than our good friend Mike oversaw this project. I know, not exactly the Apostolic Palace, high ceiling, beautiful frescoes and all, but then, painting on his back all those years has taken its toll, but we're very pleased with the results. He's at the chiropractor now for lower back pain, so I said, Mikey, take the pills, please, but no, he wants to try acupuncture, smoking alfalfa sprouts, gorging on those funny tasting brownies, of course none are covered by insurance, so I said, Mike, those old sandals offer little arch support, try orthotics, think he'd listen? Noooo."

"Please stay on task, dear," says Beatrice.

"Yes, sorry, dear," replies Dante.

"Mike? Do you mean…" says VC.

"Yes, none other, Michelangelo," answers Dante. "And FYI, our other good friend Galileo helped streamline the journey beyond the stars, and for that he got the prestigious Five Star Award and a paid sabbatical after he returns from his river cruise."

"Happy to know, where is he now?" asks VC.

"Who?" asks Dante.

"GG," replies VC.

"GG? Galileo Galilei, clever, VC, but don't push it. Well, likely stargazing somewhere, good thing he listened to his father and went to university instead of joining the priesthood, a fine kettle of fish that would have made…"

"Dante!" exclaims Beatrice.

"Sorry, dear. Tell me, VC, are you of the flat or round earth society?" asks Dante but doesn't wait for an answer and continues, "Moving on, and in keeping with familiarity, you will soon meet your gifted friend Pirandello. He helped restructure and better co-ordinate the mirror book thing, and of course, tried to recreate himself many times over in the process, but NCD, that's short for no-can-do, not allowed here. Brilliant fellow, and so loved, but you know, he's so out there. He and GG are good friends, for obvious reasons, I may add."

"Thank you, Dante, as you know, Pirandello holds a very special place in my work, and I so look forward to meeting him."

"I'm certain the feeling is mutual, but a word of caution, please don't be a rogue scholar like your very clever friend Pirandello. He has tenure, you do not."

"You'll get no trouble from me, I'm just eager to be reunited with Mo and Aila and continue our journey together, and I'm prepared to do whatever I need to do to stay the course," replies VC.

"So now you're ready," says Dante, "the question is not what do I need to do *now*, the horses have already left the barn, VC, or is it sheep? I'm sure it's horses, sheep more aptly apply to organized religions, another human invention whose sole purpose is…"

"Don't go there, Dante, please."

"Very well. VC, if I may, the question is what should you have done differently to help you better prepare yourself for this encounter? You, as with all the others, should have given that question considerable thought *before* you got here. Once here, there is no quick way to redemption VC, no quick way. Did you not read the sign on your way in?"

"I'm sorry, what sign?" replies VC.

"The sign that says, *'There Is No Quick Way to Redemption!'* It's in fluorescent yellow, like school crossing signs, in big letters, easily visible even in foggy weather, how could you possibly have missed the sign? But then I could say, humans have missed more than a few signs along the way."

"Sorry, Dante, but I didn't see it."

"Which way did you come in?" asks Dante.

VC shrugs his shoulders and says, "Not sure, but it wasn't a big door."

"Was it a white, wooden screen door with a broken latch?" asks Dante.

"Yes, it was, why?"

"Trades. Anyway, that's the back entrance and it's normally used for deliveries. However, corrupt politicians, dictators, greedy corporate big wigs, ruthless bankers and other such unsavoury characters use that entrance trying to sneak in among the vegetables, as if we can't tell one head of cabbage from another. Really."

"Vegetables?" asks VC.

"Yes, we're big on fresh fruit and vegetables here, organic of course, not cheap, anyway, these slippery characters are so dumb and to show you just how dumb they are, the delivery guys carry big boxes of cabbages while the boxes these slippery types carry are a few small packs of wild blueberries, easily noticeable of course. Not only that, but they do so wearing their expensive suits, what, no t-shirt, jeans and tattoos of mom? Really. Also, they come in wearing black socks and polished black shoes, what, no white socks and approved steel-toe boots? That is such a no-brainer. I must tell you, we will be replacing that rickety old door with a new, reinforced steel one and guard it twenty-four seven."

"Why guard it?"

"To prevent serious offenders from dodging the buckshot. You see, where they're going is like a lobster trap, once in, takes a lot to get out, and they know if they don't, well, it'll be from the trap to the eagerly waiting boiling pot, in a manner of speaking, surrounded by hungry cannibals no less," replies Dante.

"Aren't we getting a little off topic, dear?" asks Beatrice.

"Just enlightening our guest, dear, but you know, while we're on the topic of food..." Dante says.

Beatrice subtly rolls her eyes, and says, "Dante, we just had brunch, and against better judgement you ordered that calorie-ridden trucker's special."

"Yes, the special, quite filling really, eggs, sausages, bacon, whole wheat toast with those little tubs of marmalade, and those yummy pancakes ... artificial syrup unfortunately, definitely not from Quebec, but I did hold off on the whipped cream, petroleum-based, likely not even edible but sinfully delicious ... so they say, and the fruit cup on the side with those innocent-looking maraschino cherries, organic, I hear. I again ignored the calorie chart, dear, sorry," replies Dante.

Beatrice turns to Dante and says, "Time has come my dear," then turns to VC and says, "It's been our pleasure meeting you, VC, your friend will be here soon to actually answer whatever questions you may have."

"On that note, VC, determining the future nature of your journey is a very, very serious matter here, very serious," says Dante, "And the reason you were not able to open the last book is because that story is yet to be fully told."

"Thank you, Dante and Beatrice, it has indeed been a pleasure."

Dante takes Beatrice's hand and as both begin withdrawing their presence from the hall, VC immediately asks, "Wait, wait, who are you?"

"Really, VC. We are who you see, Dante and Beatrice," replies Dante.

Walking on cobblestones approaching the quartier culinaire irresitible, Dante says, "I rather enjoyed extolling the virtues of humour back there, and actually liked practicing it, rather charming in a way, uplifting, and perhaps something doctors should consider prescribing. Do doctors exist?"

"Not sure, I heard tax collectors and sinners do," replies Beatrice.

"Are they not one and the same?" asks Dante with a smile, adding, "Let's do more clever fun," he replies.

"It may very well suit you, Dante."

"We have voluntarily returned to assist, and have done so superbly, but I do miss our Festivals, our collective glow, don't you, Beatrice?"

"I do, Dante. Time to set sail towards that most cherished of horizons."

"Indeed, and let's do so with *joie et exubérance*."

"This is the time to rejoice, my love," says Beatrice. He holds her hand tightly, looks at her and smiles, and after a brief silence says, "What say you of our most recent young family?"

"No shortage of grief, but abundance of love, they'll be fine."

"I think so too. Perhaps a little more love of self, and little more forgiving of self with VC, think you not?"

"I do, Dante."

"Now, speaking of a late lunch," he says.

"I didn't say anything about lunch."

"I know, but we're in the dining district, and I was reading about this little Italian place that just opened, with food to die for, sorry, poor choice of words, food to savour, want to try it? I really feel for a bowl of pasta all'arrabbiata, and the more arrabbiata the better," he says.

"Pasta arrabbiata, definitely suits you."

"Pasta, yes, but as know my dear Beatrice, my passion for you is never arrabbiata, never, ever angry, rather a slow yet feverishly craving of your sensuous body … to gently caress every…"

"I'll just have a salad, thank you, cold water for you, and lots of it," she says while walking and laughing.

"Apparently their pasta and savoury sauce concoction is grandmother's recipe, not sure whose grandmother, but grandmother's nonetheless, glass of wine or two, espresso or two, a pastry or two…"

"One," she says.

"All right, one, and we're off to the races."

"Races?" she asks.

"Yes, and we can take turns driving the car," he replies.

"Driving the car? Do you know what cars actually are? Besides, you need a permit."

"What's a permit?" he asks.

Beatrice looks upward and rolls her eyes.

"I can ask our friend Leonardo," he says.

"He's into forging documents now?"

"No, no, never, he's as honest as they come, besides, no one can get him away from working on that strange assemblage of numbers he's got going, some kind of a code thing, I think he calls it a c-a-l-c-u-l-a-t-o-r. He's also working on what he refers to as a, get this, h-e-l-i-c-o-p-t-e-r, something resembling a large, propped-up tin box with a huge, strange-looking cross on top that when it spins like crazy will lift the box in the air so it flies like a bird, imagine that, yeah right, Lenny, good luck with that invention."

Beatrice looks at him and says, "Please button up your shirt collar, we're here."

"Don't you just love the painting of his mother?"

"It's not of his mother," she replies.

"No?"

"Button up your shirt, please."

"It's too tight."

"Been telling you to lose some weight, now button up, both preferably."

Dante, after some effort, buttons up his collar and as they enter the restaurant says, "All those carbs, I'll need a long nap after this meal."

"You are such a mensch, you know that, don't you?"

"Yes, but a nice mensch."

"Ever since we met Mo, Aila, and most recently VC, I have been struck with such a note of familiarity that I could not identify until now," says Beatrice.

"And what would that be, dear?"

"We all have so much in common, particularly you and VC," she replies.

"Oh, really?" he replies, eagerly waiting for her answer.

"Yes, you're both into pain and suffering."

THE CHAMBER OF ROADS TRAVELLED: VC

Standing next to VC's last book is a person he promptly recognizes. A person whose intellect has no bounds; a person whose magical powers helped mere mortals become larger than life from the merely written; a person that captured the essence of what it meant to be real and magnified it; a person that believed, as he did, that indeed multi-dimensional realities can exist and do flourish.

"Greetings, my good friend," the person says to VC.

"And a warm greeting to you, my friend. You, here? Hard to believe I am now face to face with a most creative and refreshing mentor," says VC while energetically shaking hands.

"Finally, we meet face to face. Please sit."

They sit on one of the decorative iron benches, face each other and he says, "I know your journey hasn't been without darkness, VC, and you've been less than kind to yourself, but you never strayed from the virtues and values that you and Mo revered."

"Mo brought me life, Luigi, and the meaning of life, and without her there has been such an absence of joy, of fulfillment, of order, just loneliness and chaos, but I always kept her splendour in my heart, the only thing that kept me going, and the only thing that keeps me going now is finding my way to her and Aila. That guiding beacon I so love, seems so far away, but I so desperately want to get to it, so how do I get to it, Luigi? How?"

"I, within what is permitted, will assist you, VC. Do know, however, there are limits."

"You are such an invaluable friend, Luigi Pirandello, if you can help, I will forever be indebted."

"Again VC, please know there is little of your journey I can alter, what I can tell you is that you will ultimately be reunited with your soul mate and with your family."

"I understand, Luigi, Dante and Beatrice were very helpful and I am grateful, can you help me put more of my journey and that of Mo's and Aila's in a perspective I may more clearly understand?"

"The Great Earth is the place where everyone's love journey should begin, and for a great number it does, as with you and Mo. Love renders eternity and the reason for encouraging such a journey of true companionship on Earth is that the union can begin living the life of love as early as possible. Also, the essence of true love can inspire others to stay the virtuous course. A loving life on earth makes the path to the Constellations much, much richer."

"How is anyone to know?"

"Really, VC? How did you and Mo know? Love of self, of others, of the planet, the possibilities are limitless. We simply need to open our eyes and listen to our hearts. We had hoped Earth humans would by all accounts have evolved from the needs of the physical to those of the emotional and ultimately to the spiritual, but a significant number did not and many, many more will not."

"What I learned from Mo is that home is and should be, first and foremost, of the emotional and spiritual kind."

"Precisely my point, VC. Humans credit themselves to be of an evolutionary nature, yet ironically, resist evolving into the spiritual." After a brief pause he continues. "There is a rhythm to life, to all life, regrettably, humans seem to be the only ones out of synch with it. Why? Because there is a growing log jam in the human heart, VC, and it seems the concept of interconnectedness is being increasingly tossed aside."

"Maybe the way things are done need to be re-examined," says VC.

"Before humans destroy another beautiful planet with everyone on it?"

"What do you mean?" asks VC.

"Some loud, self-serving voices will have you believe that there are many planets, much like Earth, out there, somewhere, that can sustain life. Others, with louder voices, will have you believe that those non-habitable planets can, in the future, become habitable. They can, and may again. However, one of the principal truths, conveniently ignored, is that those now barren, lifeless, unproductive planets were once quite habitable and thriving. Those infertile planets are the result of reckless human behaviour. They are post–human habitation, VC, not pre-human."

"Hard to believe," says VC.

"Hard to comprehend when those once beautiful and giving planets, gifts to all lives on Earth, were so exploited by humans in their quest for false immortality in the most secular and iniquitous places. Currently, similar pursuits by humans on Earth have again placed themselves and everyone else at a high risk of extinction."

"It saddens me deeply as well, Luigi, but I know you are not Luigi, nonetheless, how will you and others of your prominence prevent human emotional Armageddon on Earth?"

"Emotional and civil Armageddon are often the precursors to a global Apocalypse, and the Doomsday Clock has again reached midnight. To your question, will they be able to roll it back in time?"

"And what will you do if they can't or won't," asks VC.

He pauses, then quietly adds, "Much to consider, much to consider."

VC then asks of Mo and Aila.

"They will be waiting for you in the Chamber of Enhanced Understanding and Wisdom."

"I am more than prepared to make amends, and will do what I must to be reunited with them."

"I know you will."

"Answer me this, if you can, why was Aila taken so early from us?"

After a brief silence, Luigi says, "The early flights of the young are always the most difficult to comprehend, VC. Their passing shatters all known beliefs to the core. Of little comfort, perhaps, but do know, we all live with eternity in our hearts. As well, it may seem that Aila's passing was way, way too early, but do know that her particular journey on Earth was coming to a close. She had reached that exceptional level of knowledge and understanding, that all-encompassing wisdom and compassion, most essential for her spiritual journey. As devastating as her passing may seem, and as difficult as it may be to fully comprehend and integrate … and as heart-wrenching it was for us to bring her home, please know that her bright light will continue helping us make others' brighter. Aila passed young by human standards, but I'll have you know, she's an old soul, and her radiant spirituality will always be a guide."

VC remains silent. He briefly nods, not to indicate agreement, but perhaps now, with increased understading of Aila's and Mo's mission and early passing, he could begin to forgive.

Looking at VC's perplexed expression, Luigi says, "We create life, VC, we do not take life. We are not responsible for diseases, famine, disparity, inequality or wars. Humankind in its constant dismissal of the truth is responsible. Humankind creates division. We urge unity, kindness, benevolence. Humankind destroys the earth in search of glitter and then wonders at the resulting consequences like hurricanes, temperature fluctuations, unbreathable air, undrinkable water, unproductive farmlands, sicknesses, plagues. The day of reckoning is again upon us, and frankly, we are out of planets for new beginnings."

"Thank you for opening my eyes, Luigi, I am now closer to understanding humankind's evolution within the cosmos than ever before. I am reminded of one of Mo's prophecies if you will, 'Once you lose hope, you will lose your way.' That happened to me, my friend, now that I understand its power, I will never lose hope again. One more question, if I may."

"Yes, of course."

"What of the locked book?"

"A tale in search of a proper ending, VC," he replies, then says, "Walk with me."

They walk to the last mirror and as VC approaches the mirror, Luigi says, "Stand and look closely."

The mirror gradually changes into clear glass and Mo and Aila appear. The three of them immediately begin speaking, but they could have been a million miles apart, they could not hear each other.

Mo and Aila place their hands on the glass and VC matches their handprints with his, but it was all too brief, their images soon recede.

After a long silence, VC takes his hand away from the mirror and says, "They are my most cherished family and their hearts are my home, Luigi."

"That's what they said of you, VC."

"My only wish is for the three of us to return to where we once were. I want to watch sunrises with Mo, relive the splendour and brilliance of those sunsets long into the good night. I want to be a good father to Aila."

"Returning to the state of being of which you ask, to that particular time and place on Earth, without any recollection related to here, is unthinkable. It will never be sanctioned by the High Tribunal, as journeys travel in only one direction."

"Traditionally, perhaps, but we're visionaries, and we have pushed many an envelope and we can create within creations. I wish none other than to live and love Mo as I knew it. All I ask is for our small family to be as it once was, surely there must be something we can do."

"I'm sorry, VC, the paradigm is unchangeable, everyone must stay the course; what you and countless others ask is simply impossible to bestow. Mo and Aila have preceded you for a reason, you must accept it and be patient. You will be reunited, and your journey together will continue."

After a long, silent pause, VC says, "I understand, what do I do now?"

"Walk to the end of that corridor, sunshine and blue skies, breathe deeply through the flower garden and sit by the waterfall. I have much to do, but will join you later."

"One last question, if I may," says VC.

"Yes."

"Are you God?"

Luigi looks at him, smiles and replies, "Aren't we all?"

VC takes several steps towards the corridor, turns and says, "I must tell you, you are all I ever envisioned and now as I face you, speak with you, you are much, much more. You are that rare, luminous teacher that inspires even with silence. You give not just life to the word, but also hope to the creations. I am humbled by your presence and forever indebted."

"Thank you, VC."

Suddenly a familiar voice to both interrupts and says, "Signor Pirandello, come stai? How are you?" asks Dante.

"Bene grazie amico, e tu? E la signora?" replies Luigi, asking of Beatrice.

"Stiamo bene grazie, we are well, thank you," says Dante. "And you, Kid?"

"I'm fine, Dante, hello, Beatrice," replies VC.

"Our Supreme Deity and friend," says Dante. Luigi glances at VC staring at him, then looks back at Dante and says, "As you, my friend."

"It has been an honour, and we thank you for the opportunity to serve. We have learned a great deal, and it will serve us well in our journey. We are most ready and came to bid you farewell," says Dante.

Luigi looks at VC standing at the entrance to the garden and says, "I need a few minutes with my friends, VC."

"Yes, of course," replies VC, then thanks Dante and Beatrice for their invaluable assistance and bids them a successful voyage.

"And wishing you unmatched success with your endeavours, friend," says Dante.

"I thank you both, dear friends," says Luigi while embracing them. "You continue to enlighten me, Dante, as you, Beatrice."

"You are the latitude and longitude of all that is and shall be," says Beatrice.

"In bocca al lupo," says Dante as he and Beatrice leave the Chamber.

While walking, Dante asks Beatrice if they have time per un spuntino, a snack.

"Is this the last comedic hurrah?"

"Promise," he replies.

"All right then, listen carefully," she says while rummaging through her purse. "I have the piece de resistance of snacks, I have carrots and celery sticks for me, and for you my dear, a man of most discerning palate, I have none other than a peanut butter and jelly sandwich on semi-perforated white."

"Pardon?" says Dante.

She takes it out of her purse hands it to him and says, "Here, see."

He takes it, unwraps it and says, "What in the world is a peanut butter and jelly sandwich on semi-perforated white? And why is it cut in triangular shapes? Is this actual food?"

"Food? Not sure, but it won't kill you, unless you have peanut allergies, do you?"

"What's peanut allergies?"

"I knew I should have taken the EpiPen with me."

"What's an EpiPen?" asks Dante.

"EpiPen stands for epinephrine auto injector, it's a medical device that wives conveniently leave at home when their husbands suffer from fatal allergies."

"I see, does it help?"

"Only if he's insured."

"Pardon?"

"Just eat it and be thankful."

Dante cautiously bites into it and says, "Not bad, Bea, but what's with this bread, it feels as if I'm eating marshmallows."

"So now you know marshmallows?" she asks.

"Not really, but I like the way it sounds, but must pucker up for the correct elongated mallowww sound."

"Pucker up, as in say, a kiss?"

"Yes," he replies and kisses her on the cheek. She smiles and says, "I like maarshhhmellows," and returns the kiss.

"You know what would have been out of this world, dear? A pastrami on rye."

"So, now you know pastrami on rye too?" she asks.

"No, but I read somewhere that there is a deli in New York City that makes a mean pastrami sandwich. Where exactly is New York City?"

"Not falling for it, Dante. By the way, Mr. World Traveller, is our will up to date?" asks Beatrice.

"Why do you ask?"

"In case you have a fatal reaction to peanuts."

"Thanks, Bea, ask me after I finished the sandwich, why don't you," he replies.

They look at each other and amidst the laughter, they tell themselves they love each other.

"But what if I am allergic?"

"Don't be silly, peanuts haven't been made into spreadable butter yet," replies Beatrice.

"So, what exactly was in that sandwich?"

"Tofu spread, and no more questions."

"Very well, on another note, how do you think that VC fellow will do?" he asks.

"His voyage towards enlightenment has not been without challenges, but he's a good man, his heart is in the right place. They will do right by him."

"Do you know something I don't know?"

She looks at him but remains silent.

"C'mon, Bea, lend me your ears."

"My ears are not to lend, Dante; besides, you misquoted an author who hasn't been born yet. You should have prefaced that line with something like, Friends, Romans, countrymen, etcetera, etcetera, etcetera, not eh buddy, can you hear me."

"How do you know these things?" asks Dante.

"Really, Dante? How long have we been together now? I know things. Whose idea was it to send Virgil to the rescue? And who suggested adding two more Circles, greed and treachery, because seven were not enough to accommodate all those sinners. While we're at it, who cleverly suggested a hidden Tenth?"

"Yes, yes, but please not so loud," replies Dante.

Beatrice looks at him and says, "Dante, you're an exceptionally gifted individual, whose intellect, whose vision awes even me sometimes, but everyone should know that behind, in front, beside, wherever, every successful man stands a brilliant woman."

"All right, all right, the usual redemption?" he asks.

"Yes, the usual," she replies.

"I call this blackmail," he says.

"No, I call it dinner, and this time French please, and a tall glass of Cabernet. By the way, how will you be paying for dinner? I'm not waiting for you to wash dishes again."

"I came prepared," he answered while jiggling coins in his jacket pocket. "See, some men can step up to the plate."

"You know baseball?"

"What's baseball?" says Dante.

Beatrice looks at him and smiles.

"You know, Bea, you've often said that females are all knowing, enlightened and bearers of life. Women know the truth, live the truth and know the way of the truth. And you also remind me and my friends that the Earth is round, not square, and contrary to our personal and collective beliefs, we males are not at the centre of it."

"Correct, what's your point?"

"Just a discussion."

"For the record, Dante, men know little outside of themselves and their own needs."

"Not sure I agree," he replies.

"All right then, tell me, how long does a woman have after her water breaks."

"Water breaks? As in a dam?"

"You could say that, see? Men. There is never enough blood diverted to their small brain," replies Beatrice.

"Speaking of food," Dante says.

"I rest my case," replies Beatrice while entering the restaurant. After a delightful dinner, while sipping brandy, Dante looks at Beatrice charmingly and raises his eyebrows several times.

Beatrice looks at him, smiles and says, "Try coming to bed more often instead of working on that Inferno narrative if you want to feel real heat."

"Please, not so loud," he replies.

"Very well, next topic."

"Yes, next topic, would you know if, you know, the Most High Ones have read *The Divine Comedy*, *La Divina Commedia*, from cover to cover, from beginning to end, and from the end to the beginning? I mean really read, reread, take notes and all."

"You are referring to that cheerful little piece of yours, correct?"

"Well, not meant to be cheerful but yes."

"Yes, to reading it end to end, backwards and forwards, even upside down, and some have told you so. You know, Dante, I regret telling you to include the word 'comedy' in the title, it's not a comedy. It's confusing, and sales are low. I mean, how often have you seen people walk into a bookstore, ask for a book on humour and are directed to *The Divine Comedy*? Not many. I must say though, it's a brilliant piece of work, you have outdone yourself, my love, and the literary world will forever be indebted. So imaginative and so, so intense but so ugly."

Dante looks at her fondly and smiles.

She leans over, smiles and kisses him on his cheek and says, "We've had a good run of sunshine, have we not, my love?"

"A few rainy days, but a very good run indeed, and nothing but brightness ahead," he replies, turns to her and asks, "By the way, did you remember to bring your sunglasses?"

"Pardon?" she replies.

He looks at her lovingly and says, "I love you, Bea."

"Love you too, Dante."

After dinner, they walk arm in arm up the long and winding staircase towards their designated location of departure.

"It has been a most enlightened stay, hasn't it dear?"

"Yes, it has, Dante, and I feel so much worthier and better prepared to carry on with our journey."

"As I."

"We have each other and our journey of enlightenment continues, then why is it that I am not as rejoiced as I should be?"

"A compromised jubilation for me as well, Bea. I feel a deep note of sadness for humankind. I fear the darkness hovering over the planet will, in the not-too-distant future, be unleashed with such force that it may well extinguish all lights on Earth."

"I also fear such a doomsday development, Dante."

"The records in the Tribunal Archives we examined seem to indicate we are a dominant but rudderless species. It'll take a miracle for humankind to find its true purpose; sadly, there may soon be none left on which humankind can draw."

"What I was able to surmise from my readings of the Archives is that humankind seems to be increasinly abandoning their faith in the good scriptures, the good books, texts, in each other, in their leaders, spiritual and otherwise, begging the question, why? and in whom or in what are they placing their faith? Begging another question, how can humans walk with love and allow malevolent forces to so easily take them off course?"

"VC seems to have done just fine," says Dante.

"I agree, but let's not forget, VC had, shall we say … timely intervention. Seems to me, Dante, the sandstorm of power and greed and, strangely, their insatiable appetite for man-made things, things produced from ravaging our precious Earth's resources, will completely blind them one day. They just don't seem to get it. Although many do, sadly they're in the minority."

"Of late, the Earth has been sending messages. Too little, too late?" asks Dante.

"Not if humans take heed, but time is of the essence, and I do hope They will rethink their strategy on how to best redirect humanity onto the good journey."

"You mean, how to best save a world of humans that subconsciously resists being saved?" asks Dante.

"Perhaps, but I have faith, Dante."

Almost at the top they stop, Dante looks at Beatrice and says, "After all the sadness in the Archives to which we have been privy, one small consolation, certainly too frivolous to mention in view of the state of affairs, and I apologize, but you know, Beatrice, had we not been so bold as to explore those writings, we would have never known different foods, baseball, marshmallows or a place called New York."

Beatrice takes his hand and quietly leads the way to the top. They board their own illuminated globe and sit down. Accompanied by the lights of nearby stars, their globe soon reaches speed and seamlessly joins incalculable others in the Festival of Lights. Beatrice moves closer to Dante, points straight ahead and says, "This is where all the journeys from all the galaxies begin reunification, imagine the grandeur, the accumulated wisdom and the depth of it all, Dante."

Dante looks at the splendour ahead, takes her hand and kisses it softly. Looks directly into her eyes and sees the reflection of the eagerly anticipated myriad of flickering lights drawing near.

"What do you see?" she asks.

"Eternity," he replies.

She moves closer and whispers, "Our love's journey continues, Dante."

"Indeed, my love."

Love enriches, the journey soothes, discussions dwindle and silence shelters the hearts.

THE CHAMBER REVISITED

The entity most recently known as Luigi to VC transforms into his Deity persona, sees Moreen standing next to the station of the locked book, walks up to her, places His hand on her shoulder and says, "Our valiant and heroic Daugther with a fearless and indomitable spirit."

"Good to see you Father," she replies. They embrace and she asks of Mother.

"She will be here soon." Looks at her and says, "We have all read your proposal with keen interest, it has great merit and is most timely."

"Thank you, Father."

"I must inform you, however, some of the Elders of the High Tribunal move cautiously, not out of fear, rather out of exhaustion."

"You have all tirelessly endeavoured to enlighten and done so gallantly, but the future of humankind is often untenable and anything but predictable. Humans need us more then ever, and they require immediate active guidance, if this last of the pale blue dots in this galaxy is to survive. We were brought home way too soon, Father."

He has no reply, instead asks, "Will you be addressing the High Tribunal in your human form?"

"Yes, father."

"Very well."

Slowly a stately figure of a woman appears, embraces Moreen, looks directly at her and says, "Our hearts sing."

"As does mine, Mother."

"I can see it in your eyes," She replies.

Moreen returns the smile and the three enter the Assembly Room of the High Tribunal where members sit around the long, oval table. The Father and Mother take their respective place and Moreen begins her address.

ADDRESSING THE HIGH TRIBUNAL

"Deities of the High Tribunal, Esteemed Councils of Souls Pristine," Mo says in her opening statement, "thank you for the rare opportunity to revisit Planet Earth as a Soul Pristine, although I have no recollection of being such an entity while there, other than being an enlightened human. As such, I have returned with much to share.

"As you know, humanity's life's compass is becoming increasingly directionless, and hearts laden with conflicting emotions bloom slowly, if at all. We bestowed the gift of a bright, resilient glimmer in their hearts at birth, and left it to develop into a radiant beacon of hope on its own. As we all know, success with that approach has been sporadic. The light in the human heart is increasingly under attack by the forces of instant gratification. A considerable number of humans are forgoing future benefits we have to offer, for less rewarding but more immediate earthly possessions. Regrettably, that is now the new norm.

"Long, long ago, this Tribunal, respectfully, made the decision not to actively intervene when humans on earth chose to journey off-course, sincerely believing that an enlightened, human-driven correction would emerge and reset direction. Sadly, it never did materialize as broadly as anticipated. Will guidelines of long ago suffice to resolve issues of a contemporary nature?

"History continues to tell us we must be more actively involved in maintaining the integrity of their journey while they walk the Earth, not wait until they arrive here. We know, and have known for some time, humanity's sun is again fast losing its brightness, their moon is becoming less poetic, and the heart less able to safely carry love to its final destination.

"Threatening eternal damnation does little to change hideous behaviour, neither is the promise of eternal life a sufficient motivator to help humans continue walking a wholesome path. If we are to solemnly help humans readjust their compasses, we must form a much more compelling partnership, visible or otherwise, with every, man, woman and child while they're on Earth."

Following a brief silence of reflection, she continues. "Imagine what could be achieved if humans and Souls Pristine walked side by side on Earth. VC was going down a road overrun with darkness and uncertainty, and would not have found his way home by himself. Our hearts spoke, and we got him back onto the road he was meant to travel. What would VC's journey look like without our direct and timely presence in his heart? One can only speculate, but we do know that, when Aila and I were taken from him, his guiding light went dark, his world became lusterless, and he lost his way.

"Must we all fall in love? It would certainly make life richer, but we know that it is not possible for everyone, nor is it the only way of helping humans reconnect with what's in their hearts.

"It is my belief that an increased presence of Souls Pristine on Planet Earth, as enlightened partners of humans of all ages, particularly with those humans whose lights are dimming, would be a most practical way of helping them stay connected and on their journey. If we are to, directly or indirectly, consciously or subconsciously, guide humans towards becoming more enlightend beings, our guiding light must shine brighter than all the competing others, and our warm touch must be felt more deeply. We must take their hand and solemnly walk with them, until they can all reconnect with their own light, as well as with the light in each other. When we are assured they can genuinely feel and advance the goodness of those lights, we know they can successfully find their way home.

"In completing my presentation, I would be remiss if I did not address the needs of the banished. Exiling them to the Sublunary Place of Darkness, away from the Constellations, without the hope of ever seeing light again, may be warranted, but I respectfully ask, how will these loveless souls ever be able to rekindle their light without being able to love?

"We know the light in many of their hearts, however dim, can still be rekindled, and we can successfully guide them out of their darkness. As we all know, no journey is without peril, but we owe it to all our brothers and sisters, and to ourselves, to help safeguard everyone's journey home regardless of where they may be. I thank you."

Moreen looks around, exchanges soft smiles and leaves the Chamber. The High Tribunal deliberates. After many days and nights, a unanimous decision is reached.

THE WATERFALL

Father walks down the corridor leading to the splendor of the garden, sees VC sitting on the bench and stops. He considers approaching him, now totally captivated by the images in the cascading waters, but doesn't; instead, he silently observes.

He thinks of VC as the embodiment of every human trying to make sense of who they truly are and where they actually fit in the ever-complicated cosmos. Thinks of Mo's presentation to the High Tribunal, of Aila and of their long journey home, then thinks of the wisdom yet to be whispered. Walks up, VC promptly stands, both look at each other and shake hands. No words were spoken, but VC felt the same inspiring energy as when he held Mo's hand on that first day of school ... when her warm touch immediately became his guiding light, and asks if he is in the presence of God. A compassionate smile, a gentle holding of VC's hand with both of His, a slow setting free, a bow.

He then turns and walks towards the Chamber. VC quietly says, "Thank you," and watches until He is no longer visible.

He stands in front of VC's imageless mirror and slowly moves His hand over the book. The thin book unlocks and opens to the last page. He reads the last entry and gradually places His hand on the opposite blank page. The page fills, He closes the book, stands back, looks at the new image in the mirror, and smiles kindly.

He feels a warm, loving presence behind Him. A most precious hand rests on his shoulder, a warm whisper, and He knows it's His lifelong Companion. He places His hand over Hers and both look at the image in the mirror as it slowly fades. They leave, the lights dim, the Chamber returns to its peaceful silence, and serenity soothes.

THE TIMELESS HOUSE: A NEW DAY

Walking back to the house from having had breakfast in the garden, Aila on VC's shoulders asks, "Can we go for a drive in your car, Mommy?"

"You mean in the Boss?"

"Yes, the Calypso car," replies Aila and laughs.

"Beautiful day for a drive, honey, should we take Daddy too?" asks Mo.

"Yes, he can sit in the back," replies Aila.

"Too small for him, besides your seat is back there."

Aila pinches her father's cheeks with both hands and says, "Okay, Daddy, you can sit in the front."

"Thanks, Angel," he replies.

Before entering the house, he stops and looks at his surroundings. Aila asks if he's looking at something special. VC looks at Mo, lifts Aila from his shoulders and coddles her in his arms, and says, "Yes, you and Mommy."

Once all settled in the car, VC cleans Mo's, Aila's and his own sunglasses, hands them back, smiles and says, "You should always clearly see where you're going."

"Thank you, as if," she replies, smiling, followed by a brief laugh from Aila. Mo drives slowly on the gravel road, but once it hits the asphalt, she floors it, the Mustang bolts, tires chirp just enough for an enthusiastic laugh from Aila, then slows to the posted speed and cruises the tree-crowned back roads.

The drive seems quieter than usual, Mo and VC occasionally look at each other, VC at Aila, at the clear sky, and wonders what Earth looks like from outer space. He asks Mo and Aila says, "Like a heart, Daddy, it looks like a heart."

"Not round?" he asks.

"No."

"And how did you come to that conclusion, may I ask?"

"Mommy told me."

That evening, Aila asleep, Mo and VC in the garden by candlelight, she asks, "I have this feeling, a heartwarming feeling, dreamlike yet so real, that we recently had a stay somewhere far yet close, but can't quite place it in space or time. Do you know to what I'm referring?"

"Not exactly, yet also warm feeling. I feel the same benevolent aura when you're near me, always have, and I like the caring and considerate sentiments you bring out of me and out of all the people that know you. You must be a Saint, because I'm a better person from being with you, Mo, and am forever in your debt."

She stands, opens her arms and says, "Let's dance."

"I thought you'd never ask," he replies. He stands and asks, "Who's leading?"

"I am," she replies.

"Of course. Any particular song in mind?"

"Yes, *From a Distance*, celestially soft. Hold me tightly."

He embraces her tightly, looks up at the sky and says, "Every star has a name, you know."

"You don't say," she replies.

"I do say."

"Do you know any of them personally?"

"I may," he replies.

She smiles, pulls him closer and says, "I love you, VC," to which he replies, "Love you too, Mo."

Their bodies embrace and move in slow motion like a night tide caressing its adoring shore. She glances at the exceptionally immense sky and says, "The stars appear to cover the entire sky tonight, yet don't look like stars, strangely active for this time of the year."

She looks at the sky more intensely and says, "Look, VC, look, they're separating into distinct groups as if following different paths, never seen that before, ever, wonder what that is? Mysterious yet comforting in a way."

He looks up and says, "I see what you mean, never seen that phenomenon before either, is that a good thing?"

"What?"

"This illuminated sky bursting with such a grouping of uniquely shaped lights never seen before and … and travelling different paths? Is that scientifically possible?"

"Yes, it's a good thing, and no, not scientifically possible," she replies. "Not in our book. That's another class you missed."

She rests her head on his shoulder, continues singing quietly and both end with the lyrics, "*It's the hope of hopes.*"

Mo looks at VC, their lips touch ever so softly, they hold each other's hands tighter and look at the engaging sky.

"It seems the universe is undergoing a reawakening."

"A rebirth?" he says.

"It feels more like a revival," she replies.

She takes his hand, begins walking towards the house and says, "What say you of a new file?"

"Yes, of course, and what shall we title it?" he replies.

"The Book of Books," she replies.

"Intriguing. I like it, and the first entry?"

The natal heavens deliver, and the postnatal starry sky rests. The night in each other's arms is long, and dawn will soon visit their window ledge.

The following morning, the sun gradually emerges, warms and comforts.

VC carrying a tray of breakfast delicacies to the two most precious women in his life, both wearing sunglasses and eagerly waiting in the garden. He hears the sound of farming, looks up the road and sees Murray ploughing the fertile fallow field, with the seagulls following closely. Muriel's two loads of laundry on the line flap gently in the breeze with a third in waiting. The young man on the tractor pulling a soon-to-be-loaded hay wagon drives by and waves.

Extended growing season, predicts the *Almanac*, maybe, just maybe long enough for a second harvest.

Mo and VC, sitting across from each other, Aila on her way to the kitchen to get more jam, he asks, "Do you think there will be a second harvest?"

"More plentiful than the first, according to the wise, and Murray is never wrong," she replies.

Sun rays find their way through the small opening in the grape vine canopy, and cast light where Mo is sitting. She looks up through the opening and says, "Look at the endless blue, VC, not a single cloud, anywhere."

He moves closer to her, places his arm on her shoulder, looks through the same opening, and says, "The Old Norse used to refer to it as the Abode of God."

The rays continue to shine through, and the light expands. Aila is on her way back with homemade jam. Murray stops for the lunch Muriel had waiting, and the seagulls feast. The day evolves in Earth time and place. The sky holds blue but will eventually heed the call of twilight, and the old stars embrace the new moon.

The Epic Journey of Our Inner Light

One

One Love One Light One Soul

The Supreme Glow

The Unification of the Glow

The All-Encompassing Festival of Souls

The Great Constellation of Souls Pristine

The Constellation of Healing Souls

The Constellation of Restored Souls

The Festival of Lights

The Emerging Glow

The Constellation of Healing Lights

The Constellation of Restored Radiance

The High Tribunal

The Chambers of Enhanced Understanding and Wisdom

The Chambers of Amendments

The Tribunal

The Great Hall and the Chambers of Roads Travelled

The Journey Begins

Emerging Light Entities and the Great Planet Earth

With reverence ...

... to those on whose shoulders of wisdom we stand ... to those from whose creativity we draw ... to the adoring hands we hold ... to the soft lips we kiss ... to the tender hearts we touch and are touched by ... to the tears we shelter and the ones we shed ... to the long nights found, lost and found again ... to what it was and to what is to be.

—V.A. Colucci